THE
FOULEST
THINGS

ALSO BY AMY TECTOR

The Honeybee Emeralds

THE
FOULEST
THINGS

AMY TECTOR

A DOMINION ARCHIVES MYSTERY

KEYLIGHT
BOOKS

Keylight Books

an imprint of Turner Publishing Company

Nashville, Tennessee

www.turnerpublishing.com

Cover design by Emily Mahon

Text design by William Ruoto

Library of Congress Cataloging-in-Publication Data

Names: Tector, Amy, author.
Title: The foulest things / by Amy Tector.
Description: Nashville, Tennessee : Turner Publishing Company, [2022]
Identifiers: LCCN 2021056455 (print) | LCCN 2021056456 (ebook) | ISBN 9781684428830 (paperback) | ISBN 9781684428830 (hardcover) | ISBN 9781684428854 (ebook)
Subjects: GSAFD: Mystery fiction.
Classification: LCC PR9199.4.T393 F68 2022 (print) | LCC PR9199.4.T393 (ebook) | DDC 813/.6—dc23
LC record available at https://lccn.loc.gov/2021056455
LC ebook record available at https://lccn.loc.gov/2021056456

Printed in the United States of America

To my mother

OTTAWA, 2010

CHAPTER ONE

"QUICKLY, JESSICA," OLIVER HISSED, TUGGING ME ALONG THE THICKLY carpeted hallway. The deep pile absorbed the snow and salt melting off our winter boots, and I was already overheating in my parka. "We're late." His round face was nearly purple with the effort of hurrying down the corridor.

"Calm down," Louise said. "They won't have reached our lot yet." Sixty-eight years old with close-cropped gray hair springing from her head like the bristles of a well-used toothbrush, my colleague Louise could have retired years ago. I think she mostly stuck around to annoy Oliver.

We could hear the auctioneer's booming voice: "Sold to the gentleman at the back."

I bit my lip. We were late because I'd left my backpack in the taxi. I'd had to chase the vehicle down Sussex Drive, slipping on the hard January ice, until it stopped at a light by the American embassy.

The auction room was like the rest of Van Cleef's Auction House, elegantly appointed in muted colors and expensive finishings. Heads turned as we tugged off our heavy coats, Louise stomping the snow off her combat boots, but the auctioneer's smooth patter didn't falter.

We sunk into three chairs near the back of the room, and I caught my breath. Forgetting my backpack had been so stupid. I was on a one-year contract with the Dominion Archives, and I needed a ringing endorsement from Oliver to be hired permanently. So far, as Shania sang, I hadn't impressed him much. Oliver made me nervous. Archival techniques that I studied for years flew from my brain when he was around. I hadn't helped matters last month by spilling coffee on the white cashmere cape he wore instead of a coat.

He checked the catalog. "Thank goodness, they're not at our lot yet."

This was my first auction, and I had been looking forward to it all week. Things that people in the past touched and loved were being bought and sold like bags of potatoes or boxes of hair dye. This mixture of the romantic and the prosaic fascinated me.

I stared at the front to see what was on offer. Some canvases leaned against an easel, but I couldn't make out details. The auctioneer opened bidding at $2,000.

A brunette in a red suit raised her hand with the elegant grace of a dancer.

"Twenty-five hundred?" The auctioneer nodded at a burly man with a thick neck and a nose that looked like it had been broken more than once. He could be a villainous thug from a James Bond movie, maybe a disaffected Communist carrying a couple of nukes in a suitcase.

I grinned. These were the types of glamorous figures I imagined at an auction.

"Three thousand?" the auctioneer asked.

The man in front of Oliver lifted his hand. I noticed his shoulders were covered in a generous layer of dandruff.

Maybe they weren't all glamorous.

The action quickened now, and the auctioneer's smooth voice slid swiftly between the bids, like a hockey puck passed between sticks.

I leaned toward Louise. "What are they bidding on?"

She shrugged. "Nothing much." A Quebecer, Louise had a strong French accent, pronouncing *nothing* as *no-ting*. "Amateurs always get too excited." Her voice was husky from years of smoking, though she'd recently quit, hence her deep crabbiness. She pointed to the entry in the catalog: "Lot Three consists of eight oil paintings by various twentieth-century artists from the estate of Andrew Jarvis. Subjects include portraiture, streetscapes, and landscapes. Reserve Price, $1,500."

I tuned back to the bidding in time to see Scarlet Suit raise her hand.

Dandruff Shoulders frowned as the price climbed, and when he shook his head at $4,500, the crowd breathed a collective sigh. Now it was between Scarlet Suit and Burly Communist.

Scarlet turned slightly, so she could see Burly. Her lips parted with excitement. He looked anxious, but determined.

The rising tension seemed to make the room hotter. I tugged off my cardigan, yanking my arm up to pull the tight sleeve.

The auctioneer, noting my gesture, pointed his gavel. "We have a new bidder at five thousand."

Oh my God. My head swam, and for a second I thought I was going to pass out. I swallowed hard. Oliver's face had gone a deep shade of tomatoey red, and even Louise looked startled.

The auctioneer's voice seemed to come from underwater. "Do we have another bid?"

Everything moved in slow motion. I stared at Burly Communist, willing him to raise his hand. He glared back, obviously annoyed that I was entering the bidding so late. I turned to Scarlet Suit and nearly cried with joy when I saw her hand flutter.

"Fifty five hundred for the lady in red," the auctioneer said.

I sank back in my chair with relief.

Oliver wheezed beside me, clutching his chest. "You gave me heart palpitations," he hissed.

I was too ashamed to say a word.

"You would have put the Dominion Archives in an extremely difficult position," Oliver continued. "We do not have money to waste on frivolous jokes."

"It wasn't a joke," I whispered back. "I was hot and took my sweater off."

Louise leaned across me, not bothering to whisper. "Câlice, Oliver, relax. No harm done." She fanned herself with the catalog. "I don't blame the kid. I'm hotter than a whore in church."

Her comment drew stares from our neighbors. Oliver ignored us both, turning his attention back to the sale.

I focused on the auction, willing back tears and hoping my latest blunder wasn't going to end my career.

At $8,000, Scarlet Suit bowed out. The auctioneer banged his gavel, dabbing his forehead with a white handkerchief. "Sold to the gentleman for seventy-five hundred."

Burly Communist grunted in satisfaction.

"Ciboire," muttered Louise. "That idiot dropped a pile on a bunch of junk. I hope he doesn't bid on our ledgers, or he'll fuck us."

I flipped through the catalog to read the description of our lot: "Business records belonging to Henry Jarvis, cabinet minister during Prime Minister Bennett's term. Lot consists of 116 leather-bound ledgers pertaining to farm business. Material is in excellent condition and comes from the estate of Henry Jarvis's son Andrew."

As starry-eyed as I was about archives, even I could tell that this purchase wasn't likely to cause a bidding war. My suspicions proved correct, and the only competition we faced was a couple of telephone bids from the University of Alberta, which apparently already held most of the Henry Jarvis collection.

Louise whispered advice on bids to Oliver, and we easily won the lot. "Stealing the ledgers right from under those Alberta cowboys," Oliver said.

After the bidding, we were ushered to the office, a small space tucked between the reception and auction room. We crowded around the desk as a clerk wrote up the purchase and gave Oliver the receipt.

"I'll take the first box now, so we can get started immediately," Oliver said to the clerk. "Send the rest to the Conservation Facility for barcoding." The facility was our state-of-the-art storage and preservation building on the other side of the Ottawa River in the province of Quebec.

Business done, we waited in the reception area for the cab. I tried to make up for my earlier blunder. "Oliver, I'd love to work on the Jarvis material."

He frowned. "You proved today you're not equipped to process a collection. You're not quite ready for the triple axel, my dear. Best to stick to toe loops."

My heart sank. Oliver was a keen figure skating fan and was eagerly awaiting next month's start of the Vancouver Winter Olympic Games. He would never remove me from the drudgework I'd done since starting in the Political and Cultural Affairs section. I spent last week exiled to the Conservation Facility, examining hundreds of fragile glass lantern slides for an image of a "lady in a hat," which Oliver needed to illustrate an article he was writing. I had to start doing real archival work if I was ever going to be hired permanently.

"I think it would be a great learning opportunity for me to work with a collection from the moment it enters our possession."

I could tell by his face that I hadn't persuaded him and was about to try again, but Louise interrupted with a cough. "I wouldn't let you handle this anyway, kid. Political material is my turf."

I was hurt. Louise was the only coworker to show any interest in me.

Oliver's cheeks reddened. "In case you are forgetting, Louise, I am the manager of our section," he said. "I will determine workloads. As a matter of fact, Jessica, I think processing these ledgers would be an excellent opportunity for you."

I beamed.

"Begin work on the first box immediately, and order the others once they're barcoded," he said.

The taxi arrived, and Oliver rushed outside. Louise held back. "Sorry about that, kid, but I knew he'd give the ledgers to you if he thought I wanted them."

I grinned. I didn't know what was better, getting a shot at real work or knowing that Louise was on my side. "Thanks so much. That was nice."

She shrugged. "Not really. I'm sure there's nothing important in them, otherwise I'd process them myself. I'm a greedy old bird, don't forget it."

"I'm grateful. This might be my chance to finally impress him."

"You know, you don't have to rely on Oliver to get a permanent position."

"What do you mean?" I asked.

"The institution encourages academic work. If you can publish a scholarly article in a peer-reviewed journal, even that ass would have to hire you permanently."

Before I could question her further, Oliver gestured impatiently from the taxi.

◇◇◇◇◇◇

FIFTEEN MINUTES LATER, I WALKED DOWN THE HALL TO MY OFFICE AT the Dominion Archives' Wellington Street headquarters. I deposited the box of Jarvis material on my processing table, which covered most of the room's right wall. A computer with an ancient monitor sat on a cheap desk on the opposite side of the room. Above it hung a Successories poster of a kitten tangled in a ball of yarn with "You Can Do It!" emblazoned across the bottom. It belonged to my predecessor, who retired months before my arrival. As embarrassing as it was to admit, I left it up because I found its message encouraging.

I opened the box. I felt like a kid looking out on the first snowfall of winter. Four hardbound ledgers and the stale scent of old stationery greeted me. My job was to go through the box, flag documents that needed conservation treatment, and read every scrap of paper so I could write a comprehensive description of the material for future researchers.

I pulled out the first ledger and leafed through it, noting its contents and date. I worked steadily for an hour before pausing to stretch my back.

Louise was right. The material was uninteresting, consisting of accounting records from an Albertan cattle ranch, but I was still happy. I loved taking someone's messy, complicated life and imposing a structure on it. Undoubtedly, my passion was due to my own chaotic childhood, with my mother taking in every stray and street kid she came across.

I took out the next ledger, still thinking about my mother, who disapproved of my "musty, boring" profession. It was our ongoing argument, and thinking of it made me open the ledger too forcefully, tearing the delicate leather binding. Shit.

Fortunately, it wasn't a large tear and wouldn't require expensive conservation treatment. As my finger traced the small rip, I felt a slit on the inside cover. I pulled the desk lamp closer to examine it. Someone had deliberately sliced an opening, which you'd never notice unless you were staring at the incision.

Careful not to further rip the old leather, I grabbed a letter opener and slid it into the space, meeting with resistance. My heart beat faster. Hooking the opener under the obstruction, I eased it out.

It was an old envelope addressed to Victoria Jarvis, General Delivery, High Plains Alberta. The return address was for Jeremy Crawford, 19 Avenue de Clichy, Paris. I swallowed hard. Even if the letter was nothing but a gossipy note between friends, it exemplified what attracted me about archives: the physical sense of touching a part of history. It was what I could never articulate to my mother. Now I held such tangible evidence in my hands, and it was obviously something that had been deliberately hidden.

CHAPTER TWO

I EXAMINED THE ENVELOPE. IT WAS SLIT OPEN AND CONTAINED A LETTER on brittle, yellowed paper.

August 2, 1914

Darling Victoria,

I have finally arrived in Paris. It is said that this is a city for lovers, and I am bereft without you. You promise there is comfort in knowing that one day we will be reunited, but I lack your faith. Your father shows no sign of relenting; indeed he is now exiling you as well! I cannot imagine you on a dusty Western ranch, attending to your uncle's dreary bookkeeping, surrounded by cowpunchers and roughnecks. Instead, I remember the moment I first saw you, floating into the ballroom at the exhibition opening, your filmy white dress a perfect complement to your angelic expression. The electric lights glittered in your golden hair, making a veritable halo. Yet you, that angel, noticed me, the awkward artist in the corner.

Enough! I can hear you scolding me to stop my moping and channel my despair into something constructive. I shall tell you about Paris. It is good to be settled after the whirlwind of London and Amsterdam. I have rented a small flat. It is dingy and cramped, but it is in Paris, and that is enough. Simply to read the street names— Rue du Chat-qui-Pêche, Boulevard Sébastopol, and of course, the Champs-Élysées—thrills me. I have spent two days wandering, trying to absorb it all: the lights from the cafés pouring out onto the wide boulevards, the people laughing and tumbling from theaters. I feel like a dazzled country boy, and I realize how raw and youthful

Montreal is. Paris is an old city, so old you can feel its ghosts seep into your bones. Even the Seine is a refined, subdued river, nothing like our noisy St. Lawrence.

A sound in the hall made me look up. Ginette Noiseau, a co-worker, sauntered by, looking curiously into my office. Heart in my mouth, I shifted my body so she couldn't see what I was doing. She moved along. I turned back to the letter.

Yet Paris is also modern. The Eiffel Tower is a thrilling example of originality. Remember poring over last year's Armory Show catalog? Well, many of the artists who showed at that exhibit live here: Duchamp, Braque, Derain . . . I am soaking in the same atmosphere as they, imbibing the ideas and creativity that crackle through the streets. Indeed, I have already met some young artists—students at the Beaux-Arts. Like me, they are experimenting with color and form.

I won't abandon everything I learned at the Art Association, however. Heaven knows I paid hours of homage to the old masters while in London and Amsterdam. I have studied canvases by Titian, Caravaggio, Rubens, and Rembrandt. The sheer number of masterpieces in Europe makes me realize how meager our art heritage is. I laugh to think of how absurdly proud our museum directors are of their great "treasure," the Learmount Rembrandt. Why, it is only a drawing! At the Rijksmuseum, they had dozens of Rembrandt's oil paintings—beautiful, luminous things that force you to face truth, if only for the moment you stand before the work.

Don't fret over the rumblings of war, darling. I am safe here. France is mobilizing, but it is surely only a precaution. The Germans will not risk the might of the British Empire. This talk is nothing but the business of lawyers, diplomats, and newspapermen eager to sell more copies.

I hope this letter cheers you in your lonely farm life. Undoubtedly you will miss Montreal's energy and intellectual stimulation. Please, reassure me that you are not too unhappy. We shall be reunited. I will make a success of myself and return to Montreal in triumph. You will see. Your father will see.

I miss you. I love you.

Jem

My hands shook as I placed the letter on the table. I felt like I had peeped through a door and glimpsed another world. I rubbed the old paper gently between my fingers and reread it. Who were Jem and Victoria? What happened to them? I wondered if I was the first to touch the letter since someone slipped it into Henry Jarvis's account book. Was that person Victoria herself? It seemed a likely explanation.

I pulled out the other ledgers from the box, looking for more slits. There were none, but I wasn't discouraged. If there was one hidden letter, there might be more. I emailed the circulation staff, requesting the remaining boxes be delivered in the morning.

Too excited to settle back to processing the ledgers, I checked the Reference and Tracking Database to see if we held any information on Victoria Jarvis or Jeremy Crawford. I hit the jackpot when I located descriptions of four of his sketches in the Art Vault at the Conservation Facility. The Dominion Archives owned some Jeremy Crawford originals.

I wanted to keep the letter in my possession, but I'd be violating a hundred different rules if I brought it home. I bit my lip; it would do no harm to photocopy it.

I was surprised to realize it was past quitting time when I walked to the photocopier near Oliver's office. It pleased me to think most people had gone home. Jem was my discovery, and I wasn't ready to share him yet. Copying done, I put both the original and the reproduction safely into a file folder.

Now that my excitement was fading, I could think about the ramifications of my discovery. The letter contained many promising

research leads, including Jem's references to the art scene and descriptions of Paris before the war. If I found more letters, I could write a
scholarly paper about them and, according to Louise, guarantee my
future at the Dominion Archives.

Oliver emerged from his office and bustled toward me, his white
cape flapping behind him as if he were the Phantom of the Opera.
"Jessica, you're precisely the person I wished to see."

He talked as he walked me to my office, and I kept the folder out
of his sight. "The chief archivist's office informed me that the Belgian
prime minister is visiting Monday. We want to show him something
from our collection related to his country. There is a congratulatory
card from the king of Belgium to the prime minister over our 1964
Olympic gold in bobsleigh. Given Canada will soon be hosting our own
Olympiad, I think it's an appropriate talking point. Pull the document
from storage tonight, and prep it for Monday's consultation, please."

"Sure thing," I said, my heart sinking. Getting to the Conservation Facility wasn't simple at the best of times. It would take me
at least forty-five minutes in Thursday evening rush hour, and I
had dinner plans.

Oliver handed me the email. "This has all the details. Now, unfortunately my secretary is gone, so you can't get taxi chits. Keep your
receipts, and we'll reimburse you."

Keep my receipts? It would probably cost a hundred dollars to get
there and back. That was two weeks of grocery money. "I'm happy to
do it, Oliver."

"Marvelous." With a swirl of his cape, Oliver flounced off into the
"Music of the Night."

I stared after him in frustration. Then I remembered the letter. It
was my ticket out from under Oliver's thumb. I turned to the box of
ledgers. While I should have placed the original letter in a dated and
labeled acid-free file folder, instead I eased it back into the slit in the
ledger where I first found it. I wasn't quite ready to process it yet, and
I figured it would be safe in its original spot, while I determined what
to do. I popped the copy into my filing cabinet.

Next, I called Adela to cancel our dinner plans, but predictably, she didn't take no for an answer, instead cajoling me into going out. Since I was dying to tell her about the letter, I didn't need much persuading. After all, it would be just as easy to retrieve the document tomorrow morning before work. Oliver would never know the difference.

◇◇◇◇◇◇

THERE WASN'T MUCH TRAFFIC AT SIX THE NEXT MORNING, AND THE TAXI zoomed through the quiet streets of Gatineau. I was tired. Dinner with Adela went late as we talked over my discovery. She'd then gone into a detailed analysis of our chances in Vancouver. Hosting the Olympics for the first time in years, the Games were a hot conversational topic. Our discussion devolved into a wine-fueled debate about who was sexier: Team Canada hockey captain Sidney Crosby (an adorable moron, according to Adela) or any member of the men's speed skating team (have I seen the size of their thighs?). I'd crawled into bed quite late.

The taxi pulled up to the Conservation Facility. Built of shiny glass and steel, it looked completely out of place in the surrounding snow-covered fields, like a spaceship dropped onto the plain.

After I paid the exorbitant fare, the driver sped off before I remembered to ask for a receipt.

Pushing away my annoyance, I entered the building. The glass walls of the main hall sealed the interior from the elements, protecting the five floors of vaults that squatted like heavy cement animals in the building's center. Glass, steel, and concrete were the primary construction materials because they were fire-, dust-, and parasite-resistant. Everything was designed to protect the archival records stored here. A series of offices were perched, five stories up, atop the vaults, and above that soared the roof of the building. It was a cathedral to preservation.

I flashed my pass to the sleepy commissionaire and pushed through the door behind his desk, which controlled access to the first floor of vaults. Glancing at the email Oliver had given me, I walked down the concrete hall to Vault Seven, where the Belgian document was held.

Directly across the hall from Seven was the Art Vault, where I had toiled on Oliver's lantern slide research. It dawned on me that Jeremy Crawford's work was housed there. If they hadn't revoked my access since last week, it would be easy to have a look at his sketches.

Without giving myself time to reconsider, I crossed the hall, swiping my pass through the lock. The green light came on, and I heard the click of the door opening. I pushed my way into the Art Vault.

People associate archives with moldering secrets in dark, dusty basements, but this room was carefully climate-controlled and aggressively well lit. The conservation station to my right consisted of a white table covered with complicated-looking machinery, lamps, and magnifying glasses. The bulk of the room held rows of specially built metal shelving, stretching up to the ten-foot ceiling. The shelves were on rollers, allowing them to be pressed closely together when not in use, thus maximizing space.

Painters were grouped alphabetically, which meant that the Crawford sketches should be in the closest couple of rows. I went to the first set of shelving and turned the small handwheel on the side, which caused the shelves to separate, generating a narrow alley. I turned the wheel again. Usually you could create quite a big space, but this time the shelving wouldn't squish together any further. I heaved on the wheel, but something stopped me from widening it.

I sidled down the narrow aisle, which ended at "B." Crawford must be in the following row. I stepped out and was about to turn the next wheel when I noticed that the shelves of the "C" aisle were not pressed tightly together. Something large was wedged between the stacks.

I turned the wheel to open the aisle. The stacks moved apart, widening the row and releasing the thing that had been trapped.

Heart racing, I watched as a body flopped down in a bizarre parody of liveliness. The back of the man's head hit the concrete floor with a smack, and for an illogical moment I worried he had hurt himself. A metallic tang reached my nostrils, and I noticed that his chest was covered in blood. I fought down the urge to retch, absurdly thinking that the conservators would not appreciate the cleanup.

Then I started screaming.

CHAPTER THREE

MY SCREAMS QUICKLY CHOKED OFF AS FEAR INVADED. WAS THE MUR-
derer still here? I was in a soundproof vault with two feet of solid steel
between myself and safety. Lurching away from the dead man, I tripped
on the edge of the shelving, falling to my knees. My fear turned into
panic, and I stumbled to the door, pushing at it and sobbing with frustration when it wouldn't budge. Finally, I remembered it pulled open, and I
scrambled for the handle. Yanking as hard as I could, I opened it and ran
down the hallway to the commissionaire's desk.

"Call the police," I yelled.

The commissionaire leaped up. "What happened?"

"There's a body in the Art Vault. The killer might still be here.
Call the cops!"

"That's not funny," he said. The commissionaire was about sixty-
five, chubby, and white-haired.

I glanced behind me. "I'm not joking. Call the police, please."

The guard must have seen the panic in my face. "Well, something
spooked you, but if you think I'm calling the cops, you're crazy." He hesitated. "I can't leave my post, but I'll have someone take a look." He pulled
out his walkie-talkie. "Hi, Cameron, can you go check out the Art Vault?
We've got an archivist here who thinks she's seen a body."

I stared at the door to the vaults, barely listening to their conversation. The commissionaire chuckled and said something about
bookworms and their active imaginations.

I didn't care what they thought of me. The dead man's slack face
and bloody chest swam before my eyes. Breathing deeply, I fought
down nausea.

It took Cameron a few minutes to get to the vault, but when he did the walkie-talkie crackled to life. "Abdel! It's true, call the police!"

The commissionaire cast an apologetic look in my direction and punched in 911.

Moments later, Cameron emerged, ashen-faced, from the vaults.

"I've got bad news," he addressed Abdel. "It's Paul Thibodeau."

"What?" Abdel sat down on his stool, absorbing the information. "He wasn't even on duty last night."

"Who's Paul Thibodeau?" I asked. Now that there were three of us standing together, my fear had abated.

"He's a commissionaire here," Cameron said.

"Oh, I'm sorry." The man had looked familiar; I must have seen him on the desk last week. Putting a name to the body made his death more personal. Paul had worked here. He had a job, a life. "Does he have a family?" I asked.

Cameron and Abdel looked at each other and shrugged. "He didn't talk much," offered Abdel.

We strained to hear police sirens, but all was quiet. "Do you think the killer is still here?" I asked.

Cameron, Abdel, and I looked toward the vault door. The silence was thick and ominous as we listened for the sound of approaching footsteps, but none came.

Fifteen minutes later, we were still waiting for the sirens, and now I was pissed off. Gatineau wasn't a big city, and surely a homicide merited a speedy response. A man was dead, a murderer was on the loose, and the police couldn't tear themselves away from their doughnuts to put in an appearance.

On some level I recognized that my anger was displaced fear, but on another it felt good to be mad at the cops. My whole life, my mother had hated the "pigs." Growing up, I had tried to distance myself from her attitudes, but now, when I felt most vulnerable, blaming the police was actually comforting. Not for the first time, I cursed my mother's ability to worm her way into my subconscious. I took a deep breath and tried to cultivate an attitude of mindfulness and serenity.

The cops arrived five minutes later, and the Conservation Facility was soon filled with police. I gave a statement to a uniform and was told to wait for the officer in charge. It took another hour and a half before I was called into the makeshift command center, an unused office not far from the vault entrance.

Daniel Lemieux was a short man with a large chin and a head of carefully gelled black curls. A few tenacious chest hairs crawled up over his tie, promising that he was a hairy little man indeed. He spoke rapid French to an underling, and I couldn't follow what he was saying.

"Dis-moi quand t'as des nouvelles." He handed a folder to the uniformed cop and dismissed him. Then he turned to me. "Alors, Mademoiselle Novak." His French accent was stronger than Louise's, but I'd heard him speaking to Abdel and knew his English was good.

"Yes, Detective?"

"Should we go over the events once more?" He smiled, his teeth even and gleaming like Ricky Martin's.

I was tired and desperate to leave. "Don't you have everything you need?"

"Indulge me," he said.

I squirmed. My strange protectiveness over the Jem Crawford letter had extended to my statement to the first officer who interviewed me, and I'd told a white lie about why I'd entered the Art Vault. Now every time I repeated it, I got more uncomfortable. Still, my mother always said that if you had to lie, it was best to commit 100 percent to it. "I came to the Conservation Facility this morning to retrieve a document for my boss. When I got here I remembered that I'd left a notebook in the Art Vault last week. I went in to look for it, and that's when I saw the body."

"You're very calm for a girl who stumbled across a murder. Usually people who have contact with the police, even for small things"—he pronounced it *tings*—"these people are nervous, but not you."

"Calm?" I laughed shakily. "I'm not calm. I discovered a dead man. I was alone with it, with him, in that vault. The killer might have seen me, might have been watching me the whole time." I shuddered.

Lemieux stared at me impassively. "Let's go back to the moment you found the body. You disturbed the crime scene, is that not correct?"

"What?"

"You opened the shelving. You moved the victim. Why?"

I blinked at him, trying to understand what he was getting at. "I moved the row to see what was there. I didn't know it was a body."

He leaned forward, his voice hard. "Come on, mademoiselle, you couldn't tell it was a man?"

"No!" I protested. "It was a shape. A thing. It was wedged into the stacks, like a piece of meat." My eyes welled up, but I was damned if I was going to cry in front of this insensitive man.

"Nevertheless, you tampered with the crime scene. That is serious."

Whether it was leftover emotion from this morning's discovery or my anger with the cops' lackadaisical response, I found myself snapping back. "I'm sorry if I ruined your day by finding a murder victim, but I didn't tamper with your crime scene on purpose."

Lemieux drew in a breath and moved to another line of questioning. "Where were you last night?"

"I was with a friend at May Lynh's. It's a restaurant in Ottawa."

"Can she verify your presence?"

"Sure. So can the waitress and the bartender. We were there until about midnight."

He raised an eyebrow. "That's late for dinner on a weeknight."

"We had a lot to talk about."

I gave him Adela's contact details and the restaurant's address. He closed his notebook with a snap. "Thank you, Mademoiselle Novak. Can I have an officer take you home?"

I shook my head. "I'm going into work."

"What?" he asked, displaying the first trace of human emotion. "You should probably go home, get some rest." His voice now exuded warmth. Was he trying to be both "good cop" and "bad cop"?

"No, I don't want to sit around staring at my walls. If I do, I'll only obsess about what I saw. It's better if I'm busy."

Lemieux nodded. "You're, how do you Anglos say, a tough biscuit."

I smiled for the first time that morning and stood up. I had been dismissed and didn't need to be told twice.

◇◇◇◇◇◇

"TELL ME ABOUT THE MURDER."

It wasn't often I got to enter Oliver's plush office, but apparently discovering a body had its privileges. I was seated in a hard-backed chair opposite his large desk. I hadn't pegged him for a prurient man, but I found myself being pumped for all the scandalous details.

"There's nothing to tell," I said, blocking out the image of the man's body falling forward.

As always around lunchtime, Oliver was especially hyper. He wriggled excitedly in his chair. "Apparently the guy was a commissionaire." His eyes darted.

I frowned. "How do you know that already?"

Oliver waved a hand in a jerky movement. "It's all over the news."

"Really? Did they mention my name?"

"No, no. They said that a Dominion Archives employee discovered him. There was also an interview with the lead officer."

I wasn't surprised. Lemieux struck me as a man who'd love the limelight. I was relieved my name hadn't been released. The murderer was still out there, and I wanted to stay off their radar.

"Did the news say if Thibodeau had any family?"

Oliver paused, as if he hadn't even considered the question. "Poor bugger, I don't know. They didn't mention anything." Suddenly all professionalism, he said, "I think the more important question is, what was an off-duty commissionaire doing in the Art Vault? This won't look good for the institution. It reveals holes in our security. The police need to resolve this quickly. Why do you think he was there?"

"I have no idea."

Oliver stood and began pacing. "Come on, Jessica, think. Did you see anything unusual when you found the body? Maybe a clue?"

I was irritated that Oliver wanted to play CSI. My facial expression must have conveyed my thoughts, because he stopped probing and sat down, clearly annoyed I wasn't going to gossip.

"The crux of the matter as it relates to you is that you failed to go to the Conservation Facility last night as I asked. What's more, you made an unauthorized foray into the Art Vault. What were you doing there?"

I hesitated, but if I could lie to a cop like Lemieux, with his hard stare and skeptical attitude, I could certainly lie to Oliver. "I left my notebook there last week when I was doing your project and decided to look for it."

"You should be more careful with your belongings, Jessica. You also should not have been in that vault. Access is carefully controlled for very good reasons. It houses enormously valuable paintings. If anything is missing, you are going to be in very hot water."

I hadn't considered that something might have been stolen, but it seemed a likely motive for murder.

"Stephen Nguyen called me this morning, and he's furious. He wants to speak with you personally," Oliver said.

Stephen was the chief art curator, and a heavy hitter within the institution. I'd met him a couple of times last week as I toiled over the lantern slides, but in the normal run of events my small orbit would never intersect with his. I was beginning to realize that my unauthorized trip could have a serious impact on my career. I had to mend fences with Oliver.

"I'm happy to talk to him. Obviously, I made a stupid mistake."

Oliver smiled. "Yes, you are quite the little novice, aren't you? Still, you will have to make nice with Stephen and explain what you were doing in there. Now, I understand the Belgian material hasn't been prepped for viewing?"

I gaped at him. "No, I didn't manage to prep anything after I found the dead man." Damn, that wasn't very fence-mendy.

"I sympathize with your feelings, Jessica. I do. Still, inability to finish tasks shows a distinct lack of professionalism. The Belgian contingent is coming on Monday, and we need a document to show them."

My voice came out in a high-pitched squeak, and the excuses poured from my lips. "I don't even know if I can go back. I'm sure the police have sealed everything off. Like you said, it was murder." All morning I had tried to block the memory of the vault discovery from my mind, but now I was once again under its fluorescent lights, the stacks emitting a small sigh as they pulled apart, revealing the corpse. I didn't want to return to the Conservation Facility ever again.

Oliver dismissed my desperate arguments. "They can't be interested in the material we need. It's in a different vault. The chief archivist asked for a viewing, and I expect something for Monday morning."

"But, Oliver," I continued, "I can't go back to that place. You don't know what it was like . . . the body, the murderer . . ."

"I understand, Jessica. It must have been terrible." The kindness in his voice surprised me. "I'm not a monster—I can appreciate what you have gone through. Nonetheless, you came into work today, and I can only assume it was because you felt you could handle your responsibilities. I want to hire you on permanently, but I need to know that you're committed to the institution. I'm giving you an opportunity to prove yourself to me. Can you do that?"

"Yes." Dread churned my stomach. I knew it was irrational, but one part of me feared the killer was still there, waiting for me.

"Excellent." He turned to his computer. As I rose, he said without looking at me, "The email system is down again, and I need everyone's reference statistics for the month. Pop around to all of the archivists' offices and collect them."

"I thought I had to go out to the Conservation Facility?"

Now he turned, and all compassion was gone. "You don't think

I'm sending you on company time? You should have done the job last night, so you can go this evening. Ask for a taxi chit from my secretary."

After getting the chit, I marched back to my office. I grabbed a pen and paper and pushed the horrible thought of a night trip to the Conservation Facility from my mind. I had a job to do.

CHAPTER FOUR

MUTED CLASSICAL MUSIC DRIFTED OUT FROM UNDER GINETTE NOISEAU'S closed door, and my knock was answered by an imperious "Entrez." Her office was an oasis of calm, painted a rich blue, laid with thick carpeting, and decorated with tasteful souvenirs of her many trips to Asia, including wooden Thai masks and a watercolor of a rice paddy.

Hair cut in a sleek bob, expensive suit clothing a well-maintained body, Ginette seemed out of place in the shabby, casual-dress archives. She frowned when she saw me. "Yes?"

"Sorry to interrupt, Ginette, but I need your reference stats."

"I'm too busy at the moment." She waved me out the door.

Barry O'Quinn, a big-bellied archivist responsible for the papers of governors general, was talking into the phone when I entered his office. I didn't know much about gambling, but it sounded like he was placing bets on something.

I mouthed my request to him, and he scrawled down the number of reference inquiries he had answered that month on a piece of paper.

Louise wasn't in, so I passed by her closed office.

I went to Mike Roy's office next. In his forties, tall, wild haired, and always faintly befuddled, Mike was the closest thing to an eligible bachelor the archives had to offer. His office was crammed with books in every conceivable space, including carefully balanced on his computer monitor. Piles of papers were strewn about, making precarious towers on the floor, his desk, and the windowsill.

I explained what I was after, and he put down the book he was reading. He stood, saying, "I'm sure I've got the stats here somewhere . . ." He stared around in despair. "I have no idea where the damn things are. In fact, I don't remember ever paying attention to my reference statistics. Why don't I invent something? Will you mind?"

I couldn't keep the listlessness from my voice. "I don't care."

He looked at me with concern. "Hey, do you want a drink?"

That snapped me back to attention. "What?" I stuttered.

"Close the door, and I'll break out the good stuff."

Was this old guy coming on to me? I took a step back and put my hand on the doorframe. "No, that's okay. I've got statistics to collect, so I'll get—"

"I didn't mean to scare you," he said quickly. He ran his hand through his thick, curly hair, and a pencil fell out. "That's where it is," he muttered, stooping to pick it up. His knees cracked loudly. He smiled as he stood, and a dimple appeared in his left cheek.

I smiled back, and he cleared a pile of books, a shoe, and an old coffee mug from a chair. "Sit, sit." He closed his office door and yanked a bottle of Jameson's from a desk drawer. I noticed a couple of other bottles rattling around in there before he slammed it shut. "You probably need this after the morning you've had."

I was surprised he knew about the murder; I wouldn't have thought that Mike was connected to the grapevine. Louise had told me that since his wife's death a couple of years ago, he had become a bit of a recluse.

He poured the whiskey and handed me a chipped coffee mug with "Art Rocks!" emblazoned on it. His hands shook as he passed me the mug. I recognized the signs of a dedicated drinker from the months when I was seven and Tom, a homeless friend of my mother's, had lived with us.

"I don't usually do this," he said, "but I thought you could use it."

"It's been a strange morning." I sipped the whiskey, enjoying the warmth as it slid down my throat.

He sat back behind his desk. The sun poured in behind him, glinting on the silver in his hair. "It must have been terrible for you." His voice cracked with compassion.

I wanted to shrug, but instead my shoulders started to shake and my face crumbled. The sobs came quickly, and I realized as the tears streamed down that I had been fighting this reaction since first finding the body.

Mike rushed around the desk, took the shaking mug from my hands, and patted me awkwardly on the back. "There, there," he said. "It's been very tough for you. I shouldn't have brought it up."

Eventually the tears subsided. "Do you have a Kleenex?" I sniffed.

"Yes, of course." He seemed grateful to have something to do. He rummaged over the top of his desk and then opened some drawers. He came back with a napkin bearing a logo for the Maple Leaf Pub.

I wiped my eyes and blew my nose. "I'm sorry," I said. "Finding that body was awful. I keep thinking about that guy tumbling out from between the stacks like a deadweight . . . I know it sounds stupid and obvious, but there was no one inside there, you know? There was nothing left of him."

Mike shuddered. "Let's not dwell on that."

"No," I agreed. I knew if I kept talking about it, I would start blubbering again. I took a deep breath, anxious to change the subject. "What are you working on?"

"I was reading the new Edward Hauver biography." He gestured to a thick hardcover book lying atop a pile of papers on his desk.

"Wow. I didn't think it was out yet." Edward Hauver was a great modernist poet. He fit all the stereotypes—hard drinker, heavy smoker, and profligate sex life.

"It isn't," Mike said. "The author sent me an advance copy. I helped him out with his research. I'm in the acknowledgments." He couldn't mask the note of pride in his voice, but his bragging didn't irk me the way Oliver's did.

"I didn't know we had his papers."

"Yup. They were one of the first things I acquired when I started here. In fact, Hauver is the reason I became an archivist."

"Really?"

"Yeah, it's a good story . . ."

There was a knock on the door, and Ginette poked her head in. She looked from Mike to me, and her nostrils flared as if she could smell the whiskey. "I have those figures for you now, Jessica."

Ginette's appearance reminded me that I was still on probation, and getting caught drinking in a colleague's office was not the best way to secure a permanent spot on the team. I stood. "I'll get them right now." I turned to Mike. "Thanks for listening to me. It helped."

He smiled and waved a hand. "My pleasure."

I got Ginette's numbers, added in some invented ones for Mike, and dropped the statistics on Oliver's desk before returning to my office. My stressful morning faded away as I saw three boxes of Jarvis material sitting on my processing table.

There was a note from the circulation staff: "As a probationary employee, you are not entitled to order the twenty-eight boxes of the requested accession. Probationary employees may order only three boxes of archival material at a time. Please consult Staff Procedure Seventy-Six for more information." Damn. At this rate it would take a couple of weeks to go through all of the ledgers.

I opened the first box and pulled out the four registers, examining their bindings for the telltale slit; none had it. What if that one letter had been a fluke? Could I write a whole article on one flimsy note? Each ledger was about twenty pages, and they followed one another in chronological order. Luckily, I struck gold in the second box. One register was slit with a letter hidden inside. I pulled it out. It was the same kind of envelope, the same handwriting. It was addressed to Victoria Jarvis and had been sent from Paris.

September 20, 1914

Darling Vic,

I am safe, and the Germans' seemingly unstoppable war machine has been halted. For a few fearful weeks, it did look like the Boche would take Paris. Indeed, at several points in early

September I could hear the artillery fire from Avenue de Clichy. But as you know, the Germans were thrown back. They're calling it the "Miracle of the Marne," but whispers in the streets claim that the victory is not due to divine providence but to the Boche's love of wine. You see, the Marne is in champagne country, and apparently when people returned to their vineyards after the battle, they found thousands of empty wine bottles scattered about the fields, orchards, cellars, living rooms, and even bedchambers . . . In short, the Boche were too soused to fight. That should give the temperance movement pause!

In your last letter, you pleaded with me to flee Paris, and I must admit that during those dark days of early September I wished I had sought a safer haven. Still, the sound of shells has receded now, and Paris is a different city. The newspapers aren't publishing anymore, the government has decamped to Bordeaux, and most stores are "Fermé pour la cause de mobilization." If the patron himself hasn't been called up, then certainly his clerks have been sent to the front. I had to walk a mile before I could find somewhere to buy a loaf of bread. The streets are devoid of carriages and motorcars, and civilian movements are limited, but the boulevards swarm with soldiers. They are mostly French, although the tattered remains of the Belgian and British armies are also about.

You will think me mad, but I am glad I stayed. I find it quite exhilarating. Momentous things are happening, and I'm at the center of world events. I feel alive and fairly tingle with excitement. The only comparison I can draw is that first kiss we shared, when we skated together that magical evening. Feeling your soft lips upon mine and the quick patter of your heart against my chest, I was filled with exhilaration, fear, and joy. You bewitched me that night, my love, and I have been besotted ever since.

Now tell me of home. You write disgustedly of the war hysteria, the "squeaking journalists braying for Prussian blood," and the long lines of men eagerly enlisting. I have a confession to make, darling, and one that will not please you. In the heat of the attack, when the German triumph seemed a foregone conclusion, I attempted to enlist. I know you feel this war is misguided and that we have no place in it. Intellectually, I agree with you, my darling. When the guns were shaking Paris, however, I forgot those pacifist ideals. Instead, I was driven by an atavistic need to join my fellows in facing danger. How could I consider myself a man if I did not sign up? Like you, I had heard the rumors of German atrocities in Belgium, the bayoneted babies, the dishonored women. I was determined to play my part, even though I knew my actions would distress you terribly. I can confess this all to you now with equanimity, because I was rejected by the French Army—my lungs too weakened by the consumption I suffered from as a child. I will not be going to the front.

Now that things have settled down again, I am glad I did not enlist. You are quite wise, I believe, to discount those atrocity stories. I do not believe them either. After all, as much as the Germans are vilified, we come from the same stock. We have the same ideals, religion, art. If the Germans can be guilty of such barbarity, then that means that such a capacity is within us as well. But perhaps that is the greatest lesson to be gained from the war: we are all capable of great evil.

Jem's words brought me crashing back to the present. I had seen great evil this morning—and would have to return to the same place tonight. I pushed that thought away and picked up the letter again.

While I am not inclined to believe the most outrageous stories about German cruelty, the plight of the refugees is heartbreaking. They are a steady, tragic stream now, pouring in from the east. I wish I could convey to you the expression of their faces—it is a look of dumb horror at what they have seen.

The other day I came across a family of these poor souls selling some possessions by the side of the road. They were a wretched-looking lot, their clothes in tatters, signs of hunger pinching their faces. The man said they had fled Flanders steps ahead of the kaiser's army. They had arrived in Paris hoping to find work, but of course no one is hiring. He told me they were destitute. I explained that I did not have much money myself, but the look in his eyes was so compelling that I gave in and examined his goods. He was selling a dirty portrait of an older man. The brushstrokes were lovely, and the painter played wonderfully with light and shadow. The Belgian told me the painting had been in his family for generations. I told him I had only a few francs, but he settled up quickly. Poor bugger was starving.

When I got the portrait home, I realized that it was even better than I had first thought. I've cleaned the dust and muck off and have propped it beside my bed. I'm taking comfort and inspiration from the image. It reminds me of many of the beautiful paintings I stared at for hours at the Rijksmuseum. The painter has done a tremendous job in capturing the old fellow. His eyes are calm and soft, the irises picking up the light beautifully. Even the wrinkles covering his face look real.

Enough of my prattle. Let us turn to serious matters—you, my dearest one. I laughed aloud at your description of your aunt Therese: "Trying to get a smile from her is like squeezing sunshine from a cucumber!" Keep squeezing, darling. You are too adorable not to love wholeheartedly! It is late, and I must sign off now.

I miss you,

Jem

I sighed with pleasure. Jem's voice was coming through, and I felt like I knew him well. The letter itself was excellent and would be very useful for an article, containing as it did an artist's perceptions of Paris in the First World War. I looked through the remaining boxes but didn't locate any other letters. I photocopied the one I found and placed the original back in the ledger. I put all three boxes on my book cart and sent an email to circulation asking them to send me the next three boxes in the Jarvis series.

Only when I had finished all of my tasks and noticed the hour did the sick feeling from this morning come back. It was time to return to the scene of the crime.

CHAPTER FIVE

I GRABBED MY BIG BLUE COAT AND SHRUGGED INTO IT. THERE WAS A hard, nauseating knot in my stomach as I thought about returning to the facility. I decided to go home first, cowardly putting off the inevitable. I'd have some dinner and climb into comfy clothes before going back. My thirty-minute walk home was how I usually unwound from job stresses, and I could feel my body unclenching as I crossed Bay Street and entered the Garden of the Provinces and Territories.

The city had put flags at regular intervals celebrating the Vancouver Olympics and the colors of the Olympic rings were a bright splash on a gray evening. Passing by a stand of trees, I breathed deeply. The wind seemed to blow away my fears, and I felt better than I had all day. It was good to be outside, despite the cold.

Growing up in a house that was always overflowing with strange people, I spent a lot of time outside. Even in the dead of winter, my sister and I would roam around Toronto's wild ravines, pretending to be Shackleton leading his men through the Antarctic ice floes.

It was getting dark, and an icy wind howled down from the north. I burrowed my face into my scarf and walked on. Moving away from the park, I crossed a vast, windswept parking lot. In the far distance, a few civil servants scuttled into their cars, but there was no one near me. After the park's sheltering trees, I felt exposed as I pushed against the strong wind.

To distract myself from my feeling of vulnerability, I turned my mind to Jem and Victoria. Did his painting career take off? Did they marry and have a passel of kids? I would have to do some serious research tomorrow.

After walking across the parking lot, I approached my neighborhood. I lived west of the city center, in Hintonburg, a working-class area where I rented the first floor of a tiny house. The neighborhood was bisected by Wellington Street, the main shopping thoroughfare. I lived north of Wellington, in the decidedly less prosperous part. Ninety-year-old row houses huddled together, their tired front porches drooping. I passed a diner, Capital City Canteen, and a couple of deserted lots. A few buses rumbled past, but otherwise there was remarkably little traffic. Indeed, it was strangely quiet. I could even hear the crunch of someone's feet on the snow behind me, walking at my pace.

At a stoplight, I turned. Half a block back, a large figure muffled in a heavy dark overcoat, thick scarf, and large tuque walked toward me. The light changed, and I crossed the street.

I could hear the person behind me jogging to make the light. We walked on along the empty sidewalk, and I was acutely aware of the sound of his boots in the snow. Was he getting closer? The image of the commissionaire's body floated back to me. I walked faster.

Was it my imagination, or did the person pick up the pace? I moved even more rapidly, and I could hear him hurrying to keep up. Adrenaline zipped through my veins. The figure was close now. I could hear his labored breathing. If he wanted to, he could reach out and grab me. For a moment, all I could see was the dead man from this morning—the congealed blood around his wound, his waxen face.

Then I remembered some advice from the self-defense workshop my mother had dragged me to at sixteen: if you seem tough, you are less likely to be attacked. I stopped, turned around, and walked back toward the person, willing myself to stare calmly at him. He looked down, concealing his face, and kept walking. We passed each other on the sidewalk.

Feeling a little queasy and not wanting to be outside anymore, I hurried back to Capital City Cantine. As soon as I was seated, a comforting cup of coffee warming my hands, I was able to think more rationally about the encounter. I was jumpy from discovering that body. The murderer didn't know who I was and had no reason to be interested in me, anyway.

Nonetheless, going out to the Conservation Facility right away seemed smart. If I left now, there might still be some conservators working late. At least it would be better than sitting at home, listening to the wind howl. Using my flip phone, I called a cab and waited inside until it came. Then, for the second time that day, I headed over the provincial border.

◇◇◇◇◇◇◇

THE TAXI PULLED UP IN FRONT OF THE IMPRESSIVE SWEEP OF THE CON-servation Facility. The North Star shone strong and sure overhead, and the building's crystalline hull gleamed eerily in the night.

The morning's feelings of panic rushed back to me as I walked into the lobby. I took a deep breath, flashed my work badge to the commissionaire behind the desk, and then headed toward the vaults.

"Hang on, missy."

I stopped. The commissionaire, a man in his mid-sixties with light-brown skin, shuffled toward me. "You can't go in there. There's been a murder."

"I know," I said tiredly. "I'm not going to the Art Vault. I have to go to Vault Seven."

The commissionaire was short and very slight. His frailness was accentuated by the wispy white hair standing up all over his head. "No, no. The cops have denied access to that vault too. It's in lock-down." He said this with a dramatic flourish, obviously thrilled by the excitement of the situation.

"Why would they seal Vault Seven?" My voice quavered. "They didn't discover another body, did they?"

The commissionaire led me back to his desk, his eyes alight with gossip. "Only the one. A young lady found it this morning."

"I know. That was me." I regretted the words the instant they left my mouth.

"You!" This seemed to please him enormously. "Tell me everything!"

"I'd rather not talk about it."

The commissionaire's eyes softened. "Of course, you poor, poor girl." He extended a hand. "Name's Ernie, by the way."

I smiled and shook. "I'm Jess."

Despite his sympathy, it didn't seem like Ernie could keep from talking about the murder. After a moment of contemplative silence, he launched back into it. "I saw on the news it was Paul Thibodeau who got killed. It makes me a little nervous. What if there's a serial killer out there who's got a beef against commissionaires?"

I seriously doubted that the graying legions of commissionaires, usually retired army vets who hadn't seen boot camp in decades, would be targeted by a serial killer. Remembering my conversation with Oliver, I hypothesized, "Maybe he stumbled across a theft and tried to stop it."

"I don't think so. They inventoried the major works this morning and didn't find anything gone. Anyway, I doubt Thibodeau would have taken a bullet to stop someone from stealing. More likely he was the one doing the robbing."

I was interested in spite of myself. "What do you mean?" I asked.

"I don't like to speak ill of the dead," he demurred.

I felt embarrassed to be gossiping about a murder victim, but before I could change the subject, Ernie continued. "Thibodeau had some pretty rough friends."

"Really?"

"I think they might have been in a biker gang. I know Thibodeau used to hang out at that scuzzy bar in Mechanicsville with them."

I knew the place. Leo's Tavern was only a few blocks north of my apartment and seemed to attract a clientele of large men in leather.

Ernie continued, "They showed up on huge motorcycles once as I was starting my shift. I was a little late, because the wife was sick. Paul was so mad at me, he cursed me out! Then these two big guys— leather jackets, prison tattoos—came to get him. They weren't from a quilting bee, that's for sure!"

"Whoa, so you think maybe Thibodeau was giving them the lay

of the land? Setting up a plan to rob the vault and something went wrong?"

"Who knows? I can tell you one thing, though. Thibodeau wasn't the ringleader. One of his friends would have been the brains."

"Why do you say that?"

"Thibodeau wasn't very bright. I remember once in the staff room we were talking about how the paparazzi killed poor Princess Diana. He said that he didn't understand why the opera singer was chasing her in the first place."

It took me a second to get it, and then I laughed. "Have you told the cops all this?" I asked.

"No one's asked me anything yet."

"Isn't that typical?" I couldn't help saying. "They grill me this morning, and I know nothing, meanwhile they've got a guy sitting right under their noses with insider information, and they haven't even bothered to talk to you!"

"Insider information," Ernie repeated with a grin.

"Now they've sealed off all the vaults. How's that going to help them catch the killer?" I continued venting my annoyance. "I'm not going to be able to get my document tonight." I was going to have to make a third damn trip out here, probably early on Monday morning. The taxis were going to bankrupt me, and if all didn't go well it would put me on very thin ice with Oliver.

CHAPTER SIX

"ACTUALLY," ERNIE SAID. "ONLY VAULT SEVEN AND THE ART VAULT ARE closed. Everything else is open."

That didn't help. Vault Seven was where I needed to go. I must have looked grim because Ernie said, "Do you have anything you could do in the other vaults? I'd hate for you to have wasted a trip."

My impression from Oliver was that any Belgian document would do for the delegation. The problem was that there were literally millions of records stored behind the vault walls. Narrowing my search down was impossible without looking at the catalog. "Do you have access to the reference and tracking database?" I asked Ernie.

"I'm pretty sure I do. Want to use it?"

"That would be awesome!"

We moved over to the computer. I watched as Ernie squinted at the screen, typing in two-fingered hunt-and-peck fashion. He logged on and scrolled through the programs. "We've got all kinds of stuff on here that the cops looked at."

"Yeah?" I asked. I was anxious to get to the database.

Ernie wasn't a man to be rushed, however. He pointed to the program on his screen called Vault Access.

"The cops have been using this one all day. It records the pass number of every employee who goes into every vault and their time of entry." He scrolled through the program, and vault numbers next to lists of names and times of entry flashed by.

"Well, that should make it easy to catch the killer."

"Under regular circumstances it would, but there's no record of anyone entering or leaving the Art Vault for the twenty-four-hour period around the murder."

"How is that possible?"

"Best they can figure is that someone who knew the system shut it down. It's easy to do, and apparently untraceable. They had computer people here all day trying to figure out who did it."

"So is my entrance to the vault the first one recorded for the day?"

"You're not on there. The tracking stopped sometime on Thursday afternoon and it didn't come back online until we realized it had been tampered with, after the murder."

I recalled the cameras that were dotted throughout the facility. "What about the video? Can't the cops use that?"

"Someone shut it off for the period in question."

"Shouldn't Abdel or another one of the commissionaires have noticed that the video to the Art Vault was turned off?" It had been pretty easy for a murderer to sneak in.

Ernie bristled. "We've got a lot on the go, here." He pointed to a television screen where a shot of Vault Fifteen's steel door appeared. Color photographs were stored there at a chilly three degrees Celsius and in carefully controlled humidity levels. After five seconds, the shot changed, and it was Vault Sixteen's door.

"The images from the security cameras scroll through like that?"

"Yup. No one noticed that the Art Vault wasn't coming up."

"Maybe not the best system, in retrospect."

Ernie snorted. "You're telling me. We used to have a bank of screens and could watch every vault. There were budget cutbacks, and they got the chop. I think we're going to have a major security overhaul now that Thibodeau was murdered."

I shuddered, and Ernie belatedly remembered that I was the one who had made that discovery. "Sorry, dear."

Ernie was still bumbling over the computer, trying to close the Vault Access system, scrolling up and down through the program.

"What's that?" I asked as he passed a group of names highlighted in red.

"Oh, those are people who have blanket access to all vaults. We added a dozen names to it today, so the police can get in everywhere."

I nodded thoughtfully. Oliver's name was on that list.

"Here we are," said Ernie. He double-clicked on the reference and tracking system and stepped out of the way. I typed in some key words and began reading file descriptions for records. I found what I needed pretty quickly: a box of External Affairs documents from 1970 containing letters between the Belgian and Canadian prime ministers. While it wasn't the Olympics document that Oliver requested, there might be something there to satisfy the delegation's half-hour visit.

I jotted down the location information and thanked Ernie before heading off. Vault Twenty was on the second level. Because it contained only paper records with no prestige or monetary value, my general access pass would open it. Its entrance was at the other end of the Conservation Facility, and I was glad I wouldn't have to walk down the Art Vault corridor again.

Despite my hopes of bumping into colleagues, the building felt deserted. I knew it was probably swarming with police, but there was no one around. My footsteps echoed as I crossed the vast entrance hall. There was no elevator to the second level of vaults. Instead, researchers used a long, gradually inclined walkway along the west side of the building that brought them up to the second floor without even realizing it.

The concrete mass of vaults was to my right, but on the left was an eight-story glass wall soaring up to the roof. The swirling wind blew the snow in gusts outside, their eerie shapes dimly illuminated by the distant streetlights.

The snow reminded me of the nights I spent winter camping and telling ghost stories with my Girl Guide group. The scariest was the tale of the windigo, the Cree legend about the spirit who haunts lonely places, preying upon travelers. It teases them, whispering in their ears but never appearing. Eventually, the windigo will drive a person so mad, they will run into the frigid wilderness to die alone, totally separated from their loved ones.

Something smashed against the glass. I yelped, staring at the window. The wind had thrown a dead branch against the building's wall.

I hurried up the rest of the walkway, which ended in an open exhibition space housing a show on the history of postage. I felt safer here. This was where I'd eaten my lunch while working at the Conservation Facility—not because I was interested in postage, but because there was never anyone else around. Not a lot of tourists made the long trek out to Gatineau to see something they could buy at the post office for fifty-seven cents.

A discreet green light above a steel door was the only indication that this was the entrance to the second-level vaults. I pushed through the entry to a long hallway of vaults. Finding number twenty, I swiped my card, and the heavy door swung open. I was greeted by yawning darkness. A now-familiar feeling of panic clawed at my throat, but then I remembered that the vault lighting was on motion detection. Taking a deep breath, I stepped into the room's dark mouth, and the fluorescent lights flickered on. I moved quickly, trying not to think about dead bodies.

The shelf I needed was to the left of the door. I found it and turned the wheel to open up an aisle. I sagged with relief when the mechanism moved smoothly, creating a wide space. My hands shook as I pulled the correct box from the shelving. I schooled myself to calm down; the last thing I wanted was to spill its contents and have to spend more time in here cleaning up a mess.

I found the file and leafed through it until I located something interesting—a letter from the Belgian prime minister talking about the last time he skated on the Rideau Canal. That would play well with everyone. I pulled the document, flagged the spot I took it from, popped the box back in its place on the shelf, and then put the original document into an interim box, jotting down its barcode number. My work was done.

I marched back along the walkway, no longer nervous about the white shapes swirling beyond the glass. Instead, my attention was drawn to the gray walls of the vaults. What had gone on in there last night? Who killed Thibodeau, and why? Something nagged at my mind about the murder, but I couldn't pin it down. Maybe talking to Ernie again could jog my memory.

I rounded the corner and stopped short. The cop from this morning, Daniel Lemieux, was talking to Ernie. Damn. I'd had enough chats with the officer in charge for one day. I turned around, but he saw me.

"Bonsoir, Mademoiselle Novak," Lemieux called out. "You're not running away from me now, are you?"

CHAPTER SEVEN

I GRITTED MY TEETH AND WALKED TOWARD LEMIEUX. "HELLO, OFFICER.
Still at work?"

"Oui oui. Murder investigations take much time. We don't stop
until we catch our killer." He gave me a hard stare.

I was pleased to see him looking a bit more disheveled this evening. His gelled curls were a little fuzzier, and his loosened tie revealed even more chest hair. He seemed tired.

"Did you get what you needed, miss?" Ernie asked.

"Yes, thanks. I put the document in a viewing box, and I'll get circ
to move it on Monday morning."

Lemieux interrupted. "So, mademoiselle, what are you doing here?
Surely it's late for you?"

"I had to come back to finish this morning's job."

Lemieux made a show of flipping through his black notebook.
"Retrieving a document for your employer?"

"Yeah, that's right. Though you guys made that difficult for me."

"How so?"

"You didn't need to close Vault Seven. I had to get in there and
couldn't."

"Ah, of course! But that's exactly why we closed down that vault.
Your interest in it made it interesting to us."

"You think I might have had something to do with the murder?
That's crazy!"

"We must be thorough." His smile was friendly, but he sure as hell
wasn't. Until this moment, the fact that I was a suspect in a murder
case hadn't fully sunk in. I realized I could be in serious trouble.

"At any rate, we have gone over Vault Seven carefully and have found nothing suspicious. I have authorized its reopening."

I wondered if I should go back and retrieve the Olympics document that Oliver originally requested, but I was too tired. My fear at being a suspect struggled with my annoyance. If Lemieux was a better cop, he would be catching the damn killer instead of complicating the lives of innocent people like me. "I told you I'm not the murderer."

Lemieux lost the smile. "Where exactly did you go in this big, empty building?"

"I was on the second level, trying to find a document to get my boss off my back."

"It's true," Ernie piped up. "She was in Vault Twenty the whole time." Ernie pointed to his computer. My name and pass number were on the screen with the time I entered and left the vault.

I knew I should be conciliatory, but something about Lemieux made me combative. "See. Like I told you. Shouldn't you be pounding the pavement, catching the guy who actually did this?"

He didn't seem to notice my attitude. "We're using all the data available to us and are confident in our abilities to make an arrest."

"Great sound bite. Now, if you don't need me, I'm going to head home. Ernie, can you call me a taxi?"

"Why don't I give you a lift?" Lemieux asked. "I'm heading into Ottawa myself."

I hesitated. Given that I was a suspect, I doubted his offer was entirely altruistic, but I could handle myself. I nodded.

Lemieux and I faced the biting cold as he led me over to his car, casually parked in the spot specifically reserved for the chief archivist. It was a sports car, a low-slung black thing. He opened my door and then hurried around to his side. I sunk into the soft leather upholstery as he made a show of carefully knocking his boots against the car's side before getting in. He glanced reproachfully at my feet, which were already depositing snow and salt on his pristine floor mat.

He started the powerful engine with a roar, and the car filled with the sounds of the Quebec alt-folk rockers La Bottine Souriante. He moved to turn off the music.

"No, leave it. I like them."

"You know Quebec music?" His tone was surprised and he turned down the volume a little so that we could talk.

"A bit. I like La Bottine. They've got a good beat."

"Most Anglos don't know anything about Quebec culture." We turned onto Maloney Boulevard, a busy four-lane road that cut through Gatineau.

"My mother always tried to get us interested in different types of music. I've got an encyclopedic knowledge of Indian sitar playing too."

Lemieux grinned. "Your mother. I've done a little research on you since we last met."

My heart sank. Being Cassie Novak's daughter had never brought me anything but grief.

"She's a . . . How do you call it? A 'shit disturber.' She got a lot of cops in hot water down there in Toronto."

My mother, an investigative journalist, had exposed some major police corruption back in the nineties. The cops paid her back by harassing her for years. They pulled her over on bogus speeding charges, hassled her about the help she gave to prostitutes and street kids, and once even arrested her on a trumped-up solicitation charge. "I think those cops got themselves in trouble." Probably not the smartest thing to say.

"She must be a brave woman," he said.

"More like a pain in the ass," I replied.

"It's not always easy living up to our parents, is it?"

His attempt at subtle interrogation was irritating, and I began to wonder if I wouldn't have been better off in a cab. "No, that's right. That's why I randomly murdered a security guard this morning. Because of my issues with my mother."

He laughed. "You're pretty *défensive*." He pronounced the word with a French accent. "Anything to concern me?"

I wasn't handling this well. I sighed and spoke truthfully. "You're right about my mother. I get prickly talking about her. She can be hard to deal with."

Lemieux merged the car into the flow of traffic on Autoroute Fifty, and we hummed along quietly for a time. He broke the silence, speaking with studied casualness. "Anyway, he wasn't murdered in the morning. It was sometime yesterday evening."

"Should you be telling your prime suspect this?"

He smiled. "I misled you earlier. You were a suspect until about an hour ago. Then we received confirmation from the restaurant, May Lynh's, that you were there until midnight. Too late to kill Thibodeau."

I spoke sourly. "Why'd you close Vault Seven if you knew I wasn't the killer?"

"Like I said, we must be thorough. Anyway, don't worry about it. You're off the cook."

I stared at him in puzzlement until I realized what he meant. "Hook," I corrected. "The expression is 'off the hook.'"

"That makes more sense." He laughed.

I didn't join in, resentful of the trouble he put me through. "It sounds like Thibodeau's buddies were pretty shady. You should look there."

Lemieux glanced at me. "What do you mean?"

I regretted opening my mouth, but it was too late. "Well, my source tells me that Thibodeau might have some biker gang connections."

I was disappointed in Lemieux's reaction. Either he knew this information already or he had an amazing poker face. In any event, he didn't pursue that line with me, instead saying, "You seem awfully interested in the case."

I shrugged. "I'm not Nancy Drew-ing, if that's what you're worried about."

"Nancy Drew?"

"Yeah, girl detective—drove a convertible, had strawberry blonde hair and a sexless boyfriend named Ned Nickerson. It's not important. I meant I'm not trying to solve this case. People talk is all."

"Anyone say anything about how Thibodeau might have accessed the vault?"

I knew I shouldn't continue this line of conversation, but I was cursed with my mother's curiosity. "What do you mean?"

"He got into the building by bypassing the retinal scan at the back door. Then, he or someone else shut down the tracking system, not to mention the cameras. None of which is that hard to do, as it turns out."

Why was he telling me all of this?

As if in response to my unspoken question, the answer came immediately. "His murderer must have also been aware of the security measure. What we're trying to figure out is how many peoples would know that kind of thing."

"Know what, exactly?"

He sighed. "About the Conservation Facility security. The outside camera caught two figures going into the building through the loading bay around eight o'clock last night. We think one of them was Thibodeau and the other was his murderer. They kept their faces covered when they passed the camera and timed their entrance to avoid the commissionaire's walk-through. A half hour later, only one person left, wearing a shapeless coat and a scarf muffling his or her face."

Fear tightened my stomach and widened my eyes. Lemieux had described the person following me earlier that evening. I opened my mouth to tell the detective but thought better of it. It was freezing and three-quarters of Ottawa's population wore big coats and scarves. It might all be a coincidence and I didn't want to give Lemieux any reason to take further interest in me.

"It would be helpful if you could tell me if these methods of getting around security are *connu*—known," he said.

I shook my head. "I didn't know any of that, but I've only worked here for a few months. It sounds like Thibodeau and the killer knew each other. Maybe he told his murderer about the cameras."

We were off the highway now and passing through Hull, an older part of Gatineau. Lemieux turned onto the Chaudière Bridge, and we crossed to the Ontario side. For a moment I wondered how he knew where I lived, then realized he probably knew a lot about me. He pulled onto Pinhey Street, and his eyes darted down its length. He grunted. "This isn't a good neighborhood."

Lemieux wasn't wrong, although Pinhey Street was on the edge of a slow gentrification. The neighborhood a few blocks south had transformed into a haven for Volvo-driving golden retriever owners. Unfortunately, Pinhey wasn't quite there yet. We passed an abandoned home, windows boarded up, roof sunken in. Despite its desolate appearance, light seeped out as someone wrenched open the door and scurried in. "Yeah, but the crack houses keep the rents down," I joked.

Lemieux pulled up in front of my place. "It was good talking to you, Mademoiselle Novak."

I smiled, relieved that I had made it home without saying anything too stupid. "Likewise, Detective."

I have to admit, although he was a pain in the ass, it was nice to know that Lemieux sat and watched me get safely through my door before pulling away.

◇◇◇◇◇◇◇

MY APARTMENT WAS TINY AND SMELLED FAINTLY OF WET FEET, BUT IT was all I could afford on my probationary salary. There were four messages from Adela on my machine, and she came over as soon as I called her. Adela's parents were immigrants from El Salvador who moved to a tiny Northern Ontario community when she was two. Although we came from very different backgrounds, we were assigned the same dorm room in our first year at the University of Western Ontario and had clung together through a boozy and bewildering frosh week. That had been enough to cement our friendship and we'd been best friends ever since. Adela had a steely determination that I both admired and feared.

It was a huge relief to talk about the past twenty-four hours with her. By the time I'd finished going over it all, my dread and panic faded. I could understand the events more rationally now, and the horror was lessened.

Adela was all business when I told her about my potential stalker. After staying the night to keep me company, we spent Saturday morning making my apartment more secure. At her direction, we bought a new dead bolt for my door and light bulbs to replace those that had burned out on the porch and in the hall, and we programmed 911 into the speed dial on my landline. Adela next called my deadbeat landlord and browbeat him into promising to fix the loose catch on the window in the bedroom. She left only after she was satisfied that I was completely and totally safe.

CHAPTER EIGHT

ON MONDAY MORNING, I ENTERED MY OFFICE DELIGHTED TO SEE THAT circulation had already replaced the previous boxes of Jarvis material with new ones. Before opening them I checked my email. Oliver had sent me a note reminding me about the Belgian delegation and tersely hoping that all was in order. I didn't know how he was going to react to the fact that I had provided a different document to the one he'd requested. It was funny, but only a few days ago, such concerns would have been my biggest stress. Now I pushed the worry away and turned to my boxes. I opened them quickly and was rewarded with another letter.

> October 5, 1914
>
> Dear Vic,
>
> I miss you too, sweetheart. My desperation to see you grows with each day that we are separated. I feel a piece of me is absent, that part where my courage and strength reside. You have stirred a glow within me that no other woman has succeeded in kindling.
>
> Let me assure you once again: I am safe. News is not always reliable, but I believe there is heavy fighting in Antwerp at the moment. If the city falls, it will make Britain that much more vulnerable to invasion from across the Channel, but I cannot believe it will come to that. In fact, I cannot believe that this insane war will continue for much longer. There has already been so much death and destruction. It will end soon.
>
> Ironically, wartime Paris is enchanting. Indeed, now that they are enforcing the blackout, the city is particularly lovely. The moon

shines down upon the boulevards, marble monuments, and ancient squares, its glow unrivaled by automobile lights or streetlamps. The play of starlight on the Seine glitters like fireflies on the river's surface.

This is not to say that the city is quiet. During the day the streets are alive with activity. The great department stores are open for business once more. It is interesting to note that while patriotic French women abjure the theatres, tearooms, and concerts, they cannot resist the lure of the store's sales and reductions.

My friend André was one of the first men mobilized, and a wound to his shoulder has already returned him to Paris. It is in talking to him that I realize how profoundly this war is changing our civilization, our way of thinking. Where once he talked of Picasso, Braque, and the new cubism, now he can speak only of what he saw on the battlefield. According to him, the human element has been all but eliminated. It is a war of machine against machine. Great guns strafing the ground, shells exploding from the sky. It is nothing like the glorious test of manhood the newspapers would have us believe.

In a way it is just as well that André lost interest in his old manner of painting. There is a great outcry here against "degenerate" art, which is what they call anything nonfigurative. The ignorant feel that cubism and its ilk are inventions of the Germanic mind and are highly suspicious of experimentation. I shan't give into such attitudes, however. I have embraced the new style and will persevere despite any censure.

From your letter it seems that the war is bringing out the worst in our small, narrow-minded country. I commend you for remonstrating with the Red Cross lady, but darling, is there any point? Attitudes such as these, especially in farm country, are ingrained. You are having a difficult enough time with your aunt and uncle as it is; perhaps it is best to keep your pacifist thoughts to yourself?

What am I saying? I am like King Canute, trying to hold back the tide! You could no more stifle your thoughts on peace, women's suffrage, or socialism than I could stop painting. You are my beautiful radical, but perhaps you won't have to keep fighting with your aunt and uncle for much longer.

Have you noticed anything different in this letter, my darling? A hint that despite all of the horror around me, I am feeling optimistic? Ah, you always were perceptive! I will not hold you in suspense; indeed, it has been difficult not mentioning it until now.

Remember the painting I told you about buying from the refugees? I became curious about it last night, so I popped it out of its frame and examined it more carefully. My heart nearly stopped when I saw the signature: "Rembrandt." I know it sounds unbelievable, but the autograph only confirmed what drew me to the painting in the first place—the extraordinary use of light and shadow and the superb brushstrokes. I had not spent days studying his great works in Amsterdam to come away blind to the master's style. I have been doing some research, and there do appear to be some "lost" Rembrandts. As mad as it may seem, I have stumbled across one!

Flanders is neighbor to Holland, and the refugee who sold it to me told me the portrait had been in his family for generations. It is perfectly conceivable that the family never even realized what a masterpiece lay concealed in plain sight!

I thought of you as soon as I read that signature. I will sell the painting. Rembrandt's work fetches large sums of money, enough for us to live comfortably until my career takes flight. We can both return from banishment and resume our lives. We can attend all of the dinners, dances, summer picnics, and winter skating parties we desire; only this time I shall be standing proudly by your side, rather than skulking in shadow. Your father will be forced to approve.

Think of the possibilities! The Rembrandt gives us freedom, darling. When this war is over (and it cannot last much longer!) we could go anywhere. Perhaps we need to give up on Western civilization altogether. We could move somewhere quiet and simple. Perhaps we will follow in the footsteps of Gauguin and go to some Pacific isle. The tropical light and the colors would inspire my painting.

You could spend your time educating the natives, or liberating their women! Would it not be wonderful to flee Canada's tired morality and upright stuffiness?

All I can think of is seeing you again, touching you. That last night we spent together was the most important of my life. I've never loved anyone the way I love you, and I can't wait to hold you again. I miss you, Vic. From the smell of your hair to that adorable freckle behind your left knee.

I love you,

Jem

I put the letter aside with a shake of my head. What a romantic idiot. There was no way he'd found a Rembrandt, but I jotted a note to myself to follow up. If nothing else, his delusions about lost masterpieces and running away to Tahiti were excellent article fodder. Not only did the letters reveal a wartime perspective of Paris, but they were also a powerful personal narrative. I could see the title of my paper now: "Young Love, Foolish Dreams: An Artist in First World War Paris."

I slipped the letter into an acid-free folder. I would photocopy it later. What I needed now was to find out more about Victoria Jarvis and Jem Crawford. I needed some expert guidance.

◇◇◇◇◇◇

LOUISE WAS SCOWLING AT HER COMPUTER WHEN I POKED MY HEAD IN her office. "Hey, Jess. Come in here and help me with this thing." Louise banged the side of the machine with her hand.

"Okay, okay. Don't hurt it," I said. "You'll never get it to work by being mean. What's the problem?"

"It keeps making lists when I want to write a paragraph."

I looked over at what she had done and unclicked "bullets and numbering." Her text reverted to normal.

"How did you do that?" she asked.

Louise might have been one of the most brilliant historians at the

Dominion Archives, but she couldn't work a computer to save her life. I was surprised to see her sitting in front of one. Usually she wrote everything on an enormous electric typewriter that took up most of her processing table.

"Why aren't you using the beast?" I asked, pointing to the typewriter.

"Because Oliver, that merde eater, won't pay for its repairs. He says I have to join the twenty-first century."

"He's a jerk," I agreed. "Listen, do you want to get a coffee?"

"Sure, sure."

We shrugged into our coats and headed for the café across the street. We usually tried to avoid the archives' basement cafeteria. As soon as we were on the street, Louise patted her pockets before stopping with a laugh. "I keep forgetting I quit," she said. "Damn, I miss smoking. So, I hear you had quite the day on Friday."

I didn't mind talking to Louise about the murder, and I told her the whole story as we walked to the coffee shop.

Louise looked thoughtful when I finished my tale. "Câlice, Jess. You poor kid!"

I smiled ruefully. "It was probably a lot worse for the dead guy."

"Maybe, or maybe he deserved it."

I was startled by her vehemence. "Well, the murder was all people were talking about on Friday. Where were you, by the way?"

Louise waved her hand. "I wasn't feeling so good."

I looked at her in astonishment. Louise prided herself on never missing a day of work. "The Great Louise called in sick?"

She didn't respond, opening the door to the café. The soothing tones of Norah Jones filled our ears, and we ordered from a nose-ringed server with black nail polish and a sweet smile.

I paid for my drink and turned to Louise. "Anyway, I wanted to ask you about something else. Something to do with work."

We took our coffees and walked to a table at the far side of the room. "I'm trying to figure out what to do with some letters I found in the ledgers I'm working on for Oliver."

Louise leaned forward. "The Jarvis stuff? What did you find?"

"Love letters from Paris during the First World War."

She let out a low whistle. "That could be very promising. We're always looking for the personal angle to attract attention. You might even be able to get some media coverage. The public laps up romantic stories." She paused. "Oliver doesn't know that they're there?"

"I don't think so."

She relaxed. "Good. Jess, you need to write an article on them. Publish tout de suite. If Oliver finds out about them, he'll take over and you won't get your chance."

I smiled. "I figured that's how you'd think. I need your help though. I don't know how to go about this."

"Well, you should research as much as you can about the people, get their background. Figure out what happened to them."

"I've got the letters in my office. I could show—"

Louise interrupted. "No, you have to be careful in this place. Don't trust anyone. We're all out for our own professional glory, and any one of us would shoot you in the back if it meant we could publish."

"Easy on the talk about shooting people, okay?" I pushed my coffee away, suddenly queasy.

"Merde, I'm sorry." Her voice was intense. "What I said is true. People here are out for themselves. Trust no one." The roughness of her tone made me wonder for a moment if we were talking about the letters or something else entirely.

CHAPTER NINE

I DEBATED FOLLOWING UP WITH LOUISE ABOUT WHAT SHE MEANT, BUT I let it drop. One thing I had learned about my friend was that she couldn't be pressed for information. I changed the topic. "If you needed to find out something about people from the past, what's the first thing you'd do?"

She took a sip of her coffee before responding. "Well, if you have only names and no dates of birth or anything, I'd start with official documents. Check out provincial birth and death registries, parish records, try to get a fix on when they were born, when they got married, that kind of thing."

Although I held a master's in archival science, I knew very little about research techniques. My courses had concentrated on other aspects, things like copyright and privacy laws, the best preservation methods, and how to arrange and describe material. Doing actual research was something that everyone assumed you'd pick up gradually on the job. Now I needed a crash course. I wrote everything she said down in my notebook.

"You might not have a lot of luck with those registers, though. Record keeping was pretty unreliable before World War One. If you figure out where they lived, check out newspapers from the appropriate cities. Look over the 'hatched, matched, and dispatched' columns."

"The what?" I asked.

"The birth, marriage, and death announcements. Also, if your man enlisted in the army, the records of the Canadian Expeditionary Force might be useful."

She continued talking as we finished our coffees, and my wrist started to ache from the notes I was taking.

The walk back to the office was cold. I kept my head down against the wind, which is why I almost missed the person lurking across the street from the entrance of the Dominion Archives. He wore a bulky dark overcoat, with a scarf wrapped around his face. I glanced back, but he was already gone.

"Did you see that guy?" I asked Louise.

She looked at where I was pointing but shook her head. "No, why?"

I laughed nervously. I was becoming more paranoid than my mother. "No reason."

I let Louise get ahead of me on the staircase. Why did I feel like I was being followed? Was it a hypersensitivity brought on by Friday morning's discovery, or was someone actually monitoring my movements? If the latter, then why? A memory swam below my conscious mind. I frowned trying to catch it. Something I noticed in the vault. Something to do with the body.

Returning to my desk, I retrieved the morning's letter and carried it to the photocopier by Oliver's office. He attended a senior management meeting on Monday mornings, so he was safely out of the way.

I had just closed the lid on the machine and hit Copy when a cold hand tapped my shoulder. I turned, my heart in my throat.

Oliver stood before me, adjusting his lime-green bow tie with one hand. "Good morning, Jess. What are we up to today?"

"Hi!" I said brightly, moving my body to shield the "out" tray, where the copy of the letter was emerging. He shifted to see what was in the tray. I was eager to distract him and blurted out the first thing I thought would interest him. "So, I had another long talk with the lead cop on Friday night."

Bingo. All his curiosity about the copy vanished. "What? Really? Come into my office and tell me everything," he commanded.

What to do? If I followed him, I would be abandoning the letter on the photocopier. If I grabbed the letter, I'd draw Oliver's attention to my activities. I took my chances and left the copy in the tray and the original in the machine. Hopefully our discussion wouldn't take long.

He ushered me into his office. "Sit," he pointed to a chair.

"Thanks, I'd rather stand." This way I could monitor the hall and make sure no one approached the copier.

"Fine, but close the door. It's been a hotbed of gossip here since you found that body." His tone implied that I had discovered Thibodeau to make his life difficult. "I don't want to add grist to the rumor mill."

Damn. I shut his door, taking the opportunity to peer down the hall. Empty. I stood as close to the door as I could and told him about returning to the Conservation Facility and locating the document.

Oliver interrupted. "Yes, I've already been informed. As you know, the chief archivist and the Belgian delegation viewed the item this morning. I was most displeased to hear it was not the document I instructed you to provide."

I heard a noise outside. "Oh, were they unhappy with it?" I asked distractedly.

Oliver coughed. "That is not the point, Jessica. Your inability to carry out a simple request does not reflect well on you."

I reminded myself that I wanted a job. "I'm sorry, Oliver. As I said, the police had sealed off the vault."

"Yes, well, finish what you were telling me then."

As quickly as possible, I relayed what Lemieux had discussed with me. "So, the police seem to think that Thibodeau was working with his murderer," I finished. Did I hear footsteps in the hall?

Oliver looked upset at my conclusion. "This is going to cause us nothing but headaches. They're going to ramp up security. We'll probably have to get new passes!"

Oliver was inordinately proud of the photo on his security pass. He'd shown it to me on several occasions, murmuring about how distinguished his beard made him seem. I thought it looked like a small blonde rat gnawing on his face, but I kept that image to myself.

I made sympathetic noises and put my hand on the doorknob to leave.

"That reminds me, Jessica." Oliver stopped me. "The chief curator, Stephen Nguyen, will be in the Reading Room doing some research this afternoon. He would like to meet with you there at three o'clock."

My focus on the letter abated. "About the Art Vault?" I asked, dreading confirmation.

"Why else would a senior official trouble himself with someone at your level?" Oliver smiled, obviously pleased at the thought of me being chewed out by Stephen.

Those were definitely footsteps. I couldn't think about that problem now. "Okay, I'll be there." I was out the door before Oliver could say anything else.

My heart sank. Mike Roy stood at the photocopier, a stack of papers in his hand.

CHAPTER TEN

MIKE LIFTED THE PHOTOCOPIER LID, AND I BARGED FORWARD, SNATCH-
ing the letter from the glass. Then I grabbed the copy that sat in the
"out" tray.

"Sorry. I didn't mean to leave my papers here, but Oliver called
me into an emergency meeting." I stuffed the two documents into
the folder.

Mike was bemused. "Hi, Jess. How are you doing today?"

Relief made my smile especially wide. "I'm great."

He grinned in return, and the ridiculousness of my behavior
dawned on me. It was one thing to prevent Oliver from seeing the
letter, but Mike wouldn't steal my ideas. In fact, he might be able to
give me some research pointers that Louise overlooked. "I've got a
question for you, actually."

He nodded. "Let me make these copies, and then I'll come to you."

I returned to my office and placed the original letter back into the
ledger, tucking the copy into a file folder.

Mike stopped by and sat down in my other office chair. "What
can I do you for?" he asked. As he crossed his leg, I noticed that he was
wearing mismatched socks and that his cords had a hole in the knee.
I could see blue long johns through the tear.

"I've found correspondence in some old ledgers from Alberta. I'm trying to learn more about them. I know a bit about the man who wrote them
but not as much about the woman. Do you have any tips on finding out
what happened to someone from the early twentieth century?"

Mike looked thoughtful. "Well, start with Google of course."

"What?" I pointed to my notebook. "Louise spent half an hour giving me citations for every obscure reference book under the sun. Now you tell me I can google it?"

"Louise is a phenomenal researcher, but she's a computerphobe. I'm not saying that all you have to do is google, but it's a good place to start."

"So there's more to the internet than the latest pictures of celebrity car crashes or that video of the cat flushing the toilet?" I was surprised to find myself flirting.

Mike laughed, lines crinkling pleasantly around his eyes. "That's right. You'd be amazed at what obscure historical information you can actually dig up. Even the past has entered the digital tomorrow."

"That's almost poetic," I said. "Louise mentioned provincial registers, but I'll need information for Quebec, and maybe Alberta. Would we have those copies?" Since my research budget was nil, there was no way I could trek out to Alberta to dig through records.

"For sure. The Reading Room downstairs has microfilms of all the provincial civil data. What's this woman's name?"

I hesitated, but I didn't want to suspect Mike of poaching my ideas. He'd been so nice, and I had few allies at work. "Jarvis," I said. "Victoria Jarvis."

"Hmm. That's a fairly common name. Do the ledgers offer any clues?"

"In his later life, her uncle became a member of Parliament for Alberta."

"Really? Louise should help you then—she's the political expert."

Louise was firm about not wanting to know the specifics of my project, and I didn't want to bug her more than I already had.

"Oliver's pretty good on that sort of thing too," Mike said. "But I'm guessing you don't want him to know?" He smiled crookedly, and his dimple popped into view.

My heart fluttered unexpectedly. "I'm worried he'd take me off the project and hog all of the glory."

Mike looked grim. "He's been known to do that. You're wise to play this close to the vest. I bet you could find out more about your cabinet minister in the *Who's Who*. That series often gives information about family in there too."

"You're a font of useful information! I don't know how I can thank you!"

Mike blushed. His words came out in a stammer. "Well, actually, you could join me tonight."

Was he asking me on a date? I was too startled to reply.

He rushed into my silence. "For dinner, I mean. With me. We could eat somewhere. Although you probably have plans. Oh damn it—I haven't done this in twenty years." He pushed a hand through his hair, making it stand up on top of his head.

"Mike, I—"

"I know, I know. I'm too old for you. I don't know what I was thinking. Forget the whole thing." He stood up, and in his agitation, knocked the chair over. It hit the floor with a clatter, and he stooped to pick it up. His shoulders were rigid with embarrassment. He replaced the chair and turned to leave.

"I was going to say that I would love to have dinner with you."

He stopped in the doorway. His smile was uncertain. "Really? I mean, great."

"Cool, what time?"

He pushed his hand through his hair again. "Um, let's go after work?"

"That sounds good," I said, and Mike left with a nod.

As soon as he was gone, I second-guessed my decision. Dating someone from work was not a good idea. Then an image of his flustered blush floated into my mind. He was a nice guy, and I didn't have many friends at work. What could it hurt? While I was a new and junior employee, it wasn't like Mike was my supervisor or anything. Besides, he filled out those threadbare cords surprisingly well . . .

Thoughts of Mike faded as I remembered my impending meeting with Stephen Nguyen. He was second only to the chief archivist in the institution's hierarchy. One word from him, and my career at the Dominion Archives could be over. I hoped he wasn't too angry at my unauthorized trip to the Art Vault. I cringed to think of myself trotting out my story of the lost notebook once again; I was beginning to hate that lie.

Trying to distract myself until the meeting with Stephen, I turned to my computer. It was time to do a bit of research. Following Mike's advice, I started googling. Unfortunately, both "Jeremy Crawford" and "Victoria Jarvis" were quite common names. Even when I limited the search using date fields and any key words I could think of, I could not narrow the results down to a manageable level. I scrolled through the first fifty or so of the sixteen thousand results, and after repeatedly hitting references to "Vicky J's car-detailing shop in South Beach," I gave up. I spent the rest of the day going through the ledgers.

They were thin books, containing only about twenty pages each. A day's entry, detailing the management of cattle—births, injuries, feed prices—and topics such as stock purchases and the weather, usually took up six pages. The entries were written in the same bold, scrawling hand. Remembering Jem's casual reference to Victoria's bookkeeping for her uncle, I guessed I was staring at her handwriting. If it was her task to keep the farm records, then it made sense that she stashed his letters here.

From Jem's correspondence it seemed that Victoria was a bit of an activist. I didn't know much about the suffragette movement but vaguely remembered Mrs. Banks in *Mary Poppins* singing about the need for the women's vote. I did some quick internet research and learned that suffragettes were radicals. In addition to chaining themselves to fences and hunger striking, the most active smashed windows and set off bombs. I could see parallels with today's anti-globalization movement. I wondered if Victoria's interest in the cause of women's voting rights was the equivalent of getting pepper sprayed and arrested at a rally.

Jem's references to her father's place in society made it clear that they were from different classes, with Victoria perched on an upper rung of the social ladder. Victoria was a wealthy young woman who en-dorsed radical politics and took a penniless painter as a lover. She must have been an interesting person. Her handwriting was a further clue, however tenuous, to the woman she was. The ledgers did not contain the prim, neat characters I would expect from the pen of a well-bred young lady. Instead, the strong, loping style covered huge swaths of paper, almost as if Victoria felt she deserved to take up as much space as possible. Was she miserable on this farm? What must that have been like, to leave the glamour of a cosmopolitan city to move to a ranch?

I picked up the photocopy of the letter. It was dated October 5 and was slotted into a ledger covering the week of November 12—over a month's delay from mailing to receipt. How did people carry on love affairs at that distance, with that time lag? How did they keep the spark burning and fight off jealousy and insecurity?

I'd endured enough angst in university, waiting for a boy's less-than-instant-message to come in. How did you sustain love over months of absence and long silences?

◇◇◇◇◇◇◇

THE READING ROOM WAS THE DOMINION ARCHIVES' BEATING HEART. UN-like the messy confusion of the other floors, it was a huge space filled with sunlight, clean lines, and efficient public service. Two stories high, it took up almost the entire second and third floors, with only a small section reserved for the reference archivists' offices. The room was filled with long, battered oak tables and hard-backed chairs. Stephen Nguyen, his balding head bent over a book, sat at a table by the windows.

I walked toward him, passing researchers studiously huddled around green-shaded reading lamps. Along the room's walls were security cameras. In theory, a commissionaire monitored these at all times to prevent theft or damage of archival material. Since talking to Ernie, however, I had my doubts about this.

Stephen didn't notice my approach, which gave me a chance to prepare myself. He had been kind to me last week when I worked in the Art Vault, asking me where I had studied and what my future plans were.

Once while I worked in there, he gave a tour of the vault to some high-ranking government officials from whom the Archives was hoping to garner financial support. I sat silently among the paintings and photographs and listened. The officials—gray-suited, gray-haired bureaucrats—initially hadn't seemed that interested, but Stephen was a dynamic speaker, and he was able to make the significance of a particular image come alive. He pointed out the first depiction of a canoe in a Canadian painting and the gleam in the eye of a portrait of Leonard Cohen. By the time he pulled out our 1710 oil portrait of an Indigenous chief, the group was eating out of his hand, and I had entirely forgotten my own work.

Stephen looked up as I neared. Instead of meeting me with his usual smile, he gestured to the chair opposite him.

"Hello, Jessica. How are you?" He had dark circles behind his wire-frame glasses, and his shoulders were slumped.

I sat. "I'm so sorry about the body," I blurted.

He blinked at me, and I felt like an ass.

"Why are you sorry? You had nothing to do with that business, did you?"

"No, no," I assured him. "But I know that you must be displeased."

"Yes, it's very upsetting. I love all the works in the Art Vault. I hate to see them defiled that way."

I remembered watching Stephen as he walked through the vault. His movements were always slow, almost reverential.

"Were any paintings damaged as a result of the . . ." My voice trailed away. All I could see was that body lodged between the stacks.

Stephen seemed to grasp what I meant. He waved a thin hand. "Not badly, thank goodness. Most of what is stored in those stacks is in boxes. There was some spattering"—his mouth turned down in disgust—"but nothing we can't handle."

"Well, that's good." My voice was overly cheerful because I dreaded what was coming next.

"I'm not sure if Oliver explained why I wanted to talk with you."

Here it comes, I thought. "Not really."

"Well, as you must be aware, the murder represents a huge security failure for us. So far we believe that nothing was stolen, but we're completing a thorough inventory to be sure."

I nodded vigorously, trying to indicate my approval of his methods.

"We're reviewing all of our policies around vault access. One question has come up in the highest circles: What was a probationary employee with no business in the Art Vault doing in there?"

I trotted out my well-worn story about the misplaced notebook.

Stephen leveled me with his direct gaze. "I'm in that vault every day. I would have noticed a spare notebook." His tone was mild, but I sensed the steel behind it.

I calculated quickly. Would it hurt to tell him what I was doing there? An expurgated version, of course. It was better to stay on Stephen's good side. "You're right," I admitted. "I wasn't looking for my notebook. I wanted to see some art work."

His nostrils flared, and his voice, although quiet, hit me like a sledgehammer. "The Art Vault contains priceless works. The temperature and humidity controls are affected every time that door gets opened. We can't have people traipsing in and out on whims."

"I know. I'm sorry. I shouldn't have been in there, but I was curious about this painter, and I knew we had some of his work."

Stephen cocked his head to one side, his movement birdlike. He must have sensed the truth behind my words, because my apology seemed to assuage him. "I hope this curiosity was work related. Who's the artist?"

I hesitated for a moment. My instincts told me that Stephen was far too big a fish to be interested in my old letters. He was an internationally renowned curator. He didn't need to steal academic glory from a low-level minion. Earlier I had given Mike half my information, when I told him only Victoria's name; I could do the same with Stephen, telling him only about Jem. That felt safe. Besides, Stephen was knowledgeable; he might be able to help me. "I came across references to Jeremy Crawford in some records I'm working on. He sounded interesting."

He narrowed his eyes. "Hmm. Jeremy Crawford. A minor painter of the early twentieth century. Influenced by European modernism, I believe. Used to do urban landscapes—painting streetcars in Montreal, that sort of thing. Quite derivative. I think we have a couple of his sketches and maybe an oil."

"What happened to him?" I asked.

Stephen raised an eyebrow at my eagerness but shrugged. "As far as I can recall, he's associated with only the early part of the century. That's not my field, however, so you'd have to look him up."

"Thanks. That's what I plan to do," I said, attempting to sound authoritative and knowledgeable.

Stephen's voice was encouraging. "I'm sure you've thought to start with Tapper's *Encyclopedia of Canadian Art.* You also probably know that *Canadian Modernism* is a good resource."

I smiled. "Yes, those are the two I'll start with. Thanks." I stood from the table and took a step toward the reference area.

"Jessica." His voice was quiet, but it stopped me in my tracks. "You're new, and I don't want to harm your employment record. I know how difficult it can be to get hired permanently here."

I didn't like where this was going.

Stephen met my eyes. "Nonetheless, you should not have been in that vault. I've removed your access rights to the art areas. If I hear of any further indiscretion on your part, I will be forced to formally censure you. Is that clear?"

Stephen knew an official complaint on my record would mean that I would never get hired permanently at the Dominion Archives. He was giving me fair warning, and I was determined to heed it. "I understand. It won't happen again."

He nodded sharply and turned back to the book in front of him.

CHAPTER ELEVEN

WITH A RAPIDLY BEATING HEART, I LEFT STEPHEN AND HURRIED TOWARD the reference desk. What would I do if I was fired? Working here had been my goal for years. It would be humiliating to return to Toronto. My mother would not stint on the "I told you so's." I straightened my shoulders. I hadn't been fired, only warned. It was better to concentrate on Jem and Victoria's story. They were my ticket to job security.

I smiled when I saw that Sasha was working at the reference desk. She had been an enormous help since I'd started, often lending a hand in untangling a complex or poorly explained project of Oliver's. When I first met her, she ushered me into her office behind the Reading Room, forced chamomile tea on me, and made me admire the photos of her two sets of twins, born eleven months apart. Her husband had a vasectomy after the first set was born, but it was too late; the next two were already en route. Sasha had told me all of this within the first two minutes of our meeting.

Her face brightened at my approach. "What can I do for you, Jess?"

"I'm looking for reference books. I need the *Who's Who*, *The Encyclopedia of Canadian Art*, and *Canadian Modernism*."

"Okay, what year do you need the *Who's Who*?"

I blinked. "There's more than one?"

"Sure. They put them out every year. They're a summary of all the important people in the country."

I thought back to the dates of my letters. "I guess I'm looking for volumes from 1910 to 1920."

Sasha led me around her desk into the reference area to several shelves of reference books. She stopped in front of a row of hardcover books with red bindings.

"They started publishing the *Who's Who* in 1910, and then only once every three years, with a gap during the war." She pulled out three large books from the shelves, piling the heavy volumes in my arms.

I lugged them over to a nearby table.

"I'll bring over the art books while you sift through these," she said.

"Thanks," I replied as she disappeared into the stacks. I opened the 1910 volume and flipped eagerly to "Jarvis."

Jarvis, David Augustus; industrialist. B. Derbyshire England 19 July 1870; s. Victor and Lavinia Elisabeth (Teed); m. Thyra Young (B. 1873, D. 1896); children Frederick David, Victoria Thyra. PRESIDENT AND DIRECTOR MONTREAL TEXTILES. Conservative; Protestant. Home: 526 Mountain Street, Westmount QC.

I felt a surge of affection for Victoria, seeing her neatly slotted behind her big brother. Her life was laid bare in a few words. The family's address in Montreal's swanky Westmount confirmed my suspicion that they were wealthy. Victoria's mother died, perhaps giving birth to her; the dates worked. That meant Victoria would have been eighteen in 1914.

I could see everything now. Motherless, she was raised by a stern and unyielding father. She reacted to his rigidity by pursuing an increasingly scandalous and radical path, culminating in her affair with Jem. David Augustus Jarvis's social inclinations—"Conservative; Protestant"—made it easy to imagine him as a fat, cigar-smoking plutocrat who threatened Jem with ruin and packed Victoria off to Alberta when he learned of their relationship.

I scanned the *Who's Who* but saw no entry for Victoria's uncle, Henry Jarvis. I examined the next couple of *Who's Whos*. Both the 1914 and the 1920 entries for David Jarvis remained the same, providing no further information.

By this time, Sasha had dropped off the two art books. I perused the index in the *Encyclopedia*, but I didn't find an entry for Jeremy Crawford. The modernist book yielded better results:

Crawford, Jeremy. (1893–?) Painter. b. Montreal, QC. Crawford was a student at the Art Association of Montréal. He briefly studied under James Wilson Morrice. Crawford's technique borrowed heavily from his teacher. His landscapes and urban scenes indicate a linear fluidity and saturation of color. No works of his exist after the First World War. Time and place of death are unknown.

This didn't give me much. He never made a success of himself as a painter, that was obvious. I thought about "time and place of death unknown." Was Jem killed in the war? Or maybe he'd sold the Rembrandt and he and Victoria retired somewhere wonderfully romantic. He died of old age under a setting tropical sun. I realized that my academic distance from the story was rapidly disappearing. I found myself wanting Jem's Rembrandt to be real, because then I could imagine that he and Victoria found their happy ending somewhere. If he hadn't been a successful painter, then the only way he could have been with Victoria was if he really had found a Rembrandt.

I hurried over to the art reference section, pulling down the only book the archives held devoted to Rembrandt. I flipped through the analysis of his technique, searching for something to confirm that what Jem found was legitimate. It wasn't until I reached the book's appendix on the history of Rembrandt attribution that I found anything relevant.

Until the 1960s, people believed that there were over six hundred works attributable to Rembrandt. In 1968, a team of art historians and other experts, funded by the Netherlands Organisation for Scientific Research, concluded that this number was grossly inflated. Indeed, many of the paintings attributed to the old master were actually the work of his students, and the number of Rembrandts that are currently unaccounted for is likely to be very low indeed.

I reread those dry sentences, which likely spelled the end of Jem's hopes. I flipped through the rest of the appendix in a desultory way until I came to a paragraph at the end:

> While the chances of locating a genuine Rembrandt that has escaped scholarly notice are slim, history has nonetheless yielded several spectacular finds. The early part of the twentieth century was particularly rich in the recovery of "lost" Rembrandts, as the turmoil of European wars thrust several paintings into the limelight.

I closed the book. Could Jem's Rembrandt be one of those "spectacular" finds, or was it one of the six hundred misattributed paintings? I returned the *Who's Who*s to their spot on the shelf. On impulse, I grabbed the 1923 volume. I flipped through it quickly. The David Jarvis entry was the same, but for the first time, there was an entry for Henry Jarvis. I carried the heavy book back to the table and sat down to read.

> Jarvis, Henry; High Plains Alberta. B. Derbyshire England 16 Jan. 1876; s. Victor and Lavinia Elisabeth (Teed); m. Therese Hannington, 15 July 1910; children Andrew David, Gilbert Francis. CONSERVATIVE MEMBER OF PARLIAMENT FOR MEDICINE HAT DISTRICT. Home: RR#1, High Plains Alberta.

This was Victoria's uncle, the one she was sent to live with. We'd bought the ledgers from the estate of Jarvis's son Andrew, who would have been Victoria's cousin. The entry confirmed what I already knew, but it was nice to see it all written out officially. I closed the book and reshelved it. It was only then that I noticed that the once bustling Reading Room was empty and that Sasha and her fellow reference archivist were shutting down their computers.

"Is it closing time already?" I asked.

Sasha nodded, and I hurried back to my office, pushing thoughts of Victoria and Jem aside. I had a date, and I didn't want to keep Mike waiting.

CHAPTER TWELVE

HY'S STEAKHOUSE WAS AN OTTAWA INSTITUTION. HEAVY WOOD FURNISH-
ings, secluded corner tables, and a plush red color scheme made the
city's politicos and power brokers feel at home. Hy's was the kind of
place where big deals and important policies were hashed out over
bottles of good wine and thick slabs of meat.

It was an odd choice for a first date. But this was where, stum-
blingly, Mike suggested we go. As I sat on the velveteen chair, I regretted my decision. Mike was painfully awkward. We'd barely spoken on
the five-block walk over to Hy's.

Now, as we were fussed over by the maître-d', wine steward,
and our waiter, I felt even more uncomfortable. The waiter had a
slight leer on his face, as if he recognized our age difference and
knew exactly what was going on. I'd even spotted him glance
knowingly at the wedding ring on Mike's finger and the absence
of one on mine. It didn't help my qualms that Mike was knocking
back his second scotch and soda, while I had barely made a dent
in my glass of Merlot. At least the booze seemed to make him
chattier.

"Tell me," he said, "how are you doing after all of the craziness of
the past week?"

I laughed ruefully. "Honestly, I don't know. The cops actually
thought I was a suspect for a while."

"Damn! What do they have on you?"

"Well, nothing. I mean, I didn't kill Thibodeau."

"I wasn't implying that," he said. "Sorry, I'm not very good at
making conversation."

I accepted his apology. "I guess they thought I might have some information, but I don't. The whole thing was so horrible. I wish I could forget it." I was eager to change the subject. "The other day you started to tell me how you became an archivist."

Mike swirled his drink. "When I was a teenager, I did yard work for this old guy in my hometown. He always had the best anecdotes. He'd come and sit with me while I ate my lunch and would talk and talk and talk. He'd lived all over the place—the United States, Europe, even New Zealand, where he'd worked for a sheep farmer. He'd fought in the Second World War. He told the craziest stories about the things he had seen and done."

"And that's what sparked your interest in history?" I prompted him.

"Sort of. He died when I was sixteen. That's when I finally clued in to the fact that the guy I'd always considered a funny old fart was actually a respected writer—Edward Hauver."

"What!" I exclaimed. I flashed back to last week, when I'd come into Mike's office and seen him reading the Hauver biography.

Mike took a long sip of his scotch. "If this was a novel, I would have been inspired by my connection to a great poet to become a writer myself. Life doesn't work like that, though. It wasn't his writing that interested me, it was his life." Mike leaned forward. "Where do you keep lives once the person has gone? Where do you find the shades and nuances of someone's existence? How do you capture and understand anyone after they've left us?"

Unconsciously, I found myself leaning forward as well. "In their archive," I said.

"Exactly," he exclaimed, smiling into my eyes. "You find their lives in their letters, in their diaries, in their memoirs, and even in their grocery lists." He leaned back. The sense of mutual understanding that flowed between us was almost tangible. Mike held my gaze for a long moment, and my stomach tightened.

I took a sip of wine and cleared my throat. "It's that passion that I've tried to convey to my mother, but she doesn't get my career choice."

"Oh no? Why not?"

"She's a journalist—Cassie Novak." I waited for the usual signs of recognition followed by the inevitable questions about the danger of her work and her latest investigation.

Instead, Mike shrugged. "Sorry, I've never heard of her."

Ridiculously, I was a bit offended. "She's well known. She exposed that child trafficking ring in Toronto a couple of years back."

"I don't follow the news that closely."

He didn't know her. My smile broadened and my shoulders relaxed. "Well, she doesn't understand why I'm wasting my time on 'dead' things when I could be changing the world, the way she does. She's convinced that I should be a journalist. I used to write for the university paper, but I hated it. I never felt like I could live up to her."

"That sounds like quite a burden."

The waiter arrived with our food—a twelve-ounce T-bone for me, and a filet mignon for Mike.

"Oh, it's not that bad," I said, tucking into the meal. "I think it would have been better if I'd had a father to counterbalance her craziness, but Cassie was never sure who my dad was. At any rate, he didn't stick around. I've got a sister as well. Half-sister, actually, because Cassie drove that guy away too."

"It must have been hard on her, raising two kids alone."

I stared at him. He'd obviously never met Cassie. Nothing was hard for her; certainly not single parenthood.

"Maybe," I said politely.

Mike continued, hardly listening to my reply. "I know that I've been struggling, since Mathilde died." He twisted the wedding ring on his finger. "We didn't have kids, so I don't have the challenges of single parenthood. It's terribly lonely without her, though. It's the little things you miss. She used to wrap her arms around my waist and lean her head against my back. She was small, only coming up to my shoulders, but when she embraced me like that, I felt her strength, you know? Like I could let go and she would hold me up forever." He looked away.

In a few short sentences, Mike had been more intimate, more vulnerable, and more open with me than any of my previous boyfriends.

"When did she die?" I asked.

"Two years ago. I still miss her."

"What did she die of?"

"Cancer," he said.

I reached across the table, taking his hand in mine. "I think you're doing really well," I said, squeezing his hand and letting it drop.

He stared into my eyes for a moment before he grinned, dispelling the dark mood. "Thanks. That feels good, coming from someone like you."

"Like me?" I asked.

"You know, someone young and untainted by the cynicism that gets us all."

I laughed. "Whoa, that's pretty pessimistic. Am I doomed to become bitter?"

He nodded. "Yep. Stay at the Dominion Archives and you'll be a paranoid, dried-up hag in no time."

"Well, you'd better get me while I'm still a starry-eyed idealist."

This time his smile was flirtatious. "Sounds like a plan."

We chatted on lighter topics for the rest of the meal. When the waiter came to remove our plates, I met his smirk with a steady gaze, and he was the first to look away.

After the waiter left, Mike said, "Thanks for listening, Jess. I didn't think that this evening would veer into a grief counseling session, but it feels good to talk. I don't often get the chance."

"I'm happy to listen. Anytime."

The waiter reappeared and slid the leather bill case toward Mike. He opened it and blanched. "Damn it, steaks aren't cheap." His eyes traveled down the bill. "They charged us extra for the potatoes," he yelped.

I couldn't help grinning. Wait until Adela heard about this strange date. Not only did we spend half the night talking about his dead wife, but now he was revealing himself to be a royal cheapskate.

He seemed to realize that his exclamations were in poor taste. "Sorry for that. I guess I don't get out much." He paid the bill without another murmur.

We walked back toward the archives, where Mike had left his car. The temperature had fallen several degrees while we were eating, and the office towers along Queen Street funneled the icy air into a winter tornado. We didn't speak as we walked, but this time it felt comfortable. Mike broke the silence as we neared the parking lot.

"Say, how's your research going on those letters?"

"Great. I found out some clues today. I know more about who my two lovers are, although now I'm worried that their affair might have been doomed."

"Oh no," he exclaimed, turning to me. His brown eyes and sharp nose were the only visible elements of his face above the scarf.

"Yeah. I'm afraid my hero may have died before he was reunited with his heroine. I hope not." The wistfulness in my voice caught me off guard.

"Well, romantically that might not be good, but it makes the story better. Doomed love always sells, even to academic journals."

"Really?" I asked.

"Absolutely. Academics all secretly want soap operas. The trick is to serve up the love story with a healthy sprinkling of theoretical gobbledygook. It's like ordering the Diet Coke with the Big Mac meal. It makes them feel virtuous."

I laughed.

Mike said, "I'm parked on the other side of the lot and it's icy. Wait here, and I'll go get the car."

He disappeared into the gloom, leaving me alone in the January chill. I could hear his footsteps crunching through the snow. It was a lonely sound, and the spark of flirting with him faded as I waited for his return. A light snow began to fall, and I watched as the breeze picked up the flakes and made them dance under the yellow glow of the streetlamps. In the distance, I heard the sound of a car engine starting.

My neck prickled and my body tensed. I was being watched. I turned, not wanting to believe my own instincts.

A figure stood on the other side of the street. He leaned against a building. I couldn't make out much from my vantage point, but I noted a dark overcoat. I felt a chill that had nothing to do with the weather. I told myself it was a random stranger . . . but dawdling on a bitterly cold evening? As if to put the lie to my hopeful thoughts, the figure pushed off from the building and began walking toward me. I stared, heart pounding in my ears, as he sauntered to Bay Street and crossed over. My legs were leaden, and I was rooted to the spot. This was a nightmare. I was unable to move as the figure, who I now saw was muffled in a thick scarf identical to my stalker's, advanced toward me.

CHAPTER THIRTEEN

I STARED AT THE APPROACHING FIGURE, MY MOUTH DRY, MY HEART pounding in my chest. I needed to move, but my fear kept me immobilized. A loud honk of a horn shook me from my frozen panic. I turned and Mike pulled up in a tiny, rusty Hyundai.

He rolled down the window. "What's got you so fascinated?" He looked up the street at the figure, who moved away down the sidewalk.

My throat was tight, and I could hardly speak. "Nothing, nothing." I hurried around to the passenger side and slid into the vehicle. By the time I looked up, the person had rounded the corner out of sight. I sank back into the seat in relief.

"Are you okay?" Mike asked, frowning. "You seem shaken." He stared after the figure.

I didn't want to ruin our date, so I smiled. "I got a little spooked back there," I said. "Ever since I found that body, I've been antsy."

Mike continued to frown. "Was that person bothering you?" His voice was fierce, protective. I liked it.

"No, it's me. I'm nervous these days." I gave him directions to my house and then stared out the window, my hands twisting in my lap. If I was being followed, it must have something to do with the murder. The stalking started after I found the body. Once again, a thought swam up to me, just out of reach.

Mike pulled up in front of my house, and I turned to him. "This was great. I had fun."

"Yeah, me too."

There was an awkward pause, and I thought Mike's head moved down a fraction, as if to kiss me. I moved in for a quick cheek peck, but Mike turned toward me at the same time, and our heads collided.

"Ow," he said, rubbing his head ruefully. "I meant to sweep you off your feet, not knock you unconscious."

I laughed, touching my own head.

"Is it okay?" he asked. He took my chin in his hand, turning my head toward the streetlight, so he could see if it was bruised. His fingers traced the spot on my temple where we collided. The fabric of his woolen gloves was rough against my skin, but his touch was so tender that it was a pleasant sensation. I shivered and caught his eye. His head moved down, and this time we kissed.

It was soft and fleeting, the merest brush of lip against lip, but it was nice.

I smiled at him. "This was a wonderful date. Thank you."

He grinned. "I enjoyed it too. We'll have to do it again."

"Absolutely," I agreed. "See you at work?"

"I'll be there."

Like Lemieux before him, Mike waited until I had safely entered my apartment before driving away.

The landline was ringing and I rushed to grab it.

"Hello." Snow from my coat and boots pooled onto my thin carpet.

"Salali!"

Only one person called me by my real first name. My mother had been investigating police misconduct against Indigenous people when I was born. *Salali* meant "squirrel" in Cherokee. I hated it almost as much as my mother hated "Jessica," which is what I'd chosen to be called since the first grade. My name was one in a long line of standoffs between us.

"It's after ten o'clock," my mother continued. "I was sure you'd be in bed by now. I guess Ottawa is more interesting than I give it credit for."

While my mother was the absolute last person I felt like talking to, her call did spark my curiosity. In the months since I'd moved to Ottawa, she had never initiated a call.

"How's it going?" she asked. This was also odd. In our usual conversations, my mother launched into an immediate story about her latest exploits and finished by haranguing me about quitting my job and moving back to Toronto.

"Things are fine," I responded.

"Now, don't hold out on me. You forget that I've got connections. I read about the murder at that Conservation Facility but hadn't realized that it was my own daughter who found the body until I talked to an informant I have in Ottawa."

Now all was clear. My mother, ever the journalist, was after a scoop. In a weary voice, I recounted everything I told the police about finding the body.

"And are you a suspect?" she asked when I concluded.

Trust my mother to get right to the heart of the matter. "No, Mum, I'm not."

"Are you sure?" Her voice had an edge.

"Are you asking me if I killed this guy?"

"Of course not. Although, if you did, I can get you an excellent lawyer. Don't say anything over the phone, but if you need to, call me back from a pay phone."

"Mum. I didn't kill anyone, and I don't need your 'excellent lawyer.' The police told me the other day that I'm not a suspect. My alibi checks out."

"Are you sure? Cops are wily little shits. Whatever you do, don't trust them. They might be trying to lull you into a false sense of security. I've seen it plenty of times, Salali. They're lazy, and they arrest the easiest suspect. Be on your guard."

"Sure, Mum. Absolutely." My mother had been telling me not to trust the cops since I was five years old.

"What I couldn't figure out is how you discovered that body in the first place. I thought your job involved old papers, not artwork."

"They're not old papers, mum. They're important historical records. Anyway, I wasn't supposed to be in the Art Vault. I was curious about some sketches."

There was a pause on the other end of the line. "That doesn't sound like you. You're not usually curious about anything. Certainly not curious enough to break any rules."

I rolled my eyes. In my mother's mind I was the proverbial good girl, incapable of doing anything illicit, dangerous, or wrong, much to her chagrin. "Well, I was there. I was looking for some artwork by this guy whose letters I discovered—"

My mother cut me off. "Have I told you that there's an intern spot at the *Herald*? I could pull some strings and get you an interview. Think about it."

I agreed in order to get her off the line and then hung up. I tugged off my coat and kicked off my boots. I was exhausted.

Sleep didn't come easily, however. I tossed and turned, disturbed by the memory of that figure walking toward me. It wasn't only the bulky coat that made him seem burly; he was a big guy. The thought niggled. I frowned, trying to catch the elusive thread. Something about a burly figure . . .

It wouldn't come, and I dug my head into the pillow, willing myself to stop thinking about the stalker and fall asleep. My mind obeyed, at least the first part of the command, and my thoughts drifted back to the conversation with my mother and my recounting of finding the murder victim. Once again, I saw the awkward crumple as the body fell out from between the tight stacks and remembered the glassy stare in the corpse's eyes.

I sat up with a gasp. Like the stalker, Thibodeau was a big guy. It was his body shape that caught my attention, because I suddenly remembered where I had seen him before. The murder victim was the "Burly Communist" from the auction house.

I cast my mind back to that small, bland room. He outbid the woman in red. What did he buy? Then the memory came whizzing back. On the day he was killed, Paul Thibodeau vastly overpaid for a batch of paintings. Less than twenty-four hours later, he was found dead in the Art Vault.

CHAPTER FOURTEEN

LEMIEUX AND I SAT IN WOBBLY WHITE PLASTIC CHAIRS AT A WINDOW table at the Capital City Cantine. We sipped strong coffee served in chipped brown mugs. Except for a tired-looking prostitute nursing a coffee at the counter, the place was deserted. My neighborhood diner was a far cry from downtown's expensive cafés. If you ordered "fair trade" coffee from Faizan, he'd probably think it was a scam to avoid paying for it. It was early, and the sun hadn't climbed much above the horizon. I looked out the window, watching a huddle of well-bundled people stamp their feet and puff warm breath into the air while waiting for the Number Two bus.

I hadn't told Lemieux much when I called him, only that I remembered something about Paul Thibodeau that might be useful. I asked to meet him in person because I was enjoying fulfilling my civic duty. I was working with the police, rather than flouting their authority. The fact that my mother would have a cow if she knew that I was giving away all of my good "leads" to the cops instead of her was gravy.

Lemieux took a sip and said in a drawling voice, "So, mademoiselle. What was so important that you called me at six o'clock in the morning?"

I was nettled by his implication that I was wasting his time. I wasn't some green kid who called the cops over nothing. "Why, Detective, I figured that you'd have been awake for hours, hard at work."

He nodded. "It's true, I was up and doing my exercise. Many police don't take their exercise seriously, but I'm not like them. I keep in shape." He patted his bicep fondly.

I resisted rolling my eyes.

"Now, you were up early. And I think it was not because you were doing your exercise."

Was it my imagination, or did he shoot a pitying look at my stomach? I sucked it in and sat up straighter, trying to recapture that feeling of virtuous self-righteousness. I would tell him what I knew, even if he was a preening twit. "I remembered something about Thibodeau last night."

"Yes?"

"I had seen him before finding his body."

"Yes. You worked with him. You knew him from the commissionaire's desk."

"No." I struggled to keep the annoyance from my voice. "I saw him outside of work, at an auction the day he was murdered." Briefly I recounted the sale and the bidding war that erupted over the minor artworks. "I can't remember what paintings he bought, but that should be easy to find out," I concluded.

Lemieux jotted down the details in his notebook. "Is that everything?" he asked. His tone implied that there should be more.

"Don't you think it's significant that Thibodeau was buying paintings the morning before he was found dead in the Art Vault?"

"I want to assure you, Mademoiselle Novak, the Gatineau Police Department follows up every lead in a murder case. We will look into your remembrance and see if it sheds any light upon this case."

"You don't sound like you think it's very important," I said.

"What I think is interesting is that you only now remember seeing this man, and you thought it was so urgent that you needed to meet me immediately."

What was Lemieux getting at? I stared at him.

He sighed. "We see this happen quite often, you know. Many peoples find police work exciting. They'll do anything to involve themselves in our investigation."

The light dawned. By "peoples" he meant women. He thought I was a badge bunny who was turned on by his big gun and had invented an excuse to see him again.

I kept my voice low but spat out my words. "I'm merely telling you what I remembered. When you check out the auction house, you will see that I am right. Then you might reasonably ask yourself how a low-paid commissionaire had enough money to dramatically overspend on some lousy paintings." I stood up. I hated it when my mother was right, but this time she was dead on: cops were useless.

Lemieux raised his eyebrows at my vehemence and stood as well. He was only about a foot from me, and I could smell his cologne, which was surprisingly nice—something clean and almost woodsy. "Calme-toi, mademoiselle. I said we would look into your tip, and we will. Right now we're pursuing another angle with this murder, but we don't shut our eyes to possibilities."

"So you'll check out the auction house?" I tugged on my heavy winter coat and wrapped a scarf around my face.

"But of course." Lemieux pulled on his sleek leather jacket, which looked good but couldn't offer him much warmth.

I was still irritated by his attitude, but at least he was taking me somewhat seriously. We walked toward the door, and he opened it for me. Standing on the sidewalk, he motioned to his car, illegally parked in front of the diner. "Can I give you a ride to work?"

"No, I'm fine, thanks. I like walking."

He shivered. "On a day like today?" he asked.

"I like the cold. I used to do winter camping."

"Crazy Anglo. Why would you sleep outside in the winter? It's bad enough in the summer with the bugs and the bears. In the winter? Forget it." He waved his hand dismissively.

I had a hard time imagining Lemieux doing anything more rugged than opening a bottle of wine, so I shrugged and crunched off through the snow.

◇◇◇◇◇◇

I ARRIVED AT WORK EARLY AND BEGAN WADING THROUGH THE LATEST batch of ledgers. By ten o'clock, I hadn't found any letters and was getting discouraged. My dark mood was exacerbated because I hadn't seen Mike yet. I'd heard him speaking to Barry in the hall, so I knew he was in. I could go and say hi to him, but I wanted him to come to me.

This was Adela's influence. Her mother had raised her on "The Rules"—based on the 1990s relationship self-help book. She was always telling me that I should be a "creature unlike any other," which as far as I could tell meant taking a lot of bubble baths and wearing blusher. Another cardinal "Rule" was that the man was the pursuer, hunting the woman as a lion stalks an antelope. I usually scoffed at Adela's shocking, anti-feminist relationship stance, but now that I was in the position, I was damned if I was going to be the lion.

When Louise asked me to go for coffee, I agreed with alacrity. Anything to stop waiting for a visit from my scruffy lion.

The day had warmed up, and it was sunny. I proposed that we go for a walk. The Ottawa River Pathway was down a steep flight of stairs from the archives' back door.

We strolled along the path and drank our coffees, staring at the turbulent waters of the river. The rapids here prevented the water from freezing, even during the bitterest winter. Farther to the west the river did ice over, allowing snowmobilers to cross, although in December a couple of over-eager "sledders" hadn't waited for a total freeze up, plunging to a frigid death.

I felt the beginnings of a headache, and the caffeine would probably worsen the pain. I dumped my coffee in the snow.

"Everything okay, Jess?"

I hesitated. I wondered what Louise would say about the connection between Thibodeau and the auction, but something kept me from mentioning it. I also didn't want to tell her about my date with Mike. It was best to keep any office romance quiet. What's more, Louise had mentioned that she and Mike were once friends but since his wife's death they'd drifted apart. I didn't know how she felt about this loss of friendship.

Louise noticed my hesitation and misinterpreted it. "I want to apologize for yesterday, for what I said. I think I was too harsh." Her words came out in white puffs on the cool air, like a character's speech from the comics.

"What do you mean?" I asked as our footsteps crunched in the snow.

Louise stopped, her frame overcome with a hacking cough. "Sorry," she said. Her face was pale, and for a moment she looked like she might faint.

"Are you okay?" I took a step toward her.

"I'm fine," she said in a clipped tone. She resumed walking. "I was wrong to say that we're all out to steal your ideas and that you have to watch your back. I shouldn't let my experiences with all of those branleurs poison your ideas about the place."

"Branleurs?" I asked.

"You know," Louise made the standard gesture for male masturbation, fingers encircled in an up and down movement above her crotch. "Wankers."

I looked up. An old man walking a Yorkshire terrier stared at us, appalled. I laughed. "Right. Good word."

"Anyway, it was hard for me when I got here thirty-five years ago. They didn't want women around, and they made damn sure I knew it. Any idea I ever came up with, some asshole stole. Do you know they didn't have a proper woman's bathroom on the floor when I started? I had to ask my manager for the key so that I could lock myself into the men's every time I needed to go. They did that to humiliate me." Louise's eyes glittered, and for a moment I thought she might cry, but it was anger that made her eyes shine.

She continued. "They tried to give me crap jobs—things like the history of day care. Shit they thought was appropriate for a woman. They sure as hell didn't want me to have political records, but I got them, didn't I?"

Her hands were shaking as she brought her coffee cup up to her lips. I'd always known that Louise was bitter, but I thought her anger was focused on Oliver rather than the whole institution.

"I'm sorry you went through that," I said softly.

She cleared her throat. "It's water under the bridge, Jess."

From the fierceness in her voice, I wasn't so sure.

"Anyway, it's not like that anymore. Ginette certainly hasn't been discriminated against. I let my own experience color what I said to you. So, what are you working on?"

But the habit of caution was ingrained in me now. As I had done with Stephen and Mike, I told her only the portion of the story I thought she might be able to help with. "The old letters in the ledgers are between Henry Jarvis's niece and an artist. I'm trying to find out more about the two of them."

"Henry Jarvis?" Louise asked, closing her eyes in thought. "Alberta MP. Conservative. Started serving in Borden's second term and was made a cabinet minister when Bennett became prime minister. He was in there for years. In charge of the agriculture portfolio. Very socially conservative, if I recall. Strictly religious."

I stared at her in amazement. "How can you remember all that stuff?"

"It's my job. Plus, he's one of the ones who got away, and I remember those."

"What do you mean?"

"The Dominion Archives tries to acquire the personal papers of all cabinet ministers. My predecessors weren't successful with Jarvis. Most of his stuff ended up at the University of Alberta, except for the ledgers and anything else sold at that auction that the university didn't grab."

I stopped walking. "Was the auction we went to entirely related to Henry Jarvis?"

"Don't tell me you forgot? It was material from his son's estate. It either related to Henry himself or to his son Andrew."

Thibodeau had bought paintings that might have been owned by Henry Jarvis, art that might have been seen by Victoria when she was at the farm. Could the Rembrandt have been among those paintings? Could there be a connection between the murder and my discovery of the letters?

My discussion with Louise took on a new urgency, but I concealed my excitement. "What about Jarvis's personal life—do you know anything about that?"

We reached the locks at the mouth of the Rideau Canal and turned to head back.

Louise crinkled her brow, trying to recall. "He came over from England with his brother, I think. Their father was an industrialist or something, so they had fat stakes to start life in the new world. Henry went west and snapped up huge swaths of grazing land."

I was impressed by the breadth of Louise's knowledge and her incredible memory. If that kind of recall was required, I wondered if I would ever be a successful archivist.

Louise was still talking. "I spoke to the son about five years ago. He donated some letters between his father and Prime Minister Borden."

"You talked to Andrew Jarvis?"

"Not Andrew. The younger one, Gilbert."

"The other Jarvis son is still alive?" I asked.

"He was five years ago, but I doubt he is anymore. He'd be pushing one hundred by now. He lived in Montreal in some huge mansion with an on-site nurse when I met him. He was a sweet man."

An elderly cousin of Victoria's was a lead and I didn't want to leave a stone unturned. "Do you still have his contact info?"

Louise hesitated. "I don't know, Jess. Our policy is pretty strict about guarding donors' privacy."

I stared at her in surprise. When the subject of institutional rules came up, Louise usually said that the policies could bite her ass.

She must have sensed my surprise, because she spoke defensively. "A lot of what they tell us to do is bullshit, but I respect my donors, you know? I'm sorry I can't help you with this."

I swallowed my frustration and told myself that my suspicion about the Thibodeau connection was making me pushy. Her reticence at revealing Gilbert Jarvis's contact details was reasonable.

CHAPTER FIFTEEN

BY THE TIME WE RETURNED TO THE ARCHIVES MY HEADACHE WAS POUND-
ing so hard I felt a little nauseous. I closed my office door, swallowed
a couple of painkillers, and dimmed the lights. I put my head on the
desk and waited for the pain to pass.

Thoughts from the past twenty-four hours swarmed me. I let the
images from my date with Mike, the stalker encounter, my memories of the auction, my questions about the Rembrandt, and my frus-
trations with Louise wash over me, and then I tried to let them go,
breathing deeply and evenly as I calmed my mind.

I had rested like that for about twenty minutes, when I heard footsteps stop outside. Was Mike finally coming to say hello?

Through the thickly frosted glass on my door, I could see the outline
of someone peering into my dim office. The handle turned, and I smiled.
Instead of Mike, Ginette's well-coiffed head appeared in my doorway.

I stood, and she let out a yelp. "Jessica! I didn't know you were
in here! Why are you sitting in the dark?" Ginette moved to the light
switch and turned it on with a forceful snap.

I blinked in the bright light and shielded my eyes. The headache
had almost faded away, but the fluorescent lighting was still a shock
to the system.

"Were you asleep?" Ginette asked accusingly.

I pushed a hand through my hair, hoping it didn't look too messy.
"No, no," I stuttered. "I had a headache and was resting my eyes."

Ginette looked doubtful. "We have a first aid area, you know.
There's a cot there. You shouldn't sleep on the job, especially when
you're on probation."

I quashed my irritation. "Thanks, that's good advice," I said.

"Good. Well next time try to look a little more alert. I'd hate to have to report this to Oliver." She smiled sweetly.

It was only after she'd gone that it occurred to me to wonder what exactly she was planning to do in my office when she thought it was empty.

I made sure the photocopied letters in the file folder on my desk were all there. I was nervous for their safety. Unfortunately, the battered old filing cabinet had long ago lost its key, but I pulled out a folder with "Admin. 1978" scrawled on it and shoved the copies of the three letters among the old taxi receipts and leave forms that my predecessor had filed decades previously. Then I slotted the file back into the middle of the cabinet drawer. The letters weren't secure, but at least they'd be hard to find. I made a mental note to wait until the office was quiet and make copies of the copies that I could bring home with me.

Feeling better, I turned to the boxes I'd been processing that morning. I was thrilled to find another letter in the last box.

October 31, 1914

Dearest,

It was such a delight to finally receive your letter. The long wait for correspondence from you is always harrowing, but most especially after I sent you word of my, no *our*, most marvelous find.

Foolishly, I began to entertain thoughts that you had met some strapping cowboy who turned your head, making you forget me and the painting I've discovered. I see now how easily the green-eyed monster can invade even the most faithful romance.

As happy as I was to get your letter, its tone startled me. You seem sad, dear one. I know that the narrow views and strict piety of farm life are difficult for you, but you must not let your aunt and uncle's attitudes dampen your spirit. It's that bravery and pluck that first drew me to you. I remember the shock I received when I heard you speak at the socialist meeting. It was only a few days after the museum ball, you recall? The hall was filled. Men stood cheek by jowl, most in working clothes with tobacco and beer on their breath. Then you asked your question. Your high, clear voice, like the music of a mountain stream, poured into every corner of the hall. I recognized you immediately, though you were wearing a shawl to conceal your identity. You will hate me for admitting this, dear, but I cannot remember what you asked the men on the podium. I remember only falling irrevocably in love. While I may have been stunned by your beauty at the ball, it was in that squalid little room off Atwater Avenue that I glimpsed your indefatigable spirit. In that instant, I fell for you like a boot on a bedroom floor.

That spirit is what is missing from your last letter, darling. You say you have been feeling poorly of late, and I hope it is nothing too serious. Do not pine for me darling, because I have news: I am coming home!

Since discovering the Rembrandt, I am all the more anxious to begin my life with you. The stars are aligning, and I have met someone who can help secure passage to England. Since martial law has been imposed on Paris, getting travel permits is difficult, but Teddy has connections—a wealthy aunt in London started the wheels turning. It should be only a month or so before I receive travel permission.

You would love Teddy, darling. He is young, no more than eighteen, although he pretends to be a worldly twenty-five. He is from Toronto and, like me, came to Paris to broaden his horizons (although in Teddy's case, he seems less interested in old masters and Gallic poets and more in café society, theatres, gambling, and French wine). Fear not, however; your Jem is not tempted by this vice-laden lifestyle! Instead, I have undertaken to educate Teddy and have crammed as much art into his head as I think he can stand.

Speaking of art . . . today I brought our painting to an expert in Montparnasse. He is an old Jew, one of the few dealers who has not fled the city. André had introduced us in August, raving about how knowledgeable he is. He looked over the portrait and pronounced it authentic. He said that the signature indicates that it was one of Rembrandt's later portraits. Apparently the artist added the "d" to his name only toward the end of his career. The dealer thinks it might even be a self-portrait! To think I am staring into the eyes of the great Rembrandt Van Rijn!

Remembering the sensible caution you wrote of in your last letter, I swore the dealer to secrecy about the painting's existence. He acquiesced immediately, and I feel that I can trust the old fellow. He gave me a great deal of useful advice and told me not to try to sell the painting here, while everything is topsy-turvy. I am better to bring it to New York, where this man's partner lives. He has given me a letter of introduction and promises me that I shall realize a tidy sum for it.

The one problem is that it might be difficult to get the painting out of the country. Monsieur Levy says that with the war on, French officials are particularly concerned about losing what they term "bien culturel"—cultural heritage. If officials recognize the painting for what it truly is, they will surely confiscate it, at least until the war's end—and heaven knows when that will be! I am not sure what to do, but I shall think of something by the time Teddy secures our visas.

I am so anxious to get back to you. One doesn't like dawdling in a graveyard, and that's what Europe has become. Old ideas are dead here, and I long for a change. I must admit I was surprised at your eagerness to get away from what you call "stuffy Canada." Surprised, but excited. I had only advanced a little dream, but why don't we make it a reality? My fantasy of returning to Montreal to impress your father, to "show him," seems hollow to me now. Nothing more than a child's dream of revenge. What does his opinion matter? All I care about is you, darling. It would be marvelous to turn our back on this corrupt civilization, so intent on destroying itself. Tahiti it shall be!

Yours, as always. Love,

Jem

I put the letter aside and tried to process its implications. The Rembrandt had been authenticated by an expert. Suddenly the possible connection with the murder became more urgent. Thibodeau bought paintings from the Jarvis estate—the same estate where I had found letters detailing the discovery of a Rembrandt. Had Thibodeau somehow known about this? Did he vastly overpay for those paintings because one of them was a masterpiece? Rooting through my desk drawers, I dug out the auction catalog and flipped to the description of the lot that started the bidding frenzy: "Lot Three consists of eight oil paintings by various twentieth-century artists from the estate of Andrew Jarvis. Subjects include portraiture, streetscapes, and landscapes. Reserve Price, $1,500."

Hmm. There was no way that a Rembrandt would have been mistaken for a twentieth-century work, especially when the auction house presumably employed art experts.

That seemed to be a dead end, but I couldn't shake the feeling that the auction was the key to Thibodeau's death. Van Cleef's hadn't bothered to list the painters, although perhaps they'd been announced at the start of the sale, which we'd missed.

I stopped. I had wasted enough time trying to second-guess the police about the murder. It was time to tackle my more important mystery—the one that could make or break my career. What had befallen Jem and Victoria?

Gilbert Jarvis, Victoria's cousin, talked to Louise five years ago. It was possible that he was still alive. I'd start with nursing homes. I turned to my computer and called up the telephone directory for Montreal. I was about to type "retirement home" into the search screen when it occurred to me to try "Gilbert Jarvis" first.

I was stunned when his contact information popped up. This was too easy. Gilbert Jarvis, 526 Mountain Avenue, Westmount, Quebec. Without stopping to think, I dialed the phone number provided.

A female voice answered. "Bonjour?"

Damn. I hadn't counted on French. "Oh, bonjour. I'm looking for Gilbert Jarvis. Is he available?"

There was a pause at the other end before the voice said in heavily accented English, "Monsieur Jarvis does not respond to the phone. Who calls, please?"

"Never mind. It's okay." I hung up. It was stupid to cold call an elderly man with this crazy tale of his cousin's Parisian love letters. It was a complicated story to convey over the phone. I'd established that he was still alive. I should follow up on this slim lead. Given what his nurse or maid said, I decided to write a letter:

> Dear Mr. Jarvis,
>
> Sorry to trouble you. My name is Jessica Novak, and I am an archivist at the national archives. I'm researching a minor painter, Jeremy Crawford, and have reason to believe that your cousin Victoria Jarvis may have known him. I'm writing to inquire if you have any information on their relationship that you would be willing to share. I appreciate any help that you can provide.

I included my work address as well as my home, work, and cell numbers.

It was getting late, but I nipped out and bought a card, transcribing the message in my neatest, and largest, writing. I figured someone as old as Jarvis would appreciate a handwritten note and the bigger the letters, the better.

Before leaving for the night, I photocopied the latest Jem letter and then filed the copy and returned the original to its spot in the ledger. While I was excited that Jem's Rembrandt seemed legit, I found news of Victoria's illness disturbing. I didn't want to think that the reason I could find no information on her was because she died on some distant Alberta ranch, never reunited with Jem.

I shivered. Given recent events, any thought of death took on a repellent immediacy. Thanks to that stalker, I didn't relish my walk home.

Instead, I picked up the phone. It was time to implement a little survival strategy I had figured out without my mother's help: when in doubt, go for martinis.

CHAPTER SIXTEEN

ADELA AND I WERE PERCHED ON STOOLS AT THE METROPOLITAIN, A
trendy bar in Ottawa's ByWard Market. Adela had come straight from
work, and her thick black hair was pulled into a tight, controlled bun.
Fitting her role as a tech power-seller, she wore a power-outfit: crisp
white shirt under a so-severe-it-was-chic black suit.

She sipped a bright-green apple martini, while I worked on a chocolate one. I wasn't sure what made my drink a martini, other than the
glass it was served in; it tasted like chocolate milk laced with vodka.
We talked about my date.

"Did he actually scream over the bill?" she asked with a giggle.
"He is so not a 'Rules' man."

I spoke defensively. "It was cute. He was clueless."

Adela clicked her tongue. "This guy is typical of you, Jess. He's a
total puppy dog. Why do you always go for the losers?"

True, I was generally attracted to men who needed help. In my
university days, that meant guys who could spend fifteen hours a day
playing *Call of Duty* but couldn't get it together to make it to class.
I'd write their term papers, tidy up their apartments, and force them
to eat a vegetable every now and then. Adela went for the alpha male,
men who were frighteningly handsome, terrifyingly sporty, and used
phrases like "kick ass" to describe their latest law class or MBA project. We didn't usually double-date.

"Mike isn't a loser. He's got a job, and he's respected in his field . . ."

"He also has holes in his pants. You've got a mothering fixation."

"He's in his forties. It's pretty hard to mother someone who's old
enough to be my father."

"Yeah, but you never had a father, so now you're getting to be a little girl and a mother. You're doing it all at the same time."

I laughed. "You're crazy."

Adela shot me an assessing look. "I'm not the one with the Electra complex."

One of the most maddening things about being friends with Adela was that while she didn't know everything, she certainly thought she did.

"I bet you didn't even follow 'The Rules,'" she continued. "Was radiance permeating your being from head to toe?"

"I think I dribbled steak sauce down my shirt."

"Jess!"

I wanted to move on to other topics. "The date wasn't even the most interesting thing that happened to me last night." I told her about my encounter with the stalker, my memory of Thibodeau at the auction house, and my frustrating meeting with Lemieux.

When I finished, Adela was staring at me in concern. "Jess, I think this stalker is serious. You should tell the police about it."

I waved my hand. "Lemieux implied that I made the stuff up about Thibodeau so I could be near him." My voice shook with anger as I remembered our meeting. "What would he say if I told him I thought I was being followed?"

"But you are being followed."

"What proof do I have? The fact that I've gotten a little nervous walking alone at night in the city? What woman doesn't get skittish sometimes? It's not enough."

"You've got to trust your instincts, though."

"I do. But I don't think I can go to the cops with a bunch of mumbo jumbo about my instincts. They're going to need more."

"What about the video that you said the detective described. The one where you can see the murderer leaving and he's dressed the same as your stalker?"

"Three-quarters of the city wears enormous jackets in January. Even the cool cats in here bundle up." I pointed to the coat rack by the door. Heavy parkas hung on every hook.

"First, don't say 'cool cats.' Second, the stalking started after you'd found the body. It's connected. This stalker could be the murderer."

I swallowed hard. "You might be right. Maybe the person thinks I know something or saw something in the vault."

"Did you?"

I thought back to that morning, remembering the sterile glare of the lighting, the ominous stacks of shelves, the antiseptic silence of the place. "Nothing besides feeling that I had seen Thibodeau before."

"Okay," Adela threw back her shoulders and I could see her slipping into business mode. "Since you don't think the police will help, you've got to be proactive. Take charge."

"What?" I asked. "I'm not going to get involved."

"Face facts, Jess. You're already involved." Adela's brown eyes gleamed and her voice rose. "The stalker thinks you know something or wants to scare you off. Either way, he or she isn't going to leave you alone. You believe there's a connection between the murder and the auction, and the cops don't see that. The only solution is for us to solve the murder." Adela stared at me as if what she said made perfect sense.

I laughed nervously. I knew how determined Adela could be when she had decided on something. "I don't have time to solve a murder. I've got a more important mystery to unravel. If I can figure out what happened to Jem and Victoria, my future at the Dominion Archives is set."

"Your career doesn't mean squat if you're dead."

"Adela!" Sometimes even I was startled by her harshness.

"I'm sorry, but it's true."

"Fine, how do you propose I solve the murder?"

She ignored my sarcastic tone. "Well, I think you should get more information on Thibodeau. He was at the auction, which we agree is significant. He was murdered in the vault, which we also agree is significant." Adela narrowed her eyes. "All we have to do is learn what he was doing in there."

"How are we ever going to figure that out?"

"What about that computer system you mentioned? Could we see if Thibodeau was going into other vaults. Maybe we can suss out a pattern?"

"I'm sure the police have done that already."

"Come on. Not to sound like your mother, but you're giving the cops too much credit here. They aren't looking for a pattern connected to the auction or the paintings, but maybe you could spot it."

I wanted to end this conversation, so I said with finality, "It's a dead end. Only the commissionaires can use the Vault Access system, and then only at the Conservation Facility itself."

Adela pushed her half-drunk martini away, slid from her bar stool, and shrugged into her long coat.

"What are you doing?" I asked.

"We're going out to the Conservation Facility," she said.

I stared at her, mouth agape. "No, we're not."

"Your mother wouldn't back down from this kind of challenge."

I bristled. Adela knew how to push my buttons, but I wasn't going to be manipulated. Last time I let her talk me into something that went against my better judgment, I had limped out of the waxing salon with a Brazilian. "I'm not going, Adela. No way. The cops can solve this murder without me."

"Come on, Jess. It will be totally painless."

That's what she'd said about the Brazilian. I shook my head.

"The place will be deserted," she said. "You could even have a look at those Jem sketches you told me about—the ones you never got to see because you found the body instead." Adela could tell that she had caught my interest, so she pressed the point home. "Come on . . . When are you going to get another chance to see them? I bet it would help your research."

Before I could respond, she grabbed my coat and strode through the bar. I downed the rest of my martini and stood, irresolutely. Then, as I always did when Adela made up her mind, I caved. I reached over and drank the rest of her martini in a single swallow. If I was going back to that damn Conservation Facility, it would be easier if I were tipsy.

◇◇◇◇◇◇◇

BY THE TIME WE'D PULLED UP TO THE BUILDING, MY MARTINI BUZZ WAS singing through my veins, making me feel calm and confident. Adela's plan now made perfect sense, and I was stoked to carry it out.

She eased her Mini Cooper into a parking spot near the entrance. "I can't go in with you. It would be too suspicious. I'll wait here while you see who's on duty. If your friend Bert isn't at the desk—"

"Ernie," I corrected.

"If Ernie isn't on duty, then make up an excuse about using the bathroom and leave. If Ernie's there, see if you can get him to let you have a peek at the Vault Access system. You remember what I told you to say?"

She had drilled some techno-speak into my head to con Ernie into showing me the system. I turned toward her and spoke with my newly won confidence, "Absolutely, Adela."

She sighed and rifled in her handbag, thrusting a pack of gum at me. "Chew on a couple of these, would you? I don't want you smelling like booze."

CHAPTER SEVENTEEN

I WELCOMED THE BRACING JANUARY NIGHT AND TOOK SEVERAL DEEP breaths as I walked to the Conservation Facility. The air was sharp and filled my chest with a chill. I imagined the cold pushing the alcohol back through my veins, returning me to my wits. It hadn't entirely succeeded, because when I reached the Conservation Facility door, I gave it several sharp tugs before remembering that I should push it open. I was delighted to see Ernie behind the desk. He looked up, relaxing when he recognized me.

"Hello, dearie!" he called. "What brings you here at"—he glanced at his computer screen—"eight o'clock at night?"

I looked around and was happy to realize I was neither panicked nor scared. I grinned at Ernie, approaching his desk. "Hi, how are you tonight?"

"Good, good," he replied, a bit downcast. "Things have quieted down considerably since last week."

"Oh?" I asked. "Have the cops cleared out?"

"Yes. I don't think they believe that the murder had much to do with this place anymore."

I remembered Ernie's fear of a commissionaire serial killer. "That's good, isn't it?"

He sighed. "I suppose, but it makes these nights long again."

"Who do they think killed Thibodeau?" I asked casually.

Ernie scratched his chin. "I got the impression that they're rooting around in his biker gang connections. They finally asked me what I knew about that, and I told them about those two guys who came to meet him after work that time. They were real interested, asking me all sorts of stuff. I even went to the station to pick out their photos from a mug shot book." Ernie puffed out his thin chest.

"Wow," I said. "That's pretty cool. Did you find them in there?"

"One of the guys I could pick out. I've got a memory for faces."

"Well, I guess the cops have it all sewn up." Lemieux was taking the easiest explanation for the murder. Thibodeau was involved with a criminal gang, who killed him. Lemieux probably wouldn't even follow up on my auction tip, because it would complicate his tidy little biker theory. I shouldn't have been surprised, but for some reason I had expected more from him.

"Yeah, their investigation seems to be wrapped up here. Now, what can I do for you tonight?"

"Well . . ." What did Adela tell me to say? Something about needing to check the security vectors or the internet protocols? I had no idea, but luckily Ernie was even less computer savvy than me. "Um, my boss told me to check out how the Vault Access system is working, since the murder. Make sure that there aren't any viruses corrupting the mainframe."

Ernie seemed to buy my mission. "And you came out here on a Tuesday night? That's dedication."

"Oh, I have a friend who lives nearby. I was visiting her and figured I'd drop in."

"Sure." Ernie turned toward the computer. "What do you need?"

I came around behind him at the desk and watched as he slowly searched his drive for the Vault Access system.

"Do you mind if I do it, Ernie? I'm quick with computers, and my friend is waiting outside."

Ernie smiled and acquiesced. "Go ahead. You young people are born with those mouses in your hands." He stood from his chair and gestured to me.

I sat and turned to the computer. It was a simple program, listing who accessed which vault at which times. "Just so I understand, uh, what parameters the system is configured around, commissionaires don't usually go into the vaults when they do their night rounds, right?"

Ernie nodded. "That's right. We consider them secure."

I went back one month and began scrolling through the data. Some vaults, like the one that housed the philatelic artefacts, were only rarely accessed, and then only by the curator in charge of the collection. Others, like the textual vaults, which housed the majority of our holdings, were accessed dozens of times a day by circulation staff, archivists, and conservators. I glanced through these and saw Mike, Ginette, Louise, and Barry appear on a regular basis. While archivists normally consulted holdings at their desks downtown, people often needed to come out to the Conservation Facility if there was a problem with box numbering, a finding aid, or if the material was too fragile to travel.

I next turned to the Art Vault. It was much less frequently accessed than the textual ones, and the same names appeared regularly, including several junior conservators. There was a space squeeze for workstations in the main area above the vaults; as a result, the junior conservators used the preservation space in the vault itself.

I continued through the list and was surprised to see Mike and Louise's names appear. I didn't know what either of them would need to do in the vault, since the handling of artworks was usually done only by curators and conservators. Mike was the cultural affairs archivist, so he probably had more reason than most to be in there. Louise's presence was harder to explain. The most troubling find was that Ginette Noiseau was in the Art Vault yesterday afternoon. As the business and industry archivist, I couldn't imagine why she would be interested in the vault. Could it have something to do with her visit to my office? Had Ginette found out about the letters? Had she done what I tried to do last week and gone to look at Crawford's work?

I pushed those disquieting thoughts away and turned to Ernie. "I don't see Stephen Nguyen's name here, but he goes in and out of that vault all the time."

"He's the chief curator, right? He's got blanket access, so the system doesn't record his comings and goings."

I remembered that Oliver had a similar type of access. His movements wouldn't be recorded either.

"Were the cops able to track Thibodeau's movements?" I asked, striving to keep my voice casual.

Ernie shook his head. "Apparently not." He shrugged. "The system has been glitchy for the past few months. There are blank spots where nothing gets recorded."

I recalled the day of the murder and what Ernie had already told me. "Like the morning I found Thibodeau. I wasn't recorded as entering the Vault, and neither was Thibodeau or anyone else."

"That's right. They've done a systematic review and found a whole lot of those blank spots or recording gaps. It's shocking they weren't noticed earlier. The entire system needs an overhaul."

So much for Adela's brilliant plan, there was no way to monitor Thibodeau's movements. I hadn't caught anything on her fishing expedition. "Thanks, Ernie. I've got everything I need." I moved back to the other side of his desk.

"I'm glad to help. It's always nice to have visitors out here during the night shift. It sure can get lonely."

I looked around the big echoing space and shivered. "I bet. But you're not alone here, right?"

"No, there's someone doing a walk-through, and the other commissionaire is at the back entrance. I prefer it when there's more than the three of us, though. It's good to have staff around, but no one's working late tonight."

That was good news, though I schooled myself not to show it. Now was my opportunity to initiate phase two of Adela's plan; I needed to worm my way into the Art Vault. Yes, I promised Stephen I'd never return to the vault, on pain of my job, but the knowledge that Ginette had been in there added a new urgency to my desire. What if she had seen the letters? What if she was after my story? I couldn't let her get the jump on me.

"One thing, before I leave, Ernie. I forgot my notebook in the Art Vault last week. Do you think you could get it for me?"

Remembering my conversation after I first found Thibodeau's body, I was counting on the Dominion Archives' policy that commissionaires stay at their posts.

Ernie looked regretful. "I'd love to help you, but I can't leave the desk."

"Darn," I said, casting my head down as Adela instructed.

"Don't you have access rights?" he asked with concern.

"No, the project I was working on finished, and they revoked them." A small white lie. "My notebook's important, but I guess I'll have to forget about it . . ." Adela had told me to squeeze out a few tears at this point, but I settled for an eyelash flutter.

"I really wish I could help you." Ernie himself looked like he might well up, and I felt bad for lying to him.

I had come this far, however, and decided to keep going. "Maybe I could borrow your pass to get into the vault?" I suggested. This way Stephen would never know I was even in there. "I'm sure you won't get into trouble. After all, you must be the most senior commissionaire here." I could see him softening.

"I'm actually second-most senior, but Stan is retiring soon."

"You can watch where I go on the video system. I'll only go into the Art Vault."

He smiled at me. "Okay. You're lucky, though. They're revising all of the security procedures this week. No one's going to be able to access the Art Vault anymore unless they have explicit approval from Stephen Nguyen, not even commissionaires. My pass still works, so take it, but don't touch anything in there, okay?"

"Absolutely!" I took his pass in triumph. I was Nancy Drew on steroids, Angela Lansbury without the support hose, the entire cast of every one of the *Law and Order* and *CSI* spin-offs all rolled into one detecting machine.

It was only after I left Ernie and was surrounded by the echo of my footsteps that I realized that I was returning, in the dark of night, to the scene of the murder. My steps slowed and my breathing quickened. I forced myself forward, dreading what I might encounter behind the thick steel of the Art Vault door.

CHAPTER EIGHTEEN

"COME ON, JESS. DON'T BE AN IDIOT." I SWALLOWED, TRYING TO RESTORE some moisture to my mouth. I continued down the hall to the vault, fighting queasiness as I remembered the metallic tang of blood that filled my nostrils when Thibodeau's body was released from the stacks.

I shook my head and glanced at my watch. The first part of Adela's plan might not have worked, but I didn't want to blow the second part. The thought of my friend in her car reassured me, and I didn't falter when I reached the door to the Art Vault. With a confident swipe, I ran Ernie's pass through the reader and stepped forward when I heard the door unlock.

The air in the vault, which at twenty-two degrees Celsius was a bit warmer than the corridor, reached out to me like hot breath. The room was murky and dark. Where was the light switch?

I touched the wall. The other times I was in here, the vault had already been lit. As I stepped farther into the room, the lights came on with a soft hum and I blinked in surprise. I always forgot about the motion detection. I pushed the door, and it closed with a subdued click. My instincts screamed at me to check to ensure it hadn't locked, but I refused to give in to my fear. Instead, I looked around. It was the same as it had been on Friday. I couldn't believe it was less than a week since I was last here.

I grabbed a pair of white cotton gloves from the preservation area, telling myself to move quickly. I couldn't help hesitating when I came to the spot where I discovered Thibodeau. It was a relief to see that the stacks were closed tightly, leaving no room for dead commissionaires.

More confident now, I turned the wheel on the shelving to my right, and the rows separated noiselessly. I lost my nerve a little, as I entered the narrow space. The shelves towered eight feet above me, like canyon walls. What if they collapsed and smothered me?

I located the Crawford material and pulled out the first horizontal box. I slid out one of the metal platforms from the shelf, creating a temporary work desk for myself, settling the small ten-by-twelve-inch box on it. My pulse quickened. Here was an original work by Jem. I squinted in the light.

It wasn't a painting, but a rough sketch of Montreal: Men and women, delineated by the most basic of pencil strokes, walked down a sidewalk. A streetcar dominated the foreground. Storefronts, sketched sloppily behind the pedestrians, seemed to be selling wares on the sidewalks, but it was difficult to discern anything specific. Behind them was Mount Royal, its distinctive crucifix reaching to the sky.

I looked at the signature, recognizing Jem's handwriting. I squinted at the date by his name: 1910. He'd drawn this before he'd left for Paris. Probably even before he'd met Victoria.

I pulled out the other boxes and looked through them. They were all the same: basic pencil sketches of urban Montreal scenes. The drawings seemed flat and unimaginative. Jeremy's figures were blocks, and there was no spark of expressiveness in any of his lines.

I put the last box back on its shelf, thinking about Stephen's dismissive summation of Jem's career. His art did indeed seem derivative and unoriginal. The discovery depressed me. Poor Jem. He pinned his hopes on being a great painter but didn't seem to have the necessary talent. I hoped more fervently than ever that he'd been able to get a lot of money for the Rembrandt and that he and Victoria were happy together.

In the next moment, my contemplative mood disappeared. The vault fell into darkness. The lights were motion sensor, and I hadn't been moving in the last couple of minutes. I waved my arms, but the lights didn't come back on. My shoulders tensed. The darkness was thick and bore down on me like a smothering blanket. I found it hard to breathe. Paul Thibodeau died a few feet from the spot where I stood. His blood had pooled on the floor as it seeped out of his body. I gasped for air, my rapidly beating heart intensifying my sense of suffocation.

I needed to get a grip and calmly find the door. I placed my hands in front of me and felt along the shelf. My fingers flicked over the boxes as I inched my way toward the door. My eyes were adjusting to the darkness, and I could make out gray, dim shapes.

I took a step and then stood still. Was that a footfall? I strained my ears, every fiber of my being listening for noise. There. A soft thump, coming from behind me, somewhere deeper in the stacks.

Survival instincts I didn't know I possessed kicked into high gear. Quickly but quietly, I slid out of the stacks. The red exit sign glowed like hope at the end of the long room. I hugged the concrete wall, staying as far from the shelving as I could. I imagined someone coming for me through the stacks, reaching out and dragging me into the shelves.

I strained to hear any sounds of being followed but detected nothing over the noisy beating of my heart. Passing the conservation area, I didn't notice a chair sticking out in the gloom. My hip brushed against it, and it nudged softly against the table. The noise was deafening to my strained nerves, and I abandoned my attempts at stealth.

I bolted for the door, wrenching it open with shaking hands. I pulled it tight behind me and raced back to Ernie's desk.

"What happened?" he yelped when he saw my face.

I took a calming breath before speaking. Despite my fear, I didn't want to raise any alarms with Ernie, because he'd be forced to act on them. If he followed security protocol, he would have to investigate whether someone had been in there with me. Undoubtedly, there would be forms to fill out, and it would emerge that I was in the vaults without permission. That would end my career.

I smiled reassuringly and handed his pass back to him. "There's nothing wrong. I got scared because the lights went out."

His face was sympathetic. "Oh, that happens sometimes. The motion detection needs fine-tuning. Are you okay? Do you want to sit?"

I shook my head. "No, I'd better get going. My friend is waiting."

"Okay. Take care of yourself."

"Thanks for everything, Ernie. Good night."

"Jess!"

Almost at the door, I turned back.

"Did you get your notebook?"

"What?" I asked blankly.

Ernie's kind expression turned stern. "The reason you went in there."

"Yes, thanks." I pulled out the notebook I used for Jem and Victoria from my purse and waved it at him.

His face was all benevolence again. "Oh good, dear. Have a nice night."

I wrenched open Adela's car door and sat down with relief.

"Are you all right?" she asked.

"I'm okay. Let's get out of here."

She didn't need to be told twice. By the time I relayed everything to Adela, we were pulling up at my place.

"I think you should tell the cops," she said.

"I can't. I wasn't supposed to be in the vault. Besides, I never actually saw anyone. Maybe I just freaked myself out."

Adela raised an eyebrow but didn't pursue it. "Okay, fine. What did you find out?"

I thought back to the results of my sleuthing. "Well, not a lot, actually. Thibodeau didn't show up in the Vault Access system because it's glitchy. It doesn't get us any further."

"So the trip was a waste?" Adela said.

"Not entirely," I said, remembering Ginette. "I think a colleague is trying to poach my Jem and Victoria story."

Adela took little interest in my office intrigues. "Are you still nervous? Do you want me to stay the night?" she asked.

I shook my head. "No, I'll be all right. Like I said, I'm sure no one was there. I was just tipsy."

"I'll come in with you, anyway. Make sure you get settled."

I smiled. "Thanks, Adela."

She stood beside me as I unlocked the door and watched in silence as I checked the closet and under the bed. The advantage of living in a tiny apartment was there weren't many places for an assailant to hide.

CHAPTER NINETEEN

AS USUAL, EVERYTHING FELT BETTER UNDER THE MORNING SUN. MY mood improved even more when, upon arrival at work, I found another letter from Jem in the latest batch of ledgers. I was always a little nervous that there would be no more hidden correspondence, so it was a relief to come across another one.

> December 16, 1914
>
> Dearest Vic,
>
> It was so delightful to get your letter, sweetheart. I am sorry the air on the farm is still not agreeing with you. Bundle up, dearest. I would hate for you to catch a chill before I have the chance to return home.
>
> Christmas has arrived, bearing none of the usual joy of the season. The casualty lists are dreadful, and I grimace at how naïve I was during those warm weeks of August. Could I really have believed it would be over by now? Was there a time when the names Arras, Aisne, and Ypres did not chill my veins with dismay? Yet, like you, I am not sure if it is the carnage on the front or the attitudes at home that are most disturbing. My friend André, the daring experimental painter who inspired me this summer, has abandoned all of his ideas about art. Now he paints image d'Épinale, bland classical portraits on patriotic themes. He refuses categorically to talk about his old ideals. What is truly sad is that I know he despises the images he produces. I suspect that he wants to avoid being returned to the front and hopes to escape the fighting by being commissioned as a French war artist. I certainly cannot blame him for that.

The season makes me realize that it has been five long months since we have been together. Time moves so quickly in some respects, and yet so slowly in others. For me this war is nothing but an impediment to our love. Oh, I know it is a dreadful thing to say, when young men are coming over here and dying in great numbers, but I cannot help it, dearest. All of my energies, all of my focus is now directed to getting home and being with you once again. I miss you every moment of every day. You are my inspiration, Victoria. You have unleashed something within me, and for that I will be forever in your debt.

Let me turn the subject to our old master, the seed from which our future shall grow. Your solution to the problem of getting the painting out of France is perfect! Typical Victoria—inventive, brilliant, and with a dash of audacity. I knew I could rely upon your cleverness. I shall investigate all possibilities. I do not want to damage the canvas, so I will have to discuss the issue with André and some other artist friends, but do not fear, I shall be discreet!

After countless delays, it appears that Teddy's aunt will secure the exit visas within the next week. I shall be crossing the Channel to England soon and then waiting for passage to home.

Oh, Victoria, I don't know how to tell you what I feel other than to say again I love you and leave you to guess the gestures and caresses with which I would tell it to you, if you were only here.

Jem

I stared at the letter in puzzlement. How was Jem planning on smuggling the painting out? I hoped he wasn't going to do anything foolish that damaged it. I wasn't as confident in Jem's abilities as Victoria seemed to be. From what I could gather, he was a romantic, dreaming boy who might not have had the best grasp on reality.

As I walked down the hall to Mike's office, I told myself that borrowing a book from him on painting techniques made more sense than trundling all the way down to the Reading Room. I certainly wasn't turning into an aggressive "she-lion," as "The Rules" would contend. I knocked on his door in the softest, most demure, un-lion-like fashion possible.

"Yes?" he called.

I poked my head into his cluttered den. "Hi," I said.

His face creased into a wide grin, and he jumped from his chair. "Jess!" he exclaimed. "It's good to see you."

He walked toward me, slipping on a pile of loose papers but recovering quickly. "I wanted to see you yesterday, but when I came by your office it was dark. I thought maybe you'd gone home."

"I had a pounding headache, so I shut off the lights for a few minutes. Of course, that was when Ginette tried to sneak in."

"Oh?" he asked, stepping aside and gesturing me to a chair.

I sat, and Mike leaned against his desk, looming slightly over me. "What do you mean she snuck in?"

"It was strange. She came into my office uninvited and was surprised to find me there. She threatened to tell Oliver I was napping on the job."

Mike frowned. "Be careful, Jess. Ginette's got a lot of ambition, without a lot of morals."

"What do you mean?"

"I know that she's often scooped colleagues on articles they've been working on. She's good at nosing out subjects that can advance her career. She and Louise have had a couple of run-ins."

"Really?" I asked.

"Yeah. I don't know the details, but I think Ginette might have double-crossed Louise at some point. I know Louise doesn't have any time for her."

This was interesting. In all of Louise's dark warnings to me to watch my back, she'd dwelled on what the men in the department did, rarely mentioning Ginette. "Do you have any idea why she would be in the Art Vault lately?"

"I've certainly never seen her when I've been working. Why do you think she's been in there?"

"Oh, something she said once." I was appalled at how easily I lied. "Do you go into the vault often?" I asked.

He nodded. "Yeah. I handle the acquisition of painters' papers. Generally, if they're a big-name artist, their work will be in the art galleries, but we'll take everything else. Often, a bit of artwork slips in with their records."

I hated myself for questioning him, but between Louise's warnings and Ginette's interest, I was in full paranoia mode. "Have you acquired any painters' papers lately?"

"Yeah. Last month we brought in the records of one of A. Y. Jackson's nieces. She's an artist in her own right, and we took some of her work." He coughed. "I went out to the Conservation Facility to have a look at it. Marvelous stuff. If you're interested, I could bring you out there sometime. Show you my etchings." He waggled his eyebrows.

I laughed, relieved that there was an explanation for his Art Vault forays.

"Why are you so interested in that vault, anyway?" he asked.

Again, a lie tripped off my tongue. "I've been curious about it since I found the body."

"Do you think it's tied to the murder?"

I shrugged. "The police don't. The victim, Paul Thibodeau, had biker gang connections, so apparently the cops are concentrating on that angle."

"And you think the police are overlooking something?" he asked with perception.

"Well, I don't have a lot of faith in cops. I'm sure they'll sort it out, though." I brought the conversation back to more pleasant topics. "I enjoyed our time together the other night." I smiled at him. That was definitely against "The Rules."

He smiled back, the atmosphere in the room changing slightly. "Me too. I've been thinking about you day and night."

The intensity of his words caught me off guard, and I was momentarily speechless. I could hear the wind pushing against Mike's office window, lifting up the plastic flap that covered the air conditioner.

The heat of the furnace, still pumping out warm air, caused the few strands of hair not tucked up in my ponytail to whisper lightly around my face. The hard chair dug into my back, but I enjoyed the sharp sensation, just as I enjoyed smiling at Mike. I could smell his scent—clean, like Ivory soap. I stared into his eyes and saw something in their brown depths darken as he looked back at me. My stomach tightened, and I felt a surge of warmth that had nothing to do with the furnace.

"Mike, I . . ." my voice cracked slightly and I coughed, embarrassed. I started again. "I actually came here to get some work advice."

He blinked. "Of course," he said. He leaned back from me. "What do you need?"

I bit my lip. "Well, I'm doing some research for one of Oliver's projects." My habit of secrecy was ingrained, and technically, I wasn't lying.

"Is he sending you off on another wild-goose chase?" he asked.

"Something like that. I was wondering if you owned any books on the mechanics of painting. You know, stuff about paint types, canvases, that sort of thing."

"Sure," Mike said. "Although, the real master of anything like that is Stephen Nguyen. He's the chief curator. Absolute expert."

"I know, but I didn't want to bug him. He's a big muckety-muck."

Mike acted offended. "And I'm not?"

I smiled. "No, you're not. Besides, I've got an 'in' with you."

He grinned. "You do, do you?"

"Yup. You've bought me dinner, so you're now in my thrall."

Mike laughed, a light sound that surprised me in its spontaneity and happiness. "I can think of worse things," he said, turning to his floor-to-ceiling bookshelf. "I don't know a lot about art—I'm more interested in writers and performers—but I know I've got something on technique. What's the project, anyway?"

"It's the one I told you about before. The letters to Victoria Jarvis."

"That's something to do with farming in Alberta, right?"

"Something like that," I agreed.

Mike located a book and pulled it off the shelf, handing it to me.

"*The Idiot's Guide to Oil Paints.* This looks about at my level," I remarked.

He laughed.

I turned to the door. "Well, thanks for your help."

"Jess?" he asked.

I liked the way my name sounded when he said it. "Yes?" I turned back.

"I wondered if . . . if . . . you wanted to go out to dinner again?"

Score one for the lioness! I kept my voice casual. "Yeah, but can we give Hy's a miss this time?"

He laughed. "Absolutely."

"Okay, then. Let me know when and where."

"Sure thing." He frowned. "Damn it. I forgot that I'll be in Vancouver for the rest of this week. I'm meeting with the head of a dance troupe who might want to donate. I've got to squeeze the trip in before the Olympics start and hotel prices quadruple. What about next week?"

I smiled. "That would be great." I left his office with a spring to my step. Even bumping into Ginette couldn't dim my happiness.

"Visiting with Mike again, I see." She stood in her doorway, staring as I walked down the hallway.

"I had a work question."

"Sure you did."

I was sick of Ginette and her innuendos. My lioness mojo was flowing, and I decided to go on the attack. "I didn't think to ask you yesterday morning, but what were you looking for in my office?"

Her gray eyes met mine, and I must have imagined the small flicker of uncertainty, because she spoke confidently. "Oliver wanted the progress report on the Jarvis ledgers. He asked me to pick it up from you. You startled me so much, I forgot to get it."

"Oliver never asked me for a progress report."

Ginette shrugged, a chic twist of her shoulders that dismissed me as effectively as her words. "Part of being hired on permanently is knowing your deliverables without being told. You might try to remember that." She turned and shut her door.

I stomped down the hall to Oliver's office.

I was about to knock, when I heard a flush from the nearby men's room, and Oliver emerged. The time between his flush and his appearance was so short that he couldn't have washed his hands. I added poor hygiene to his list of crimes.

Oliver had gone for a flamboyant look today. He wore a purple tunic over loose silver-flecked trousers. I glanced down, fearful that he might have slipped on a pair of curly-toed shoes. Thankfully, he resisted that flourish. He looked like a pasty, slightly sweaty genie who must have come out of quite a large bottle.

He was in one of his hyper moods as he ushered me into his office. "Ah, Jessica, Jessy, Jess. How are we today?"

I tried not to stare at him. "Fine, Oliver."

He sat, drumming his fingers against his desk. "Come across a body today? Anyone with that 'not-so-alive' feeling? Anyone who is breathing challenged?" He chuckled at his own jokes.

My response was stiff. "No." I didn't find Thibodeau's death funny, and I doubted I ever would.

He rubbed his nose. "I meant to check in on you yesterday, see how you're getting along. I was in meetings all morning, of course, and then was swamped in the afternoon. My expertise is always in demand—quite a bother." He smiled contentedly at me.

"I'm sure it is," I said evenly.

"What brings you to my humble domain?"

"Ginette mentioned that you needed a progress report on the Jarvis material?"

"Ah yes. She and I spoke about that yesterday. Rapidamente. Rapidamente. That's Italian, you know. I spent a year there in my youth. Lovely place, Italy. Filled with olives and grapes . . ." His voice trailed away, as if he'd lost his point.

I prompted him. "The progress report?"

He stood, rubbing his hands. "Yes, give me something short—say ten pages on what you've found to date and how long the rest will take. Can't have you dillydallying."

I left Oliver murmuring to himself. He was getting stranger and stranger.

More interesting than Oliver's oddness was what he revealed. He was in meetings all morning yesterday, so he couldn't have instructed Ginette to demand a progress report from me until after our encounter. What was the real reason she entered my office? Something told me I would not like the answer.

CHAPTER TWENTY

I TOOK EVASIVE ACTION FOR THE REST OF THE WEEK. I AVOIDED GINETTE, kept my office locked, and tried not to speak about the letters to anyone.

After banging out Oliver's progress report (leaving out any mention of the letters), I devoted the rest of my time to researching Jem and Victoria's story. To that end, I spent most of my time in the microfilm consultation area, a cave-like series of rooms annexed to the Reading Room.

The space always reminded me of a strange church where an alternative religion was practiced. Solitary researchers worshipped at their machines, scrolling through page after page of copied archival documents, lit only by the ethereal glow of the readers' light bulbs. The click and whir of the reels spinning through the machines and the soft scratch of pencils formed the choral music as the researchers sat in holy communion with history.

By Friday, I was thoroughly sick of the microfilm room with its dim lighting, mouth-breathing researchers, and machines that ate film. I found out very little. I'd located the birth entries for Jeremy and Victoria as well as Victoria's brother and her two younger cousins. Victoria's birth date confirmed my suspicion that her mother died in childbirth, but beyond that I discovered nothing significant.

Both of Victoria's cousins wed in the mid-1930s, but I could find no marriage or death certificates for Jem or Victoria. For a while I was convinced that there was some dark plot to expunge the couple from the records, but in discussing research methods with Louise, she explained that record keeping was spotty in the early twentieth century and entries could be located in other registers or even in other countries. This made me feel slightly better. It meant I could still find out what happened to them, if I could only figure out where to look.

My need to discover their ending was growing stronger and stronger. It wasn't only to help my article; I was invested in their happiness. I read and reread the photocopies of Jem's letters, hoping that they found a way to sell the painting and have a "happily ever after." Growing up, I saw so many depressing stories—prostitutes going back to the pimps who beat them, junkies overdosing, runaways being returned to their abusers' homes—that I craved happy endings. I loved Elizabeth and Darcy, not Anna and Vronsky. I wanted hand-in-hand walks into the sunset, passionate kisses, and a slow fade out. I wanted Jem and Victoria's story to be a romantic comedy, not a tragedy.

Unfortunately, by Friday, I had examined nineteen of the twenty-eight boxes but uncovered no more letters. This silence made me nervous. Thankfully, I didn't find ledgers with empty slits. At least no one was pilfering letters before I got a chance to see them.

I had a bit more luck with my research on Jem's Rembrandt. Mike's book was simple and didn't offer me a ton of information, so I had put in an interlibrary loan request for a few more volumes on painting and technique and was waiting for them to arrive. On one lunch break I'd hit the public library and found a helpful book on art theft. I learned that the simplest way to hide a painting was to pop the canvas out of its frame and roll it up. Thieves did something similar in an infamous art raid on Boston's Isabella Stewart Gardner Museum in the 1990s. They stormed the building and sliced thirteen paintings from their frames, grabbing a haul worth more than $300 million. In a cinematic twist, a reporter with the *Boston Herald* later claimed to have met the thieves in a darkened warehouse and watched as they unrolled a Rembrandt canvas to prove they still had it. The thieves hoped to ransom the paintings back to the museum.

It seemed likely that Jem popped the canvas from the frame, rolled it up, and hid it in his luggage to get it back home.

Despite my lack of real leads about Jem and Victoria, I walked home from work on Friday night with a spring in my step. The intense cold that gripped the city had loosened, and it was warm enough for me to walk without my usual tuque. While I loved the winter, it was a relief not to be huddled against the wind. Best of all, there had been no stalker scare since my Tuesday trip to the vaults. Things were looking up.

◇◇◇◇◇◇

IT WAS MIDNIGHT, AND TIFFANY'S "I THINK WE'RE ALONE NOW" WAS blaring from the speakers as Adela and I bopped on the dance floor. Sunday Eighties Night at Barrymore's was our tradition and always brought out the craziest fashions. Tonight was no exception. In front of me was a sea of neon jewelry, acid-washed jeans, and leg warmers.

Adela went big in everything she did. She had combed her hair into a wall around her face, slashed bright-pink lipstick on her mouth, and painted blue eye shadow all the way up to her eyebrows. She wore a billowy pink baby doll dress. I had on my usual Eighties Night garb—a pair of tight dark purple jeans, a tiny *Knight Rider* T-shirt depicting David Hasselhoff and his KITT car, and the pièce de résistance, a platinum blonde wig.

The song ended, and I herded Adela off the dance floor before she could start jumping to Bon Jovi. I had a long week ahead of me and wanted to get home.

The air outside was warm for late January, hovering well above freezing. My ears rang slightly from the bar's blaring music, my eyesight was a bit fuzzy thanks to three vodka cranberries, and my feet ached from dancing. It was a good night.

Despite the fact that it was Sunday, Bank Street was buzzing as people in turquoise and neon streamed in and out of Barrymore's. We walked north, away from the club.

A couple of diners and falafel shops were still open, and the delicious smell of greasy fries wafted over the night air.

"I'm going home," I said.

Adela shook her head. "Not yet."

"I can't believe you're not tired. You work seventy hours a week. How can you have the energy to do anything?"

Adela ignored me, hailing a cab.

"I'm not going to another club," I grumbled.

"Don't worry," she said as we climbed in. "This place is right by your house. It will take twenty minutes, and then you can go to bed."

"By my house? There's nothing near my place unless you want to smoke crack, watch a cockfight, or get a blow job. Please tell me we're not going to do any of those."

Adela laughed and leaned toward the driver. "Leo's Tavern, please."

"What!" I exclaimed. "Why are we going there?" Leo's was a no-torious Ottawa dive. It was around the corner from my apartment, but I'd never ventured in. It was rumored to be a big biker hangout. Then the light dawned. "You want to do some more digging into Thibodeau, don't you?"

Adela spoke in hushed tones. "We're going for a beer. There's no harm in having a drink. Besides, we're in perfect disguise at the moment." She waved to my outfit. "We'll fit right in."

"Fit right in? We look teleported in from a Glass Tiger video." I could tell by the set of her mouth that Adela was determined, so I tried another tack. "The cops can handle this investigation."

"Ha. I haven't heard a thing all week about the murder on the news. They aren't even close to solving it."

"Well, what do you think we can do?"

"We're undercover. We can talk to people who might have known Thibodeau. Find out what he was up to."

"You don't even know if Thibodeau went to Leo's."

"Ottawa isn't exactly swimming in biker bars. Your pal Ernie said he hung out at a bar in Mechanicsville. This is the place," Adela said decisively.

I marveled at her aura of authority. She seemed to actually believe she could solve this crime.

"Adela, why in the world would you want to do this?"

Her eyes sparkled. "Because it's different and exciting."

"Maybe for you, but you're not the one who found the dead body or thought you were being stalked."

Adela was not swayed. "I know it was hard on you, Jess, but I think you should face your fears. Wouldn't you feel empowered if you caught the guy who killed Thibodeau?"

"No," I snapped. "Traipsing into some biker bar dressed like Cyndi Lauper is not going to empower me. I'm not going in." I crossed my arms.

"Fine, I'll go by myself. Just remember, if anything bad happens to me, it's all your fault."

She had me, and we both knew it. We passed the rest of the trip in silence as I remembered all the stupid things that Adela convinced me to do over the years. Under her instigation, we faked our IDs and scammed our way into the campus bar, hitchhiked to Montreal to see a concert, and once tripped out on magic mushrooms that she bought from a friend of a friend of a friend's roommate.

The cab stopped, and we got out in front of a dilapidated building, the neon Leo's Tavern sign long since burned out. A window on the upper floor had been smashed in and boarded up, so the building looked strangely off-kilter. The cheerful hubbub of Bank Street was gone. Instead, enormous pickups and large SUVs dominated the parking lot, gleaming menacingly under the light of the streetlamps.

"It's not too late to go home," I hissed. "What do you think you're going to accomplish here, besides getting our teeth knocked out?"

Adela tried for breezy self-assurance, but the building's dingy, menacing vibe subdued even her. "Don't be ridiculous, Jess. Nothing bad will happen."

We opened the door into a room filled with large, meaty-looking men. I adjusted my wig nervously, hoping it would stay on. No one even gave us a second glance as we got our bearings, and I relaxed slightly. This place wasn't so scary. In fact, there was so much long hair and leather on the men that I wondered for a second if we took a wrong turn and wound up back by Barrymore's in Ottawa's gay village. But given the motorcycle decor—tattered posters of Harleys and handlebars mounted on the walls like animal trophies—the patrons' appearances were due to their biking days rather than an homage to the Village People.

The air was murky, and it took an instant to realize why. Ottawa enforced a strict anti-smoking bylaw, but apparently Leo's had exempted itself because a thick cigarette haze enveloped us.

We made our way to the long bar in one corner of the room, serenaded by the blaring twang of Waylon Jennings piped in through the stereo. We stood next to a tall man with an eagle tattooed on his forearm who was leaning against the bar. He turned and sized us both up before speaking to Adela.

"Where did you come from, little momma?"

While Adela started telling him she was a cocktail waitress at the Gatineau casino, I ordered a beer and looked around the room. The bar wasn't entirely filled with big men; there were also a number of short women with high hair and bountiful bosoms.

Everywhere I looked, I saw cleavage spilling out of tank tops, thrusting out of T-shirts, and pouring out of tiny little dresses. I gaped at the amount of surgery and support-engineering I was witnessing. It was comforting, however, to note that we didn't look out of place. True, our chests weren't Dolly Parton-esque, but otherwise our big hair and loud makeup didn't stand out. Adela, as usual, had been right.

Watching people laugh and drink beer, I remembered a friend of my mother's from my childhood. Nick was a member of the Hells Angels, but he had been very sweet. He used to let me sit on his bike and even wear his helmet. My sister and I loved it when he came by, because he would always slip us Mars bars and packs of gum when my mother wasn't looking. I smiled at the memory and dug my elbow into Adela's side. "I like this place," I whispered.

"Uh-huh." Adela's voice was strained.

"Hey, are you okay?" I asked quietly.

She turned away from the tattooed guy and bulged her eyes out in the universal sign for "Get me the hell out of here."

"I need to talk to you," I said as I pulled Adela away from the bar. She turned and gave her new friend a halfhearted wave.

"What happened?" I asked when we were out of earshot.

"He was coming on to me with some of the worst pickup lines I've ever heard. He said sex was a killer, then asked if I wanted to die happy."

I snorted, and she cracked a smile. She looked back at the bar. "Listen, I don't want to encourage him. He looks scary. I don't know how we're going to find out anything useful from anyone. You were right—I think coming in here was a bad idea."

It wasn't often that Adela admitted she was wrong, and I felt an ungenerous moment of pure self-righteousness. "Not quite yet," I said, relishing the chance to torture her. "I'm going to finish my drink." I turned back to the bar. As I did so, a movement caught my eye.

In the far corner, someone was shrugging into a bulky overcoat and wrapping a familiar scarf around his face. I stepped behind a large post and peeped out. It wasn't his outfit that gave him away, but how he moved as he made for the door. I'd been seeing that walk in my nightmares for the last ten days. Twelve feet away from me was the stalker.

CHAPTER TWENTY-ONE

I pulled her into the crowd as the stalker turned and looked around the bar. His face was wide, with a high forehead and close-set eyes. I squeezed deeper into the throng, trying to avoid his gaze.

He waved to a man sitting against a wall and then pushed open the door and was gone. He hadn't seen me. I sagged in relief and walked to a quieter corner of the bar.

"What's got into you?" Adela demanded.

"The big guy who left? That was the stalker."

Her mouth dropped. "Are you sure?"

"Absolutely. It was the same coat, same scarf. And the way he moved—it was him."

Adela looked into my face and must have seen my certainty. "Oh sweetie, are you okay?"

I shook my head. "I need to sit down."

She pulled a nearby stool toward me, and I sat. I waited for the fear to flood me as it had several times since discovering the body. I waited for my heart to start pounding, my stomach to start heaving, and for that panicked, adrenalized feeling to course through me. Nothing happened.

It occurred to me that I was actually relieved to have spotted the stalker. My mother always claimed that she was never nervous about dangers she could anticipate but was terrified of what she didn't know. I must have picked up that attitude, because I felt a weight was lifted from my shoulders.

The faceless monster from my nightmares was an ordinary man. If he had a face, then I could figure out who he was. He was not in charge. I didn't know how long this feeling of strength and liberation would last before my usual meek, common-sense self reemerged, but I wasn't going to wait around for "Sensible Jess" to show up. I wanted to learn who this guy was, and I wanted to do it now.

I stood up and walked toward the other side of the bar.

Adela followed. "Jess, we should leave."

I stopped and spoke to her as quietly as I could. "No, I'm staying to do what we came here to do—find out who killed Thibodeau."

"What?" she asked. "You spotted the stalker. You need to go home, call the cops, and hide under your blankets!"

I hesitated. I was already rethinking my initial bravery. It did make more sense to let the police handle it. Then I remembered the terror that this man had made me feel. My voice was fierce. "This is my chance, and I'm not going to let fear stop me." My tone softened. "Thanks for bringing me here, but you can leave if you want."

She looked surprised. "When did you get all warrior princess?"

I stared steadily back at her, and she sighed. "I'll stay, but don't expect me to wear a leather bra."

"Your outfit is good enough," I grinned. "I'm glad you're here."

"What's your plan?" she asked.

For once in our relationship, Adela was asking me what to do. It felt good. "The stalker knows that guy against the wall," I tilted my head toward the man he had waved to. "I'm going to talk to him."

"You're going to walk up and introduce yourself? What if he's in cahoots with the stalker? What if he recognizes you? This is a stupid plan."

Our entire friendship, I always went along with every one of Adela's idiotic schemes. "What do you suggest?" I snapped.

"Let me talk to him. It's safer."

"No. I want to do this."

"Jess, twenty minutes ago, I had to convince you to even come into this bar. Now you want to place yourself in serious danger? I'm not going to let you. Besides, you're not good at thinking on your feet or coming up with quick lies. That's my specialty. What if you start panicking and say something stupid?"

"I did okay with Ernie," I said.

"That guy was like ninety years old. Trust me, Jess. I can do this better than you."

I knew she was right. I nodded, and we found a quiet table to discuss the plan of action. "What do you need me to find out?" she asked.

"We want to know the name of the stalker, and it would be great if you could see if he's connected to Thibodeau or the murder."

"No prob," Adela said, standing from the table and fluffing her hair.

"How are you going to get him to talk to you?"

"I'm going to use my girlie powers—twirl my hair and giggle."

She sashayed away before I could reply. I watched as Adela approached the stalker's friend. He sat alone at a quiet table in the back of the bar. He was a short guy, his feet dangling from the tall stool, but he looked muscular. His tight black T-shirt emphasized how massive his shoulders were, like two boulders about to crush his head, which seemed small by comparison.

I saw Adela smile flirtatiously at him, and his gesture for her to sit. He flagged down a waiter and ordered her a drink. Adela touched her hair a lot and once brushed his arm. I could see he was relaxing. He leaned back and looked her over, his interest written on his face.

The longer they talked, the more nervous I became. A few minutes passed. I rubbed my face, my thick makeup feeling like a mask. What if Adela was making a mistake or putting herself in danger?

I was so intent on watching them, I didn't notice someone approaching.

"Hey, beautiful. You look lonely," a voice whispered in my ear.

I jumped. Adela's acquaintance from the bar had wandered over. I smiled nervously at him and looked back toward Adela's table. Their drinks arrived, and they were still chatting.

"Mind if I join you?" my would-be suitor asked.

"Well . . ."

He ignored my hesitation and pulled up a stool. I was actually pleased when he sat down because he hid me completely from the stalker's friend, which made me feel less exposed. If I leaned back a little, I could still see Adela and make sure she was okay.

"Come here often, gorgeous?" I noticed the guy's other forearm. On it, almost concealed by his shirt, was what looked like a swastika tattoo.

"No," I stuttered. "This is my first time."

"You're quite the sexy lady, do you know that?"

"Thanks," I said. I'd never been hit on so aggressively and was getting flustered.

We talked for a little while, and I kept my eye on Adela. I could tell by her posture that she wasn't doing much speaking. I hoped she was able to get the guy to tell her something useful soon, because my new date was frightening. He picked up my hand and stroked it. I didn't want to rip it away from him, in case I drew attention to myself. Instead, I smiled wanly and allowed him to massage each of my fingers in turn. I felt like a cow being milked.

"You should see my machine," he said. "It's a 2009 Fat Boy. I've got Screamin' Eagle exhaust and fuel injection. It's a sweet ride. Fucking winter means I have to drive some piece-of-shit truck."

"That's too bad," I murmured sympathetically. I noticed Adela writing something on a piece of paper.

"Know what I would like to do to you, momma?"

Adela had stood up. "What?" I asked distractedly.

"I'd like to take you for a ride on my big fat hog."

That caught my attention. "That's not a good idea," I said.

I looked up. Adela was scanning the bar. She caught my eye and then stared meaningfully at the door.

"There's my boyfriend," I said, pointing to a muscly man leaning against the doorway. I pulled my hand away and hurried toward him. Thankfully, my Romeo didn't try to follow. On the way out, I glimpsed the guy Adela had been talking to. He was staring at his cell phone. The feel of the night's fresh air on my skin was like a splash of water against my face, and I felt cleansed of the bar's smoky and sordid atmosphere.

"How did you get away from him?" I asked Adela as we turned away from the bar and began walking toward my place.

"I told Joe I had to get up early for a waitressing shift. I gave him my number, but it was for that Greek place we like to order from."

"Nice work."

"Let's not hang around, though," she said. We picked up the pace for the short walk to my apartment, not bothering to talk. I looked back nervously a couple of times, but we weren't followed.

CHAPTER TWENTY-TWO

AS SOON AS WE WERE INSIDE MY APARTMENT, DOOR DEAD-BOLTED, I turned to Adela. "What did you find out?" I asked.

Adela smiled. "Your stalker's name is Ray Malone."

I whooped with happiness. "How did you learn that?"

"Simple—I told Joe that his friend looked familiar and asked him his name." Adela sat down on my threadbare couch.

"Ray Malone," I repeated. "That doesn't ring any bells. Did you learn anything else?" I took a seat beside her.

"You bet I did. I'm pretty good at this, if I do say so myself."

I snorted. "Yeah, I didn't realize your alter ego was Vampy Sex-a-Lot."

"How else could I get a meathead like Joe to open up?"

"Hey, I'm not complaining, Adela. Thank you so much."

"Wait until I tell you what I learned. First of all, Malone is Paul Thibodeau's cousin."

There it was: the connection I suspected, but dreaded. I was being stalked because of the murder. "How did you learn that?"

"Joe asked me how I knew Malone. I told him I recognized him from a bar I worked at, but that I hadn't seen him in a while. That's when Joe said that Malone was keeping a low profile since his cousin was murdered."

"What else?" I asked.

"He said the cops were stupid to think that Malone killed Paul. Then he ranted about how dumb policemen are. He reminded me of your mother, but scarier."

"Malone is a police suspect," I murmured. I could see Lemieux quickly concluding that the victim's biker-affiliated cousin was behind the murder. That's probably why their investigation was no longer focused on the Art Vault. "Did Joe say he knew for sure that Malone hadn't killed Thibodeau?"

"He said there was no way that Malone would have done it. Malone loved his cousin like a brother. And he said that if Malone murdered Thibodeau, he would have been more discreet then to leave a corpse in the middle of a government building. He said Malone would have dumped the body at the bottom of some lake, where the cops would never find him." She grimaced. "It sounded like Joe was talking from experience."

I swallowed hard. "So according to Joe, Malone is a killer, but he didn't murder Thibodeau?"

"Yup. Maybe I'm naive, but I believed Joe when he said that Malone didn't do it. He sounded sincere, and he was very up-front about everything, like he had nothing to hide."

"Yeah, nothing to hide because when he and Malone murder people they throw the evidence in a lake," I said.

"I have to admit, he was scarier to talk to than I thought he'd be. Did you see his tattoos? I think they were from prison."

We lapsed into a grim silence, thinking about the danger she had skirted. My earlier exhilaration was tempered now. Learning about Malone's relationship to Thibodeau and hearing about Joe brought home how serious these men were. It wasn't a nice thought.

Adela seemed to be thinking along the same lines. "You should tell that cop that Malone is stalking you."

I rolled my eyes. It still rankled that Lemieux had accused me of inventing excuses to talk to him. "Who knows if he'll take me seriously? If anything, now it looks like I'm stalking Malone."

"But he's Thibodeau's cousin. The police will see the connection."

"Adela, you've got way more faith in Lemieux than I do. He barely listened to my tip about the auction house." I frowned.

"Come on. You're in danger."

"How would I explain to Lemieux what I was doing at Leo's?"

Adela grunted in irritation. "You've got to get over this distrust, Jess. You should go to the police. They're trying to solve a murder, and a prime suspect is stalking you."

I didn't relish the idea of talking to Lemieux again, but Adela was right. I looked at my watch. "It's nearly two in the morning. There's no point in calling him tonight. I'll do it tomorrow from work."

"Good," Adela said.

"Hey, I don't want to be alone. Will you sleep over?"

She didn't even hesitate. "Of course, sweetie."

"Should we rehydrate before bed?" I asked.

Adela answered by heading into my kitchen and pulling out my anti-hangover Gatorade stash.

I followed, dumping ice cubes into two tall glasses. "So what did we learn tonight?" It felt good to look at the situation logically, like I was categorizing and filing my fears, as I would archival documents.

Adela poured the bright blue liquid into two glasses. "We know your stalker's name is Ray Malone, and we know he and Thibodeau were cousins. It makes me wonder how Thibodeau got a job as a security guard if he was related to someone in a biker gang."

I pulled out a ramen packet and waved it at Adela. "Sustenance?" I asked.

She nodded. I flicked on the kettle and dumped the noodles into a pot. As I waited for the water to boil, I thought about my own application to the Dominion Archives. "The fact that Thibodeau's cousin is shady wouldn't have come up during his security clearance. I had to give details about my mother and sister when I applied, but I wasn't asked about extended family. If Thibodeau's criminal record was clean, they wouldn't investigate much more deeply."

"Really!" Adela said in surprise.

The kettle boiled and I dumped the water into the pot with the noodles, adding in the flavor packet. I dished up the ramen in silence, stirring my bowl of savory noodles.

"What are you thinking?" Adela grabbed her drink and bowl and walked toward the living room.

"Well, Thibodeau paid way too much for paintings at the Andrew Jarvis auction, right?" I followed her.

Adela nodded. We both sat on the small couch.

"And the night of that purchase he was murdered, correct?"

"Yes," she said.

"We believe those two events are connected, especially because at the same auction I found letters that discuss a Rembrandt painting."

Adela shifted in her seat, following my train of thought. "So you think that Victoria's cousin, Andrew, ended up with the Rembrandt and his estate sold it to Thibodeau, who was then murdered for it." She slurped up the ramen.

I considered. That's what my gut was telling me. "Yes."

Adela cocked her head. "You might be right, but you're making a few leaps. In your version, this masterpiece goes undetected for ninety years, until a not-very-bright security guard sees it at auction, recognizes it even when Van Cleef's trained experts don't, and buys it? Then some mysterious person realizes what has happened, kills the commissionaire in one of the most secure locations in the whole city, and steals the painting for himself?" She took another mouthful of noodles.

It didn't sound as plausible when she laid it out like that, but I jutted out my chin. "That's right." Something else occurred to me. "I found Thibodeau's body right by the place where Crawford's artwork is stored."

Adela leaned forward, "Okay, but you looked at Jem's stuff and none of it was even oil paintings, right?"

"Yeah, but what about the fact that Thibodeau was buying art the day he was murdered, and then was found dead in the vault?" I asked. I put my bowl of ramen on the table. I wasn't hungry.

"I know," Adela said. "It seems like an unlikely coincidence, but then again a missing masterpiece also seems unlikely. It might be that we have two separate mysteries here: who killed Thibodeau, possibly related to his criminal biker connections and your historical mystery—whether or not Jem found a Rembrandt—and if he did, what happened to it?"

I hesitated. Was my interest in Jem and Victoria's story leading me to make connections that weren't there? Yet, a voice in the back of my mind told me that there was a link, and I was learning to listen to it. My mother often talked about following her hunches and trusting her gut. I'd always thought she was full of it, but now I could see where she was coming from. Thibodeau's death was connected to the Rembrandt. I had to prove it.

CHAPTER TWENTY-THREE

I HAD EVERY INTENTION OF CALLING LEMIEUX THE NEXT MORNING FROM work, but thoughts of him flew away when I saw that Mike had emailed me. He was back from Vancouver and wanted to take me out to lunch. I grinned like a fool, and my fingers flew across the keyboard typing my acceptance.

My good intentions were again thwarted when Oliver blew into my office in a fedora, purple jeans, and clogs. There was a glitch in our online database, and he needed me to check all of the descriptive entries made by archivists in our section over the past three months. The quality assurance needed to be done by noon. The deadline was tight and the work was exacting; there was no time to make any calls. I just managed to finish up when Mike appeared in my doorway clutching a box of Rogers' chocolates.

"Hello!" I said with a wide grin.

"Hi," he said and smiled back. He stepped forward and thrust the chocolates at me. "Here you go. They're a British Columbian specialty."

"Thanks," I said. "No one's ever given me chocolates before."

"It was this or half a smoked salmon. I figured chocolates were more romantic."

"Romantic?" I shot him an arch look as I pulled on my parka.

He stammered. "I meant friendly or convivial."

I squeezed his arm. "Romantic is good."

He coughed. "How do you feel about Italian?"

◇◇◇◇◇◇

ALTHOUGH UNUSUALLY WARM FOR JANUARY, THE DAY WAS OVERCAST, and Carmello's sun-kissed color scheme of reds and ochers was a welcome change from the sky's heavy bank of gray clouds. Mike and I snagged a corner booth, and I was pleased by its intimacy.

"How was Vancouver?"

"Cold, wet, and busy." Mike looked exhausted, and his hair was even wilder than usual.

"Come on, it couldn't have been as bad as here." I gestured out the window to Sparks Street, where civil servants trundled from one government office tower to the next.

He massaged his neck. "I find acquisition trips a pain. You've got to make nice with potential donors and do a real sales job on the institution. I'm not good at either. I don't know what I'm good at, really."

I frowned. Mike was in a negative mood, and I found myself having to cajole him into smiles. He was like a grumpy child, and I remembered Adela's words; maybe I was attracted to men I could mother. The waiter arrived with our drinks—a Diet Coke for me and a glass of red wine for Mike—which he drained in one swig.

He gestured to the waiter for another and then turned back to me. "I don't want to dwell on my lousy week. What have you been up to?"

My mind whirled. Where to start? Lost Rembrandts? Murderous bikers? Growing up, my life was buffeted by the turmoil surrounding my mother's various strays. As a result, I'd made it my mission to live in an understated, competent, and self-sufficient fashion. I hated drama queens and certainly didn't want Mike to think I was one.

I shrugged. "I haven't been doing too much. I searched for my missing lovers in what feels like every single microfilm in the archives. I think I'm going to go blind or turn into a mole from all the squinting."

Mike laughed and relaxed, although I couldn't tell if it was my scintillating conversation or the second glass of wine.

"Anyway, I didn't find another dead body, so it wasn't such a bad week."

"How are you doing with that?" he asked.

"Okay, I guess. No nightmares or anything." Good, that sounded strong and in control. Nothing he needed to worry about.

"What about the guy you saw that night after Hy's? The one who scared you? Has he been bothering you?"

I was touched that he'd remembered the incident. I wavered. It would be nice to tell him about Malone, but on the other hand, "The Rules" were very clear about not appearing needy or clingy. Lions liked antelopes they had to chase, not ones who needed help getting to the watering hole. I didn't want to freak him out with my crazy stories, at least not so early in the relationship. "That guy hasn't bothered me again," I said. My statement held the added bonus of being mostly true.

"So you stared at old microfilm all week? Sounds dull."

I brightened. "No, I actually have a social life, thank you very much."

"Oh?"

I was gratified to see a spark of jealousy in his eyes. "I was out dancing last night. My friend and I hit Barrymore's for Eighties Night."

Mike groaned. "Eighties Night? Do you even remember the eighties, or is this some ironic joke you make at the expense of geezers like me?"

I laughed. "It's big fun. Great music, and everyone dresses up."

Mike looked dubious. "Great eighties music? I seem to remember a lot of crap. I'm embarrassed to say I even owned the Don Johnson album."

"You're kidding. He made an album?"

"I think one of the songs was actually called 'Love Roulette.'"

"I used to watch *Miami Vice* in syndication. I never would have pegged you as a Don Johnson fan," I said as the waiter arrived with our meals.

Mike shook his head. "It wasn't me. Mathilde loved that show. Our first date was watching the series finale in our dorm TV lounge. She was an amazing woman with phenomenally bad taste in TV."

I laughed, relieved to see Mike able to talk about his wife so easily. The sadness that seeped out of him at Hy's was still there, but it seemed fainter now. I liked to think it was because of me.

The conversation drifted to other topics, and Mike entertained me with stories of the cantankerous donors he'd met on his trip to rainy Vancouver.

Walking back to the office together, my earlier qualms about Mike faded. His kindness twinkled out from his crinkly eyes, and when our arms occasionally brushed, I felt a frisson of sexual attraction even through my winter layers.

The sun broke free of the clouds, and its rays beamed down, actually warming my skin. About a block from the office, I pulled off my tuque, shaking out my hair. "Isn't this great? Winter might be over."

Mike laughed. "So young, so innocent. It's the January thaw. There's no way winter's done with us yet. Trust me, by the time the Games start in Vancouver, we'll be back to freezing our butts off."

I closed my eyes and tilted my head to the sun. "It feels fantastic, though."

The warm light played against my face, and I imagined the three freckles on my nose pushing their way to prominence on my skin. In the next instant, the sun was blocked out and Mike's lips touched mine. For a moment, Sparks Street drifted away. His breath tasted nicely of red wine, and his lips were soft and questioning. My heart raced. I wrapped my arms around his neck, and my hand burrowed into his thick hair. I felt a thrill of possessiveness. Eventually, Mike pulled away.

My lips tingled, and I touched them with a gloved finger. "You seem to be getting better at this dating thing," I said with a smile.

"No kidding," he responded. His eyes were shiny, and he grinned at me. It was a lazy, sexy grin, one that I wouldn't have expected from rumpled, crumpled Mike.

Thrilled at the prospects that grin suggested, I smiled back.

"I couldn't resist," he explained as we walked back to work. "You looked so gorgeous standing in the sun."

Gorgeous! An old boyfriend regularly called me "Sweet Tits" and another had told me my hair was pretty, but I'd never been called "gorgeous." The word conjured up Halle Berry on Oscar night or Scarlett Johansson on the cover of *Vanity Fair*. I knew I wasn't gorgeous, but it felt damn good to hear Mike say it. I bounced back to work, basking in warm sunshine and a great compliment.

CHAPTER TWENTY-FOUR

I LEFT MIKE AT HIS OFFICE, WITH PLANS TO DO SOMETHING LATER THAT week. My good mood grew as I saw that the books on painting I'd requested had arrived. There must be something in them that would help me understand the connection between Thibodeau's death and Jem's Rembrandt.

The books offered some fascinating stories about hidden artwork, and I realized that my assumption that Jem rolled up the canvas to smuggle it from France might have been wrong.

Apparently, there were lots of options to hide a painting. A few years back, a valuable Morris Graves still life was revealed on the reverse side of an earlier canvas. It was concealed for years by the covering painting's cardboard backing.

In the nineties, the art world was shocked when a Rembrandt was uncovered beneath an overpainting by one of his students. This portrait of a Russian aristocrat floated around Europe for over three hundred years, but after being tested under x-ray and infrared technology it revealed an early Rembrandt self-portrait. That painting now hung on a billionaire's wall in Las Vegas after he paid over $10 million for it.

Another possible way to conceal art was to stretch one canvas over another. Conservators made a few happy discoveries over the years, examining one painting and uncovering two. The most famous of these was the discovery of *Girl and Three Male Heads* by Edvard Munch, creator of *The Scream*. This painting was hidden beneath another of the artist's cheerfully titled works, *The Dead Mother and Her Child*.

These stories gave me food for thought. It appeared that Jem had several options for smuggling the painting out of Paris. The question now was, which did he choose? I hoped that I would find another letter. It was over a week since I had located one, and I was worried.

Luckily, I hit the jackpot that afternoon, when Gus, the circulation guy, dropped off a new batch of boxes. I pulled a letter from a slit in a ledger dated February 1, 1915.

> January 3, 1915
>
> Victoria,
>
> As always I was delighted to receive a letter from your own dear self. I laughed aloud at your portrait of your uncle's hired hands. I confess I read that portion of your letter to Teddy, who thought their references to "automobillygoats" was too amusing. As you say, these Western "cowpunchers" have a rather fine sense of humor.
>
> Not all parts of your letter made me laugh, however. I was dreadfully upset to hear that your aunt is mistreating you. I do not know much about female concerns, but I think you are correct in supposing that her harsh words are a result of her confinement, rather than genuine feelings against you. I am glad you have stopped attending church, darling. The minister's murderous sermonizing about the rivers of Hun blood that must be spilled for the glory of Empire disgust me as much as they do you. I admit that I am surprised that your pious aunt and uncle have excused you from church so easily. Perhaps you have finally managed to persuade them that their version of "Churchianity" is not your vision of Christianity.
>
> Try to keep your little chin up, sweetheart, because you will not have to stay there much longer. After a week of feverish (and might I say, inspired) painting, I have succeeded in covering up the Rembrandt. Our old master has been thoroughly disguised. At your clever suggestion, I discussed it with Monsieur Levy. He gave me valuable advice on how to best preserve the original and has even shared the details of an expert art restorer whom I shall contact when I return home.
>
> I have mixed feelings about my success at this endeavor, be-

cause I am quite proud of the painting I have used to hide our treasure. In a way I am loath to see it destroyed, as it must be, to realize our dream. I feel this painting has changed my life in more ways than one. I have finally achieved something completely different, something new and vibrant and alive. This work will not survive, but in creating it I hope I have liberated myself from the past.

Ah, now I can see your bright eyes, alight with curiosity, eager to know what I painted. Well, I shan't tell you, but I will give you some clues: Paris inspired me, but I have not forgotten the past either. You will understand when you see the painting, dearest, that I was thinking of you the entire time I created it. Will it surprise you? Delight you? Make you laugh or move you? I'll say no more and let the image speak for itself.

I had been working so hard on the painting, I almost forgot that there was a war on. I emerged yesterday from my studio, blinking in the winter light, to cheering crowds. In my daze I thought the hubbub was for me, before I understood that there was a Boche defeat. I found Teddy and André and the rest of my friends at their usual haunt, the Café de la Rotonde, and we celebrated the victory late into the night. I have never consumed quite so much French wine before. I woke up this morning feeling like my head had been boiled, and with a prodigious thirst. Don't worry, dearest heart, while parts of the evening are a little murky I always kept you in my thoughts. Indeed, Teddy stopped by for a visit this morning and teased me about my incessant Victoria-chatter. He says it's a good thing we'll soon be headed home, because he is half in love with you himself!

Speaking of Teddy, he says there has been a further delay with the visas but that it should not be much longer now, a week or two at the most. I must admit I am chafing at the slowness of these French functionaries. I am exhausted thinking of it, and as the hour is growing late, I must go to bed.

Your own,

Jem

I put the letter down. He actually did it—painted over the Rembrandt. I couldn't decide if this was a brilliant or foolish move on his part. On the one hand, the French authorities would not stop the painting from leaving the country. Indeed, given the state of art conservation technology at the time and the fact that a war was on, they would have no way to detect what he had done. On the other hand, as I learned in my research, removing an overpainting was a painstaking task requiring enormous skill and attention to detail. It could take as much as three years for a conservator to retouch an old painting, let alone remove another painting entirely. Even if Monsieur Levy's art restorer was a genius, it could take Jem years to restore the Rembrandt.

Frankly, I didn't have much faith in Jem's patience. He seemed quick-tempered and impulsive. I suspected that Victoria was tougher and smarter. Her activities and interests revealed a woman of firm ideas and strong convictions. Indeed, despite the rough living conditions and emotional censure she seemed to endure on the farm, she didn't crumble. It was Victoria who encouraged him to get advice from Monsieur Levy, suggested the overpainting plan, and who was constantly telling the impetuous Jem to keep his mouth shut about the find. Victoria would have made sure that the restoration of the Rembrandt was done properly.

A thought occurred to me: What if Jem and Victoria never removed the overpainting? I made another leap. Could one of the modernist paintings Thibodeau bought at the auction be a Crawford, which hid the old master? Before I could work out what that insight might mean, the ringing phone interrupted my thoughts. I looked at the call display and saw a Toronto number. My mother. I let it ring. Then, curious as to why she would call me at work—I had never even given her my number—I checked her message.

"Salali, I haven't heard from you in a while, so I thought I would catch you at work. I was wondering if you had anything to tell me," she whispered into the machine, "about the investigation." Her voice resumed its normally commanding tone. "Come to Toronto next

Wednesday. Terry Reid says he can still get you an interview at the paper as a special favor to me."

My stomach clenched.

Her voice continued, "It's not too late to have a career, Salali. I know you and your sister think I'm a horrible mother, but I want you to have a life that matters. Don't you want to leave your mark on the world? Don't you want to be remembered? Don't you want to accomplish some good in this—"

Thankfully the voice mail cut her off.

I called Adela at work. Sometimes venting to a friend was the only cure for maternal angst.

Adela laughed when I told her about my mother's message. "Man, Cassie is a piece of work. My mum only gives me guilt trips about not calling my abuela enough, not about failing to save the world."

"Mothers don't deliberately mean to make their daughters feel inadequate, do they?"

"Only if they're Betty Draper, sweetie."

I wanted to tell her about what I learned about the Rembrandt, but I didn't feel safe speaking about it in the office. Instead, we talked about inconsequential things, but my mother's words nagged at me. I was viewing my discovery of Thibodeau's body as a calamity, something I had been victimized by. I'd allowed Lemieux to imply that my auction tip was bogus, and last night Adela's logic made me question my intuition about Thibodeau's connection to the Rembrandt. With Jem's revelation I had a real lead on the whereabouts of the masterpiece. My mother was right; I needed to accomplish something worthwhile with my life. I remembered how powerful I felt when I spotted Malone at Leo's Tavern. I'd loved feeling so strong, and I wanted that sensation back. I was going to take charge of this investigation.

CHAPTER TWENTY-FIVE

AN HOUR AND A HALF LATER, ADELA AND I SAT IN HER CAR, STARING AT the stone facade of Van Cleef's Auction House. Although only about ten blocks from the Dominion Archives, the ByWard Market felt a whole world away. Gone was the shabby comfort of the archives. Instead, the glass-and-steel fortress of the American embassy loomed over the district. Even at seven o'clock a few slick-looking political aides, lawyers, and business people roamed the streets, barking orders at underlings over expensive cell phones.

"It looks closed," Adela said.

I was surprised to hear the note of relief in her voice. I would have thought she would be up for another adventure, but she seemed daunted.

"The secretary told me the office closed at five but the reception area is open until seven thirty."

"There isn't an easier way?" Adela asked.

I shook my head. "We need to find out what Thibodeau bought two weeks ago. Now that we know there could be a Rembrandt under there, it's even more important. I tried calling and asking for the info, but they keep their buyers' information strictly confidential. They won't release it."

Adela sighed. "Tell me again why we can't let the police handle this?"

"The cops haven't done anything. They're lazy. They focus on one theory and can't be deflected." I was all too aware that I sounded like my mother.

"Jess, did you even call Lemieux today to tell him about Malone?"

"I forgot," I said truthfully. "I'll do it as soon as I get home. Anyway, once I tell him that Malone was stalking me, he'll double down on the biker connection and dismiss Thibodeau's attendance at the auction as meaningless."

"How do you know the police haven't followed up on this?"

"Because Lemieux didn't tell me that he did," I said.

Adela rolled her eyes. "Jess, it's a murder investigation. The police aren't going to check in with you."

In my heart I knew that Adela was right, but I also knew that the proof of a connection between Thibodeau and Jem's painting was in the auction house. Once I had that, I could present the whole thing to Lemieux.

Instead of arguing with Adela, I appealed to our friendship. "Please help me. I can't do this without you. It's important."

She met my eye. "All right, Jess. Of course." She stared at the building and a smile began tugging at her lips. "This might be fun."

I rehashed the plan I had outlined on the way over.

"Okay, the key is to keep the receptionist busy."

Adela nodded, looking more confident. "Right. I'm going to demo our data management software. I'll give her the hard sell."

"Great. That gives me a chance to slip in the side door, which is directly in front of the office." Only two short weeks ago, Oliver, Louise, and I stood in that same office signing the forms for the Jarvis ledgers. The auction clerk had placed our paperwork in a file marked "January 19, 2010". It was simply a question of retrieving the file and reading what Thibodeau bought.

"Why are you so sure that the side door will be unlocked?"

I dreaded telling Adela this part of my plan; I knew what her reaction would be. "If it isn't, I can pick the lock."

Adela stared at me as if I had told her that Michael Jackson had impregnated me with his love child. "What?"

I sighed. "One of my mum's runaways used to steal. He showed me how it was done."

It was my raging twelve-year-old crush on Kyle Wong—who looked like an Asian version of Leonardo DiCaprio—that made me such an avid student. *Titanic* had recently come out, and I would have robbed a bank if it would have impressed Kyle.

Adela's voice was admiring. "You know how to pick locks, and you're proposing a break and enter. It's like I never knew you."

"This is not a break and enter," I snapped. "I'm only peeking at a file. I'm not going to take anything."

Adela's eyes were dancing. "Jess, you're a criminal. You're a thief."

"Let's get this over with," I said.

Adela picked up her purse. "Okay. Where is this side door, anyway?"

I pointed at a narrow alley separating Van Cleef's from its neighbor. "It must be down there."

Adela straightened her hair in the rearview mirror. "Give me a couple of minutes to get my sales pitch going, and then sneak in."

"Okay," I said, swallowing the thick lump of nervousness in my throat. "I'll probably need ten minutes to get the door open and find the file."

"All right, let's do this!" Adela raised her hand excitedly for a high five.

She crossed the street with a confident stride and opened the door authoritatively. If anyone could convince someone they were there on legitimate business, it was Adela.

Through the window, I watched my friend conferring with the receptionist. It was now or never. I reached down and grabbed the tools I had taken from Adela's place: a pair of gloves, a screwdriver, and a straightened out key ring that I hooked at the end to use as an improvised lock pick. I opened the car door and slipped out. Taking calming breaths in the mild evening air, I walked casually to the alley.

As I feared, the door was locked. Glancing right and left to ensure no one was watching, I dropped to one knee and examined the lock. Thank God it was a common dead bolt, which meant a simple pin and tumbler cylinder lock. I withdrew the flat-head screwdriver from my pocket and wedged it into the keyhole. Moving slowly, as Kyle taught me, I turned the screwdriver slightly, moving the lock plug as a key would until I was satisfied with its positioning.

I had never picked a lock alone, and certainly never when my heart was jackhammering in my chest. It was harder than I remembered. I struggled to keep my hand steady as I withdrew my pick and carefully inserted it into the mechanism, straining to sense where each pin in the lock was held, so that I could lift it into its proper position.

I cleared my mind of all distractions, thinking back to those Sunday afternoons with Kyle. How cute I thought his badass fifteen-year-old self was. I had longed to stroke the slight peach fuzz that covered his cheeks and erase the pain hovering behind his eyes. Man, Adela was right. When it came to men, I really did have a mothering complex. I felt the last pin slide up into the lock housing, and I stood, my hand on the door handle. I'd done it.

Now to see if the door was alarmed. I didn't think it would be, at least not while there was still an employee in the building, but I couldn't be sure.

I pulled the door open a bit and waited. No sound. I poked my head in cautiously. No alarm.

I could hear the murmur of voices to my right: Adela and the receptionist. The hallway was in darkness. To my left was the auction room. Directly in front of me, as I remembered, was the office door. I prayed that it wasn't locked. I could pick it as well, but it would take extra time.

I tugged at the door, and it opened with a loud squeak. I paused, frozen. The receptionist's voice faltered, and then Adela broke in, speaking so loudly I could make out her words: "The best part about the software is its sales-tracking capabilities. Let me show you another brochure."

I stepped into the office, closed the door, and switched on the light. As I remembered, the room contained a big desk, numerous filing cabinets, and a large window overlooking the patio of the neighboring sushi restaurant.

I went to the filing cabinet where the clerk had placed our sales records. The files were arranged chronologically. I flipped through, looking for January 19, 2010. There was nothing there.

Damn it. My throat tightened in disappointment. We'd done all of this for nothing. The file was gone. Was the killer covering up his tracks? Maybe he'd broken in and taken it. A less calamitous thought was that Lemieux actually followed up on my tip, and currently had the folder in his possession. There was one more possibility. If he had requested the file recently, it might not have been returned to the cabinet.

There was an in-box on top of the filing cabinets. Bingo. Right on top was a neatly labeled file: "Sales, January 19." I grinned with relief and leafed through the papers, looking for Thibodeau's name. There it was. I scanned the document quickly but the murmur from the reception area grew louder. Another voice had joined them.

I turned off the office light and crept to the door. I couldn't hear what was being said, so I opened it a crack. The newcomer spoke loudly, and the familiar voice shocked me: "Mesdames, I'm sorry to interrupt, but I'm from the Gatineau PD. I need to have another look at the file I reviewed the other day."

Adela replied in a loud voice. "Oh, if you need to talk to this police officer, I can come back another time. A time when the police aren't here."

I heard the front door open; Adela must have left. I didn't wait to hear what was said next. I dumped the file back in the in-box and raced for the side door. I stepped through the exit as the door to the reception area opened. I heard the receptionist saying, "Right this way, sir."

The door banged behind me. I hauled my hood up and didn't turn around, running for the safety of the street. As I left the alley, I heard the side door open. The shouted "Tabarnak!" made me confident that Lemieux hadn't seen who I was. Adela was waiting in the car, and I jumped in.

"We did it!" Adela turned to me, her face exhilarated.

I gasped for breath, my heart pounding in my ears. My hands shook with excitement. While I was adrenalized by our near miss, I knew that my reaction was more a result of what I had read about Thibodeau's purchase in that file: On January 19, he'd bought two Jem Crawford paintings. One of them was entitled *Paris 1915*.

As the car peeled away in a cloud of exhaust, I realized I had found the Rembrandt.

CHAPTER TWENTY-SIX

IT TOOK ONLY A MOMENT FOR MY EUPHORIA TO ABATE, BUT WHEN IT DID, I noticed that we were speeding down Sussex Drive. "Hey, Adela, slow down."

She glanced in the rearview mirror and said in a hard voice, "I'm trying to shake our tail."

My stomach plummeted. I turned to stare at the cars behind us. "Our tail?" I squeaked. "Is Lemieux following us?"

Adela shook her head, merging into traffic by the grand old Château Laurier Hotel. "Nah, but I always wanted to say that."

Her grin annoyed me. "I don't find that funny. What if Lemieux identified me?"

"Relax. You said if he saw you at all, it was only from behind. Besides he doesn't have any proof."

Easy for her to say; she hadn't picked the lock. Besides, it occurred to me that breaking into the auction house could put me back on Lemieux's suspect list. "What about you? He must have got a good look at you."

"He saw a woman trying to sell some software. That's my job."

A terrible thought occurred to me. "Was Lemieux the cop who interviewed you about my alibi?"

"Nope."

"Thank God. Still, you ran away. A policeman like Lemieux will make the connection."

Adela was riding her crime-spree high and spoke without a hint of worry. "Even if he does, I wasn't doing anything illegal. What's more, you didn't take anything. At most, you were trespassing."

I was still nervous. "How did it go with the receptionist? Did she suspect anything?"

Adela shook her head. "Nope. I threw a bunch of numbers and stats at her, and she snapped her gum and took everything I said as gospel."

We drove for a moment in silence, which Adela broke. "Thanks for that, Jess."

"For what?" I asked.

She glanced over at me. "For the buzz. Doing that was a blast. It felt straight out of a movie or something."

"Are you on crack?" I thought back to my pounding heart, sweaty palms, and that queasy feeling in the pit of my stomach. Then I remembered the thrill I felt when I located the file. Some of it had been fun.

"I loved it," Adela continued. "It was like we were in *Ocean's Eleven*."

"Does that make Lemieux George Clooney?" There was a sour note to my voice.

"Well . . ."

"Adela! You can't seriously find him attractive!"

"What? You should have told me he was sexy."

"He's a wee little man!"

She waved a hand. "I don't need them burly, like you do, Jess. I like 'em lean and ready for action."

It was true. She went for whip-thin guys, whereas I liked my men with a bit of meat on them, so that I felt little by comparison—the way I felt with Mike.

We cruised along Wellington Street, past the Parliament buildings and the archives' darkened offices. I steered the conversation away from her distasteful opinion of Lemieux and discussed everything, including Jem overpainting the Rembrandt.

"So you see," I concluded, "there is a huge motive for murder and a definite link between Thibodeau and Jem's painting."

Adela ignored the triumph in my voice. "Thibodeau knew that *Paris 1915* concealed a Rembrandt, and that's why he paid so much to win it?"

"Exactly."

"Then presumably he was murdered to get the painting?"

"Yes," I agreed happily. I had practically solved the mystery. I could imagine what my mother would say. She might have exposed a couple of police kickback schemes, but she'd never single-handedly caught a killer.

"I wonder how Thibodeau, or his murderer for that matter, knew that there was a Rembrandt hidden under that painting."

My smile faded. I hadn't considered how anyone would know about it. As far as I could tell, it was a secret between Jem and Victoria. I frowned as I thought of something else. If *Paris 1915* hid the Rembrandt, that meant that Jem and Victoria hadn't succeeded in removing the overpainting, selling it, and escaping to Tahiti. The only reason they wouldn't have sold the painting was if something happened to one or both of them; the world was a dangerous place in 1915.

My frown deepened. When I told Lemieux about the connection between the letters and the painting, he would confiscate all of them as part of the investigation. He might even find new letters I hadn't yet discovered. Jem and Victoria's story would become part of the public record. My chance of a scholarly scoop and a career would be dead in the water.

"Here we are," Adela said brightly.

I said a subdued, "Thanks."

"No, thank you, Jess. This was one of the best nights of my life."

I roused myself enough to shake my head. "You're crazy."

"Yup," she said. "See you later this week?"

I agreed and then headed to the house. The motion-sensor porch light flickered on, and Adela waited until I unlocked the door before driving off.

I dropped my purse and flipped the front hall light switch. Nothing. That was weird. I was sure I had put in a new bulb when Adela and I upgraded my apartment security. A bit of light seeped in from the front window, and I could make out the room's familiar shapes. I moved toward the table by the couch, which held a lamp.

Taking that first step, I noticed something else. It was cold, like a window was open somewhere. The hairs on the back of my neck stood up, and my heart thumped loudly in my chest. My landlord had never fixed the lock on my bedroom window. I shivered and moved toward the lamp, trying to convince myself that I was being paranoid.

It was then that I noticed the breathing. It wasn't loud, but with my tension heightened, I heard it perfectly. In fact, all I could hear was the quiet inhale and exhale, even and deliberate. Someone was behind me, by the door. The person had been standing inches away when I walked in.

Blood roared in my ears, and for a moment I couldn't think. I took a breath, forcing myself to remain calm. The phone was on the opposite side of the room; there was no way I could get to it without alerting my intruder. My cell phone was tucked away in my purse in the entranceway. No, my best bet was to find a weapon.

His eyes bored into my back, watching my movements. It was an atavistic sensation, this feeling of being prey. I reached the table. The lamp was too big to use as a weapon, but there must be something else. The table held an unlit stick of incense, a photo of Adela and me at graduation, a stuffed elephant from my sister, and a glass of water. Not the nunchucks or flamethrower I could actually use. I stifled the hysterical urge to laugh.

I sensed movement behind me. I didn't have any more time. I flicked the lamp on, grabbing the glass of water in the same movement.

The intruder's heavy footfall crossed the small room. I spun around, glass in hand. No time to aim. I flung the glass toward the person with as much strength as I could summon.

It hit him on the shoulder and then fell to the floor, shattering at his feet. It didn't stop him. It barely slowed him down.

CHAPTER TWENTY-SEVEN

I STARED AT THE INTRUDER, ALL OF MY FEARS REALIZED: IT WAS Malone. The face that I glimpsed at Leo's loomed over me. His close-set eyes, stuck like shriveled raisins in his wide face, would have been almost comical in another situation. Here they bore into me with a terrifying menace.

"Fuck," said Malone, rubbing his arm. "You're a frisky little bitch, aren't you?"

He grabbed me before I could respond, shoving me hard against the table. The lamp, which had illuminated the scene in a warm yellow glow, smashed on the floor and plunged us back into gloom. He was tall and thick. A large, terrifying presence. His hand on my shoulder kept me pinned against the table, which dug painfully into the small of my back.

I opened my mouth to scream, but he anticipated my action, whipping a switchblade from his pocket. He flicked it open, pointing it at the underside of my chin.

"Go ahead and scream, honey. I doubt anyone can hear you, and on this street, I doubt they'd care."

"I have an upstairs neighbor." I didn't recognize my voice; it was squeaky like a seven-year-old's. "He'll hear all of this banging. He'll come to see if everything's okay."

Malone's mouth tightened into a thin line. "Then you'd better shut the fuck up, honey, or I'll slice your throat open."

He paused, letting me absorb the threat. He continued in an un-hurried fashion. "You made me wait tonight, and I don't appreciate that." He pressed the knife lightly into my throat. "Now, I don't want to hurt you." He stopped as if considering. "Actually, I'd like to hurt you, but I won't. At least, not if you're a good girl. Understand?"

His breath enveloped my face with a warm intimacy, and I turned my head, closing my eyes.

He dug the knife deeper into my throat, and I cried out, my eyes flying open.

"I asked you a question, honey. Are you going to be a good girl?"

I nodded.

"That's smart thinking." He twisted the knife ever so slightly. I could feel warm blood dribbling down my neck into my coat collar. "Now, what do you know about Pauly's death?"

I swallowed hard, the knifepoint edging deeper into my throat. "Nothing. I don't know anything." At least my voice had returned to normal.

He snorted. "Not sure I buy that. I've been keeping an eye on you, seeing if you were in on Pauly's scam. You're playing it cool, that's for sure."

As Malone talked, he seemed to forget that he had the knife pressed against my throat. I shifted slightly to escape the point, and he didn't notice. If I wasn't leaning so heavily against the table, I could use my legs and perhaps surprise Malone with a swift kick to the shin. I was still wearing my winter boots, and they were heavy enough to do some damage. Emboldened, I tried to find my center of gravity.

He continued to speak. "I'd started to think you didn't know shit, but then Joe told me about that chick and the questions she was asking at Leo's. Didn't take much to realize a young thing like that was probably connected to you. That's when I realized that maybe you're a better actress than Julia Roberts."

I was almost fully upright now, and if I aimed below his knee, I might be able to get to the door before he caught up with me.

Malone chuckled, not a nice sound. "I'm learning not to write you professor-types off. You're all a lot smarter than you look." He laughed again, apparently pleased with his wit.

My eyes darted. If my escape attempt didn't work, Malone would be further enraged, and I didn't know what he would do to me. I hesitated for a second too long, and he seemed to anticipate my plan. He pushed the knife more firmly to my throat, forcing me to lean farther back.

He spoke in a snarl. "Don't dick me around. Tell me what you know about the painting. Are you two working together? Is that it? Tell me, or I'll slice you open"—he paused, unzipping my winter coat—"although not before seeing what you've got hidden under all those layers."

He pulled my coat apart, staring at my thick sweater and sensible turtleneck in disappointment. "We'll have to strip you down." His face bore a dark leer, more animal than human.

Thoughts of escape fled. I was paralyzed with terror. "Please," I croaked out, my mouth dry.

His lips stretched across his teeth in a hyena smile. "'Please' what, honey? Please this?" He slid his hand up my sweater, squeezing my breast through my turtleneck. The knife wavered, and he lowered it.

It was my second chance. I leaned forward, pressing myself into his body so I could whisper in his ear. "Please don't."

His smile grew wide with anticipation. "When you ask like that, honey, I know you don't mean—"

He never got to finish the sentence, because in that moment I drove my knee into his groin with every ounce of fear, hatred, and force I could muster. My self-defense instructor had drilled it into our heads that the only time to attack a man's groin was when his guard was lowered.

Malone let out a strangled groan before dropping to the floor.

I wasted no time leaping over him and racing to my door. I flew outside, stumbling down the porch stairs, before running for the street.

I was free! I was safe!

I was caught in another set of male arms. I kicked with all my strength, but the man easily sidestepped my frantic movements.

"Calme-toi, mademoiselle." Lemieux's French accent penetrated my terror, and I stopped thrashing. "Do not fear. I haven't come to arrest you, although I probably should, given your bêtise tonight."

I don't know what Lemieux was expecting, but it was not me throwing my arms around his neck.

"What is it?" he demanded, his voice rough.

"There's someone in the house." I gulped.

Lemieux didn't have to be told twice. "Is he armed?" he asked.

"He's got a knife," I said, pointing to my neck.

Lemieux's face was grim. "Get into my car," he commanded. "Lock the doors." Without looking back, he drew his gun and approached the house. Bereft of bravery, I did as I was told and climbed into the vehicle.

I felt empty, completely numb. I told myself the story of recent events: Malone had broken into my house. He'd lain in wait for me. He would have raped and murdered me if I hadn't gotten away. These cold facts elicited no reaction. It was like I was a blank page, an empty vessel.

After what seemed like an eternity, Lemieux emerged, shaking his head. He pulled out his cell phone and dialed a number.

I unrolled the window to hear what he was saying.

"Allô, Mohammed, it's Daniel Lemieux, Gatineau PD. I've got a break-in at 212 Pinhey. Attempted assault. Suspect fled on foot. Can you send a couple of cars? I've got the victim here." Lemieux paused, listening. "Yeah, I'll do that now. No problems."

Lemieux approached the car, leaning into the open window. "He climbed out the bedroom window. That looks like the way he got in."

I shivered and wrapped my arms around myself.

"What did he do to you?"

I pointed to my chin and spoke matter-of-factly. "He held a knife to my throat."

Lemieux leaned forward, tilting my head back to expose the cut. His fingers traced the wound lightly. "Yes, that's the point of a knife. Not a deep cut, though." He released my head. "Did he do anything else? I saw signs of struggle."

I shook my head, my voice a steady monotone. "He tried. That's when I kneed him and ran."

Lemieux appraised me and said calmly, "Do you have your house keys and purse?"

"They're probably still in the hall."

Lemieux retrieved my things and locked my door. He returned to the car, sliding into the driver's seat. I could tell he was shaken by recent events, because he forgot to wipe the slush off his boots.

He pulled the car onto Pinhey. "Want to tell me what happened?" he asked. I'd never heard his voice so gentle.

I shook my head. Talking about it would break my protective bubble. We drove in silence for about five minutes, winding our way through the city's downtown. I gazed out the window. Lemieux turned onto Elgin, a street bustling with bars and restaurants. I finally roused myself. "Where are we going?" I asked.

"Ottawa PD."

This was a blow. I didn't relish reliving those moments of terror with a group of strangers. "Can't I just tell you what happened?"

Lemieux's wide smile made a brief appearance. "I am honored that you'd rather talk to me, mademoiselle, but this is Ottawa turf. I'm a Gatineau cop."

We pulled into police headquarters, and Lemieux parked his car in a reserved space.

I didn't move from my seat. I realized that my emotional defenses were brittle, and I could feel cracks spreading like fault lines. I was almost murdered tonight. My legs were weak, and I wasn't sure if I could stand. Lemieux assessed the situation and came around to my door. He opened it and extended his hand. "Come with me. I'll take care of you."

I gave him my hand and he guided me to the station. I was thinking about the ordeal ahead and spoke quite absently. "It's just as well that you're coming in, since this affects your case."

Lemieux halted, hand on the door. "Hein?" he asked.

I looked at him, surprised. In my numbed state, I forgot that he didn't know the details of the attack. It was so vivid to me, it didn't seem possible that Lemieux wasn't aware of it. "The man who was in my house was Ray Malone, Paul Thibodeau's cousin."

Gentleness vanished. "How the hell do you know about Malone?"

I stuttered, "He's been stalking me. Adela and I tracked him to Leo's Tavern and identified him."

Lemieux's face darkened like a winter sky at twilight and I was anxious to get away from him. I wrenched open the station door and hurried inside.

CHAPTER TWENTY-EIGHT

MUCH LATER THAT NIGHT AN OTTAWA PATROL CAR DROPPED ME OFF AT Adela's apartment. My friend met me in the lobby. Riding up in the elevator, I didn't recognize the woman staring back at me from its mirrored walls. Her eyes looked enormous in a pale, drawn face. Her lips were almost white from fear, and she sagged with exhaustion. I was grateful to escape my own image when the elevator reached the twelfth floor.

While being interviewed by Ottawa PD, I managed to hold it together. I calmly recited the facts of the attack. I gave the officers approximate times of events, explained exactly where Malone was standing, and told them precisely how I managed to get away. I didn't remember much of Malone's conversation, but I told them what I could recall, mentioning that he seemed to want a painting. Lemieux was present for the interview and supplied some details about Malone's possible connection to Thibodeau's murder.

The composure that I had clung to all night evaporated the instant Adela closed the door to her apartment. As soon as we were alone, she swept me into an enormous hug, or as enormous a hug as a short woman can give. It was uncomfortable, my back aching as I stooped awkwardly, but the love behind it was real.

"Come in, sweetie." Her concern enveloped me like a warm blanket.

Adela's apartment was pristine, gigantic, and almost empty. Her living room walls were white, and her furniture was black. It re-minded me of an oversized chess board where the white army had decimated the black, leaving only a few stray survivors on the field of battle: a sleek leather couch dominated one wall, a giant cube coffee table made of black glass squatted menacingly, and a minimalist chair made entirely of sharp angles jutted like a glacier. Patio doors, leading to a narrow terrace, offered a twelve-story view of the city's twinkling white lights.

She sat me on the couch, and between big gulps of air and lots of tears, I relayed what had happened since I last saw her, a few hours ago.

When I got to the part of my story where Malone unzipped my coat and touched my breast, I lost all control. My narrative stopped, and sobs welled up from the bottom of my soul. I had never cried like this before. I dimly realized it was a symptom of shock but was powerless to control it. Adela held me, not attempting any words of comfort.

My tears were interrupted by the apartment's buzzer, angry and insistent.

I stared at it in terror. Had Malone found me? I knew he was unlikely to buzz to gain access, but something as simple as logic didn't help irrational fear.

Adela pressed the intercom.

A voice crackled into the room. "It's Lemieux. I would like to speak to Mademoiselle Novak."

Adela glanced at me, a drippy puddle on her couch, and said firmly, "She's not up for it tonight."

His answer was succinct. "I don't care. Let me in immediately."

I knew that as soon as he saw Adela, his suspicions about our role in the auction house break-in would be confirmed. My friend looked at me, and I read the same thought in her eyes. My sobs faded to small hiccups. I shrugged, feeling strangely brave. "Might as well get it over with."

Adela handed me a box of Kleenex to wipe my eyes and blow my nose.

With one peremptory knock, Lemieux entered the apartment, seeming to fill the space with his presence. "Bonsoir, mademoiselle," he said to me.

I nodded at him and said, "This is my friend Adela." My voice was clear, not a trace of a wobble.

Lemieux stared at her but said nothing beyond a murmured hello. "May I sit?" he asked.

I relaxed slightly. Could he have failed to recognize her?

"By all means," Adela said, indicating the backless, armless thing she called a chair. She sat next to me on the couch, and I was grateful for her closeness.

Lemieux shifted in his seat in a futile attempt to get comfortable before he spoke. "I know you have endured a very difficult night, mademoiselle, but you held yourself up so well at the police station I thought you could manage a few questions I didn't get the chance to pose."

I sat up straighter and dabbed at my eyes. As annoying as it was to admit, I valued Lemieux's good opinion.

When he asked his next question, however, I realized that he had been keeping a tight rein on his emotions. "How could you have been so stupid to go to Leo's? What is wrong with you girls! That place is dangerous. Bad men stay there. Very bad things happen there."

I shrank back into the couch. I was in no condition to handle his angry outburst, and I felt the hot press of tears return to my eyes.

Luckily, Adela wasn't in as fragile a state. She spoke firmly. "Listen, if Jess had more faith in your abilities, we wouldn't have needed to do our own investigation. Besides, we got some useful information from Joe—we identified Jess's stalker. And we learned that Malone is Thibodeau's cousin."

Despite Adela's forceful tone, Lemieux did not back down. "First, if Mademoiselle Novak had told me about the stalking, I would have investigated it. What's more, we already connected Malone to Thibodeau. We had been following him, waiting for enough evidence to pick him up."

Did Malone stop stalking me because he knew the cops were keeping an eye on him? It made sense.

Lemieux was still talking. "This morning, forensics matched the bullet found at the murder scene to a gun that Malone used in an armed robbery a year ago. We finally amassed enough evidence to make an arrest. The only problem is that Malone gave our officers the slip. We'd been tracking him for a week, so I couldn't understand what spooked him this morning. Now I do. Your little 'investigation' to Leo's frightened him off." Lemieux glared at Adela.

I felt terrible. We had blundered, but Adela was not intimidated. "It's not our fault you guys can't do your job. You should have arrested him last week instead of letting him terrorize Jess."

Lemieux glanced over at me, and his face softened. "I am very sorry that you were attacked, mademoiselle. That is not an easy thing to go through. You handled it well."

I sniffed. "I don't feel like I did. When he showed up, I turned to jelly and panicked." My voice cracked.

Adela reached over and held my hand.

"Au contraire, you kept your head and fought him off," Lemieux said. "Malone is a very dangerous man, with a hot temper. You would have been in real trouble had you not escaped." Lemieux then addressed both Adela and I. "You must view this incident as a warning, and pay attention to it by staying out of police business."

I felt Adela bristle at his condescending tone, but it didn't bother me. Instead, I allowed his words of encouragement to cheer me up. I said with feeling, "Thanks. That means a lot."

Lemieux obviously decided I was not as fragile anymore. He spoke slowly, making sure we followed his words. "I did not actually come here to yell at you about your bêtise at Leo's. I wanted to finish what I started this evening, when I stopped by your apartment at such a fortunate hour."

I should have known he wouldn't let that matter drop. I shot a guilty glance at Adela. "What did you want to talk about?" I asked innocently.

"There was a break-in earlier this evening at Van Cleef's Auction House."

He watched me carefully. I could feel the blush creeping up my neck to my cheeks, and I willed myself to stay cool. "Oh?" I said.

"Yes. I am sure your friend"—he nodded at Adela—"could tell you all about it, since she was there at the exact time it was happening."

"Really!" Adela exclaimed in the terrible-acting tones that a seventh-grade kid uses in her school play. She fluttered her lashes at him. "I had no idea there was a break-in. I finished my business, so I left. I didn't see anything."

"And what exactly is your business?" Lemieux demanded.

Adela purred her response, "Senior sales representative at Delta Systems Inc. Van Cleef's is a potential client." She reached into her purse and handed him her card.

Lemieux snorted. "And if I called your office, they would support your claim?"

Adela busted out her sexiest smile. "As senior sales rep, I make my own target decisions. The firm has no idea what I get up to."

Lemieux looked at her appreciatively. "I bet."

I interrupted, irritated by the sexual tension crackling around me. "Did you get a look at the person who broke in?"

"You know damn well I didn't." Lemieux's voice was hard again. "You were running away."

"Was anything stolen?" I asked.

"Nothing at all."

"If nothing was stolen and you can't identify the person running away, then how do you know that anything illegal even happened?" I asked.

"I don't have to ID you to know it was you," Lemieux roared. "This is serious. You're tampering with a murder investigation. In fact, you're back on my suspect list."

CHAPTER TWENTY-NINE

I TWISTED MY HANDS TOGETHER. AFTER MALONE'S ATTACK, I WANTED
Lemieux on my side. I tried to pacify him. "I'm not saying I was there,
but if I was, it would only have been to see what Thibodeau bought
at the auction."

Lemieux spoke grudgingly. "I figured, and after what you reported
tonight about Malone looking for a painting, it seems that auction tip
of yours was relevant."

That was as close as I was likely to get to Lemieux admitting we
might have helped him. I thought back to the sales file I had glimpsed.
"Have you found all of the paintings Thibodeau bought? If I remember, it was eight canvases."

"What a good memory you have, mademoiselle. To remember
such a detail from two weeks ago." He knew I had seen the list but I
was done playing cat and mouse.

"Did you find the paintings?"

"We found all but two in Thibodeau's apartment." Lemieux consulted his notebook. "The missing paintings were both by the same
artist—Jeremy Crawford." He cocked an eyebrow at me. "Do you
have anything to tell me?"

The cops didn't know where the painting was either. I thought about
what Adela said in the car. I might be the only one who knew which
Crawford painting concealed the Rembrandt. On one hand, I wanted to
tell Lemieux everything I knew. On the other, I still had a chance to save
my article, and unravel Jem and Victoria's story myself. I hesitated.

Lemieux noted my hesitation and pressed on, his voice heavy with
warning. "Whatever you found out, you must share it. Malone is out

there, and he is not a nice guy. If he thinks you know something that would implicate him in murder, he's going to come for you."

Lemieux had taken the wrong tack. I'd had enough intimidation for one night; I didn't need him to threaten me as well. "Isn't it the cops' job to protect me from him, then?"

Lemieux saw that he'd made an error and tried another approach. "Don't you want to end this and catch Malone?"

I felt myself weakening. It would be good to hand all of the questions and problems over to someone else. Nice to walk away from the fear.

Lemieux blew it by continuing to talk, however. "Help us, instead of running around town getting into trouble doing ridiculous niaiseries like breaking into auction houses."

I realized that entering the auction house was foolish and going to Leo's was dangerous, but I felt bad enough about my actions, and didn't need Lemieux rubbing it in. For the first time that night, I got mad, and my anger felt good. "I didn't break into Van Cleef's. If you think you've got proof, I'd like to see you bring it up in court. Until then, keep your questions to yourself or get me a lawyer."

He breathed heavily. "You're a very annoying woman, Mademoiselle Novak. We're working toward the same thing here. Now, tell me how Jeremy Crawford is significant."

I glowered back at him. "I have no idea." I was damned if I was going to tell him about the letters.

From the corner of my eye, I saw Adela look at me with a start. If Lemieux noticed, he gave no sign.

He closed his notebook and stood, Adela and I following suit. "I guess I will have to learn some other way why this Jeremy Crawford is such a valuable painter, hein?"

Lemieux moved to the door, but Adela called to him. "What about catching Malone? Jess is not going to be safe until he's behind bars."

He paused at the door. "We are doing all that we can. As I said before, your expedition last night may have hampered our investigations. Happily for you, Malone has certainly left town. He is dangerous, but not stupid. To be certain, my colleagues in Ottawa have stationed a police guard outside this building and outside Mademoiselle Novak's home."

"Two cop cars? That's all you can spare? The man tried to kill Jess."

"Mademoiselle Novak should keep the Ottawa police department informed of her movements. I believe they gave her the appropriate number to call at the station."

I nodded.

"Ideally, we would have a detail following her, but police resources are tight, I am afraid. Anyway, if Malone is still in this city, we will catch him, but I'm positive he's no longer here to be caught."

"That's your hypothesis, Lemieux. Who knows if you're right?" Adela asked.

"I know I am right, because I am so seldom wrong."

His cockiness got on my nerves. "Just like you're certain Malone murdered Thibodeau?" I asked.

"Of course. That is the natural assumption."

Adela jumped in. "I'm not sure. When I talked to Joe at Leo's, he implied that someone else killed Thibodeau."

Lemieux smiled at her. "Joe Lawson? Convicted criminal and known associate of Ray Malone? You must remember the testimony of a man like that doesn't carry much weight. Especially if he's protecting his good friend."

She persisted. "As a saleswoman, I'm pretty good at reading people. I'm sure he was telling the truth."

"I'm sure you're good at many things, mademoiselle, but I doubt you're used to dealing with criminals. They all lie."

"What's Malone's motive for killing his cousin?" I interrupted.

Lemieux's mouth took on a stubborn cast. "Malone is a member of a criminal biker gang. They do many illegal things. Obviously, Thibodeau's death has something to do with the paintings he bought at the auction. Perhaps they were fencing stolen art. Perhaps forgery."

I stopped my questioning. Thibodeau died for a Rembrandt. I didn't want to clue Lemieux into that nugget of information, at least not until I found and photocopied all the letters.

"Well, if that is all, I will bid you adieu. It's been a big day for both of you."

As soon as the door shut, Adela turned to me. "Man, that guy is so sexy it almost makes up for him being such an obnoxious tool."

I sat back down on the couch. "I don't see the attraction, but he was justified in being angry with us. We messed up his case."

Adela waved a hand, coming to sit beside me again. "Come on, he said it himself, Malone is a dangerous criminal. The cops should have picked him up as soon as he was a suspect. Lemieux is trying to cover his butt by blaming us."

"They needed the results from forensics before they could arrest him," I argued. I closed my eyes and leaned back into the couch, second-guessing my decision to withhold the information about Jem's Rembrandt. Once again, I felt Malone's hand on my body. I shuddered and snapped my eyes open.

Adela zeroed in on my doubts. "Why didn't you tell Lemieux about Jem Crawford?"

"If I told him about it, he would confiscate the letters as evidence and I'd lose my chance to publish my article. It will take me about another week to examine the rest of the ledgers. Once I've seen all the correspondence, I'll call Lemieux."

"Are you sure you want to do this, Jess? You're taking quite a risk for the sake of your career."

"It's more than my career," I said. "It's stupid, I know, but I feel like Jem and Victoria are mine. I have a responsibility to them."

"To a couple of long-dead people you've never even met? That's weird, Jess."

"It's not weird. It's like they've shared their secret with me and it's my duty to unravel its ending and tell the world about it."

"Well, it couldn't have been only their secret, if Thibodeau and Malone knew about it."

"How did Thibodeau learn about the Rembrandt?" I spoke thoughtfully, trying to work it out. "I'm certain I'm the first person to see Jem's letters since Victoria slid them into the ledgers ninety years ago. Tracing the provenance of a painting is extremely complex. Without the letters as a guide, you'd need enormous research skills to figure out that the Rembrandt existed, especially hidden under another painting."

"From the little we know of him, I doubt that Malone has those kinds of skills," Adela said.

Now that I was calmer, I was able to remember the attack more clearly. Snatches of Malone's conversation resurfaced, things I hadn't remembered when the police questioned me. "The impression Malone gave me was that finding the painting was Thibodeau's scam. I don't think they were working together on it. That's why he doesn't know where it is."

"Okay, so Thibodeau was the master criminal?"

Remembering that Ernie said that Thibodeau wasn't "the sharpest tool in the box," I shook my head. "I don't see Thibodeau being capable of that kind of research and planning."

"So he must have had a partner."

I recalled something else Malone said during the attack. "You're right. I think he did."

"What do you mean?"

"Malone spoke about underestimating 'professor types' and asked me if I was working with someone."

Adela was excited. "A professor! Maybe an art history prof at one of the universities?"

"Maybe," I agreed. Another, far less palatable thought occurred to me.

"Although, maybe Malone thinks of anyone with an education as a professor-type," Adela continued. "It could just be someone smart or nerdy, you know?"

I worked with dozens of highly educated people. People who knew tons about art history. People who were textbook definitions of nerds. People with easy access to the Art Vault.

Was one of my colleagues a murderer?

CHAPTER THIRTY

I AWOKE THE NEXT MORNING TO THE LOCAL DJ'S SMOOTH TONES SLIDING out of Adela's stereo: "Well, folks, it's January thirty-first, and it's happening yet again—Ottawa's experiencing a heat wave. That's right; we're at eight degrees above zero this morning, shooting all the way up to twelve by midday. The hot, drippy weather is scheduled to continue all week. This city can't seem to catch a break—"

Adela flicked the radio off as I blinked my way into alertness from the couch.

"Rise and shine," she said.

I felt shattered and didn't want to move. "At least it's warming up," I groaned.

Adela laughed. "Yeah, poor us. We suffer through freezing weather all year, but inevitably, when it's time for Winterlude, we hit a heat wave."

I followed Adela into the kitchen, where she was brewing up heavenly smelling coffee.

"Isn't it better if it's actually mild for the big outdoor festival? You know, so people can enjoy it instead of freezing their asses off?"

"Wrong, wrong, my friend. You want it good and arctic so that tourists buy tons of hot chocolate, cider, and BeaverTails. If it's too warm, everything gets messed up. Last year they put the ice sculptures in freezers during the middle of the day. Plus, they had to shut the canal when a skater fell through. The last thing any good Ottawan wants is a balmy February."

I laughed at her vehemence. "Listen, I love the winter as much as the next gal, but you have to admit, when it's so cold your eyelashes freeze closed, a bit of sunshine isn't the worst thing."

Adela poured two big mugs of coffee and then turned to me. "I don't think you should go into the office today. Call in sick. Malone might still be lurking."

My stomach lurched, but I shook my head. "No, he's long gone. Lemieux said—"

Adela cut in. "Detective Tight Pants seems competent, but he can't give you any guarantees. You're shaken up. You need a day off."

She strode to the living room, and I trailed after her.

"I can't. I'm not sick. There's nothing wrong with me."

She rolled her eyes. "Sweetie, there's so much wrong with you I don't even know where to start. In the past two weeks you've found a dead body, been stalked, threatened with a knife, and you now think that one of your colleagues is a cold-blooded murderer."

"I can't mess up this job."

"You're making a mistake," Adela said. She had uttered these same words when I started dating the guy who kept a framed glamor shot of his mother on his bedside table.

I didn't argue any further. Sometimes, the only thing to do in the face of Adela's unwavering certainties was to shut up.

She stopped in front of the mirror by the couch and applied a dark layer of "Big Apple Red" to her lips. She straightened her jacket before turning to me.

"How do I look?" she asked.

"Terrifying," I replied truthfully. Adela's suit was a severe black, her curly dark hair was pulled straight back from her face in a high bun, and her makeup was strong, highlighting her glowing skin and high cheekbones.

"Good," she said. "A dominating woman scares the pants off the other sales guys."

Her stilettos made a sharp clack against the foyer floor as she walked toward the door. She turned, her hand on the handle. "Call in sick."

I waited until I heard the elevator ping and then allowed myself to consider her advice. If I was honest, the thought of venturing out into the streets with Malone still on the loose was daunting. I looked at my watch. It was 7:45 a.m., so Oliver wouldn't be in yet. I'd leave a message on his voice mail and then bask in a day of doing nothing.

The phone rang several times, but when his voice mail should have kicked in, a groggy voice answered. "Hello?"

"Oliver?" I asked. It sounded like I had woken him up.

There was a pause, and when Oliver spoke again it was with his usual clear diction. "Yes?"

"It's Jess. I'm not feeling very well, so I'm going to take a sick day."

Another pause. "Is that wise?" he asked.

"What do you mean?"

"A certain dedication is expected from our junior staff. We don't hire slackers."

I was about to explain Malone's attack and the reason I needed a break, when I stopped, remembering that three more boxes of ledgers were due to be delivered. There were only six boxes left in the whole collection, and events were becoming more urgent. The faster I found out the end of Jem and Victoria's story, the sooner I could tell Lemieux about the letters. "I am dedicated, Oliver. Don't worry about it. I'll take some Tylenol and be in."

Oliver's voice was triumphant. "Good, Jess. I like your esprit de corps."

◇◇◇◇◇◇◇

UPON EXITING ADELA'S BUILDING, I WAS BUOYED BY THE COMFORTING presence of a car from the Ottawa PD parked outside. If Malone was lurking, they would spot him. I walked to work, thinking I would jump at every car horn and shrink at the sight of every man in a dark coat, but the fear was entirely absent. The sun was warm on my face, and when I stopped at a crosswalk, I realized that I was actually enjoying myself. I shook my head at my own perversity. Last night I was threatened with a knife by a murder suspect, and yet today I felt alive and excited. I skipped over the enormous puddles of melted snow with elan. This was not the nervous, paranoid reaction I expected from myself. It must be a delayed symptom of shock.

When I arrived at work, the first person I saw was the circulation clerk, bringing me three more boxes of Jarvis ledgers. Gus was a young guy, always eager to chat. He unloaded the boxes onto my processing table and packed up the old ones.

"Hey, Gus. I've only got three more boxes in the collection. Is there any way you can add them to this order and bring them to me today?" I pleaded.

Gus shook his head. "I'm sorry. I'd love to help you, but Oliver gave us strict instructions—only three at a time."

I stopped him. "What does Oliver have to do with this? I thought it was policy that junior archivists could only get three boxes?"

"Yeah, but usually we let it slide. Oliver told us explicitly not to do that for you."

My pulse quickened. "When did he say this?" I asked.

Gus blinked his watery blue eyes, surprised at my intensity. "I don't know, about two weeks ago."

Was that before or after I found the body? How would Oliver even know about the correspondence hidden in the ledgers? Gus noted my confusion. "Don't worry about it. Oliver is a control freak. He usually does this with all of his new employees."

I smiled wanly.

Gus left, and I cracked open the next box. It felt good to be doing something, rather than staying at Adela's, huddled in front of the television while Oprah and Dr. Phil boomed about the trendiest diet or latest relationship hack. I worked quickly, searching each ledger for another letter. I was pleased when I came up with one:

> February 1, 1915
>
> Dearest Vic,
>
> Progress is being made. Teddy has our papers and we shall depart as soon as we find a ship to take us. I shan't be sorry to leave. My time here is over, and I have learned all I can from this city. Now that the threat of invasion has truly passed and fighting has bogged down in Flanders, Paris is returning to something like her old self.

There are even tourists again, if you can believe it. Now, not only do they visit Mr. Eiffel's tower, but they stop and gawk at the German war trophies at the court of the Invalides. Another tourist activity is to creep ever so carefully to the edge of a battle so that one can return home boasting of having heard the booming artillery. The whole thing sickens me, and I am eager to leave Europe, which seems to be collapsing in on itself. I long for the cleanliness of a new world, the world you and I shall create together.

I followed your instructions and mailed the painting last night. I admit to being apprehensive at entrusting our future to France's postal service and the U-boat infested seas. I have faith, however, that it will make it through. If the painting is confiscated, at least I shall be home and we shall be together. To be stopped with the painting, if they learned what it concealed, would certainly have landed me in hot water!

Strangely, it was liberating to let the painting go. It has consumed an enormous amount of my attention and worry since I discovered it so many months ago. Now, come what may, it is out of my hands. I know it is silly when I think of what it conceals, but I am anxious for you to see my work. As I've said before, it is a departure for me.

I love you,

Jem

The letter confirmed my fears. Jem mailed the painting to Victoria, but for some reason they never removed the overpainting. What happened to prevent them from doing so? Maybe they couldn't cover the expense of restoring the Rembrandt and abandoned the project. The more obvious answer, that both Jem and Victoria died, was one I didn't like to contemplate.

As I did with all of the others, I photocopied the letter, placing the duplicate deep within my filing cabinet. I was uneasy about putting the original back in the ledger and sending the boxes to storage. After all, anyone could call up the boxes and find it as I had done. Still, I couldn't go against my archival training. Removing an original document without carefully documenting where it was found was one of the worst things you could do. In the archival world, context was everything. Besides, I reasoned, it took ninety years for someone to find these letters; they would remain hidden for another few days.

After lunch, I returned to my office, intent on finally determining what happened to Jem and Victoria. I liked to believe that they made it to Tahiti and discovered they didn't need a lot of money to survive. They kept Jem's painting intact because they loved it so much. Maybe Jem continued painting, this time under a pseudonym to avoid Victoria's father's wrath, explaining why I could find no trace of him. He and Victoria lived out their lives in happiness under the tropical sun, secure in the knowledge that if they ever needed money, they had a masterpiece at hand. On Jem's death, Victoria could have mailed the painting back to her cousin Andrew, the child she knew when she lived on the farm, never telling him the secret of what was under Jem's image.

I smiled, pleased with the neatness of my daydream. Now it was a question of proving my hypothesis right. The tale of my archival detective work would make a fascinating journal article. I could see myself on the cover of the next issue of *Archivaria*, an archivist superstar.

My excursion to Van Cleef's gave me vital information, and I intended to follow up on it. Thibodeau bought two Crawford paintings, and while *Landscape 12* could have masked the Rembrandt, *Paris 1915* was the likelier candidate.

My intention to hit the Reading Room was delayed by a knock on my door. I looked up to find Ginette standing in the entrance, next to Lemieux.

"I was coming back from lunch, and the commissionaire downstairs asked me to escort this gentleman to you." Ginette's eyes burned with curiosity. "He's with the police."

CHAPTER THIRTY-ONE

MY FIRST THOUGHT WAS THAT LEMIEUX HAD FOUND SOME PROOF LINKING
me to the Van Cleef break-in. I hated myself for blushing; I knew it
made me look guilty in both Lemieux's and Ginette's eyes. "Thanks,"
I said to her. I stood and ushered Lemieux in, closing the door in
Ginette's face.

For such a small man, Lemieux was good at looming.

"What do you want?" I squeaked, crossing my arms over my chest.

Lemieux took in my defensive gesture, and his mouth tightened
until I thought he'd swallowed his lips.

"I want to talk without your jaseuse friend around," he said.

"Jaseuse?" I repeated, stalling for time.

Lemieux rolled his eyes and explained. "Yap yap—talks a lot."

"Do I need a lawyer?" I asked with a shaky laugh.

"Only if you have something to hide," he said, sitting down uninvited. "You're sure you don't want to tell me about your activities at
the auction house?"

"I wasn't at the auction house," I said.

He sighed and stared around my office, taking in the messy boxes
lining the floor, the old filing cabinet, and the shabby desk. He was
waiting.

"I went for a long walk," I said finally.

Lemieux snorted. "You and I both know that you broke in there
last night. Please, if you found out something that would help the
case, tell me."

His unusually conciliatory tone moved me. I thought of what Adela said about working with the police. I didn't want to tip my hand

about the Rembrandt, but I could tell him about the "professor type" without harming my own research.

"After you left last night, I remembered something Malone said."

"Yes?" he asked, pulling the other chair closer to mine, so that our knees almost touched.

"He said that there was someone else in on the plan."

Lemieux nodded. "Yes, we think it's his friend Joe. He's missing too. Maybe they were working on this thing with Thibodeau."

"I don't think so. Malone gave me the impression that he wasn't fully in the know about Thibodeau's scam. That's why he didn't know where the painting was."

Lemieux sighed. "That is what Malone would say. Just like he told Joe he didn't kill Thibodeau. You mustn't be fooled by these bad men."

I snapped. "I wasn't fooled. I'm telling you my impression. Anyway, last night he referred to someone else. He used the word 'professor.' It sounded like someone smart, or at least, educated."

Lemieux surprised me by considering my opinion. "You may be right." He pulled out a notebook. "Tell me everything Malone said."

"He talked about 'Pauly's scam,' said he'd underestimated someone he called the 'professor type' and later he asked me if I was working with that person."

"Anything else?" he asked.

My mouth twisted as I tried to recall Malone's words. "No, that was it."

Lemieux leaned back. "Okay, that's good. We can work with this. See if Thibodeau was hanging out with any intellectuals. Thank you."

I voiced my greatest anxiety. "You'll keep looking for Malone, right?"

Lemieux looked at me with that same gentleness he showed last night in his car. "Absolutely, mademoiselle. How are you doing with all of this?"

"Better than I thought I would be," I found myself admitting.

"I am not surprised. As I said before, you're a tough biscuit."

I laughed. "Thanks, I think."

He stood. "I also came by to tell you that there are reports that Malone and Joe were spotted in New York, but nothing confirmed yet. Until we catch them, keep your head down, inform the Ottawa PD of all your movements, and stop doing foolish things."

I opened my mouth to protest my innocence, but Lemieux waved a hand. "Save your breath for when you want to tell me what you were actually doing last night." He softened his words with his wide Ryan Seacrest smile, and I found myself grinning back.

◇◇◇◇◇◇

THE READING ROOM WAS QUIET THAT AFTERNOON. MAYBE EVERYONE WAS outside enjoying the warm weather, or more likely, according to Adela, cursing the sun. I glanced out the large window and saw the trees dripping water and streets filled with half-melted snow.

Sasha was at the reference desk.

"Hey, Jess. Can you believe this weather?"

"Yeah. It's great."

"Great? You're obviously not a skater. They're going to be swimming down the canal this year. Well, if Winterlude's a bust, at least we have the Games to look forward to."

"Uh-huh. Listen, I was hoping you could help me. I'm looking for information on Canadian paintings from the beginning of the twentieth century."

Sasha frowned. "Beyond the usual suspects—encyclopedias and reference books—I don't know how much help I can give you. I tell you what, Stephen Nguyen is over there." She gestured with her head. "Why don't you ask him?"

Since I had defied his order to stay out of the Art Vault, the last thing I wanted was to talk to Stephen. "No, no," I said. "I don't want to disturb him."

Sasha said, "Don't worry about it. He's been here every day for the past week. I think he's trying to avoid real work or something. He's got most of our art books piled on his table. Go ask him."

I glanced over. His thin frame was bent over a thick tome. Books were stacked all over his table like a small fortress. "Are there any worthwhile reference works that he's not looking at?" I asked.

"Well, he finished with the *Primer on Canadian Modernism* yesterday, so you could try that. There's also *Canadian Modernism*, which I think you looked at last time."

I nodded. Then I'd been looking for information on Jeremy Crawford's life; now I wanted to know about his paintings. "I'll start with those."

"Great. Grab a seat, and I'll bring them over."

I crossed the big room, picking the farthest chair possible from Stephen. Sasha followed with the requested books. When she left, I flipped to the index of the *Primer*. There it was: *Paris 1915* by Crawford, Jeremy. I turned to the page and read:

Created while the artist studied in Paris, this painting reflects the growing interest in modernist techniques. Here Crawford uses an almost cubist approach to the depiction of the Parisian street scene.

That was it—not even a photo of the painting to accompany the small amount of text. I turned to *Canadian Modernism*. It held a short blurb about *Landscape 12*, mentioning only that it was painted in Montreal in 1912 as part of a series of oils depicting the city. Just as I'd suspected; this could not be the Rembrandt.

I found more information on *Paris 1915* in *Canadian Modernism*, which contained an almost identical description to the *Primer* but also had an image of the painting. I stared at it avidly. Could this conceal my Rembrandt?

As the text indicated, the painting was an attempt at cubism. The colors were muted beiges and creams. Crude, angled shapes, rather than naturalistic forms, dominated the canvas. Nevertheless, you could clearly see the blurred figures and the shape of the Eiffel Tower. The painting conveyed a sense of warmth and movement. I smiled in pleasure. Jem was right—it was beautiful. I recalled his works that I had seen in the Art Vault. Those were stilted and unanimated. This painting, however, was vibrant and full of movement. If nothing else, Jem succeeded in becoming an artist in Paris.

"Hard at work, Jessica?"

My head jerked up. Stephen stood before me, hands on his slim hips. I closed the book with a snap, hoping he hadn't noticed what I was reading.

"Hi," I proclaimed, overbrightly.

"You've got quite the interest in modernism," he commented.

I felt the blush crawl up my neck. "Yes," I stuttered. He was looking at me strangely; did he know I'd snuck into the Art Vault?

His next words amplified my fears. He spoke slowly, in that precise way of his. "If I recall correctly, when you discovered that body it was because you wanted to look at the work of a modernist painter. What was his name?"

I laughed. "Who can remember these things?"

Stephen flared his nostrils. "I remember, Jessica. In fact, it was Jeremy Crawford's work, was it not?"

I nodded, cursing myself for returning to the vault. Stephen must have found out about my second trip. Did Ernie tell him? Maybe he'd seen camera footage of my entrance.

"I'd like to talk to you about your interest in Jeremy Crawford." Stephen's tone was firm. "I'm away for the next couple of days, but I'll meet you Friday morning. Eight thirty in my office at the Conservation Facility." It wasn't a request.

"What's this about?" I asked.

Stephen's voice held none of its usual warmth. "I think it's best if we discuss it in my office."

I nodded again and then watched him exit the Reading Room. My head was swimming. I was going to be fired. I would have to leave Ottawa, leave my job, leave Mike. What would he think of me? I'd never learn the end of Victoria and Jem's story. I swallowed a rock in my throat and willed myself not to cry. I stared at the book in front of me, but I wasn't reading.

I looked up only when the room's lights flickered on and off. Sasha approached with a grin. "We're closing, Jess. Party's over."

CHAPTER THIRTY-TWO

THE CHEERFUL CONFIDENCE I ENJOYED THAT MORNING VANISHED WITH the setting sun, and my walk back to Adela's was grim. How could I have been so stupid? One foolish trip to the Art Vault to satisfy my curiosity, and my career was in ruins. I would return to Toronto, having failed to solve the Jem and Victoria mystery, failed to solve the murder, and failed to be an archivist. Fired with cause from the national archives, I'd never get another job in my field. I'd spend the rest of my life living in my mother's long shadow. Maybe I'd steal a shopping cart and start collecting bottles. I could adopt dozens of cats and never wash my hair again. My life was over.

Although the temperature was warm, well above zero, the night was damp with melting snow. I shivered in my jacket. There was something almost eerie in this change of weather; it felt like things were off-kilter.

After Adela finished work that night, she drove me to my apartment to collect some clothes and personal things. I couldn't bring myself to tell her about my conversation with Stephen, staring instead out the window as we wound through the city streets. When we pulled onto Pinhey, the hairs on the back of my neck stood up. The street was strangely quiet—not one skinny, pockmarked teenager loitering by the crack house on the corner, no prostitutes hurrying to Wellington Street for the commuter rush. The place, while never welcoming, felt abandoned.

I realized why when my apartment came into view. An Ottawa PD cruiser sat outside, its bright white-and-blue markings an odd addition to the street's usual dim squalor.

"They're not exactly subtle," Adela said, pulling in front of the car and pointing to the cop behind the wheel. "Do they think they're going to catch Malone this way?"

I answered absentmindedly, "I guess they have to cover all their bases, in case he comes back." My attention focused on the front door I had burst out of last night as I ran for my life. I shivered, a violent body spasm I hadn't expected.

"Let's go in," Adela said.

I mounted the steps and fished the mail from my mailbox: a depressing stack of utility and credit card bills. I opened the door with trepidation. My morning's courage had abandoned me. The dark apartment had never seemed more ominous. The familiar shapes of the furniture loomed like shadowy intruders. I froze, staring at the shards of glass littering the floor. They caught the light from the porch, seeming to glitter with bright, cold menace. This was the spot where Malone nearly killed me. The faint ticktock of the kitchen clock was a harbinger of impending disaster. My feet were leaden, and I was unable to take another step.

Luckily, Adela was not so affected. She pushed in behind me with hearty bonhomie. "Let's get going." She marched over to the lamp, which lay fallen on the floor. She popped it onto the table and turned it on, vanquishing my demons with the flick of a switch. If only all my fears were so easily resolved.

◇◇◇◇◇◇

THE NEXT DAY WAS EVEN MORE DEPRESSING. THE LAST THREE BOXES OF Jarvis material arrived, and I found no more letters. I searched through the ledgers twice to be certain I hadn't missed a slit, but there was nothing. I didn't know how I would ever learn the end of Jem and Victoria's story without the help of the hidden letters. I certainly wouldn't get many opportunities to continue my research after Stephen fired me on Friday.

Ginette Noiseau's visit to my office did nothing to improve my dark mood.

"Yesterday's police appearance seems to have shaken you up," she said.

The kindness in her voice startled me. "I guess."

"It can't be easy being interrogated by the police."

My tone was defensive. "I wouldn't say I was interrogated." Although parts of Lemieux's conversation felt that way.

"What did they want?"

I looked at her sharply. I might not be able to finish Jem and Victoria's story, but I damn sure wouldn't help Ginette. Her face revealed nothing.

"The officer needed to ask me about some developments in the murder case."

"Oh?" Ginette's smile was warm and inviting. It transformed her face, and for the first time, I saw how charismatic she could be.

"I don't want to get into it," I said.

"That's fine, Jess. Do you mind if I talk to you about something else?"

She sounded diffident, tentative, and I was again surprised. "Sure," I said, indicating the other chair.

"This is a bit awkward." She gave a nervous laugh as she sat. "I know I've got a certain reputation here, that I'm tough and maybe a bit ruthless. I don't mind that, you know. Archivists are supposed to be so mild mannered, but I didn't get into this profession to be pushed around."

I couldn't imagine anyone thinking they could push Ginette around. I nodded.

"Anyway," she continued, "I probably came across too strong when I started here. I was determined to carve a name for myself, and it didn't matter the cost. I did a few things, made some hard decisions, and I created enemies of people who could have been my friends."

"Uh, okay." I paused awkwardly. "I appreciate you sharing your experience."

Ginette waved a hand. "I'm not telling you this for some touchy-feely reason." Her voice took on an edge. "I know you're working on something,

Jess. I've been watching you. I'm sure you've got a good lead on a potential article, maybe even a breakthrough of some kind. I wanted to tell you to be careful how you handle it. There are people here who don't want others to succeed, even if they claim to be friends."

Who was she warning me against? Or was this a ploy to get me on her side so I would reveal my secret? My smile was shaky and uncertain. "Thanks for the advice, Ginette."

"Pas de quoi," she said, standing. She looked strangely vulnerable when she turned on leaving and said, "I wish someone had talked to me like this when I first started." Then she, and her expensive perfume, was gone.

◇◇◇◇◇◇◇

THAT AFTERNOON I DRAGGED MYSELF TO ONE OF OUR VERY RARE SECTION meetings. Despite another warm day outside, the conference room was freezing. For some reason, the building's primitive air conditioning was on. Cold, musty-smelling air blasted up from the vents in the floor, coming straight from the bowels of the building. Frost caked the inside of the windows.

I huddled deeper into my sweater. This was my first, and probably last, staff meeting. It was hard to concentrate. The only thing I could think about was my impending meeting with Stephen. For the hundredth time, I went over our conversation in my head. Trying to banish my negative thoughts, I considered the possibility that he wasn't going to let me go. I frowned. If Stephen didn't want to fire me, why would he want to see me? He'd said something about Jeremy Crawford. Maybe Stephen was the professor? The idea was preposterous. Stephen was a quiet, kind man. He couldn't shoot someone in cold blood. Yet my mind returned to the idea. It made sense in a weird way. If anyone was professorial, it was studious, quiet Stephen Nguyen. I shivered. At least I was meeting him at his office, with other people around.

My other colleagues were also possibilities. They were all research experts. They were all passionate about history, and they all made the same lousy salary.

I examined the five people sitting around the meeting table. Obviously, they were used to the room's tundra temperatures, because they were well-bundled against the chill. I sat next to Louise, who wore her old army coat and a fuzzy pair of earmuffs, which I suspected were more to muffle the sound of Oliver's voice than for warmth. Ginette, across the table from us, was draped in a thick gray pashmina. Mike looked rugged in a fisherman's sweater and a plaid scarf. It looked like Barry O'Quinn was actually wrapped in a duvet. Oliver himself was resplendent in his cape. They were all quirky, but maybe not benign.

I clamped my mouth closed to keep my teeth from chattering.

As if sensing my discomfort, Mike unwound his scarf and pushed it along the table toward me. Out of the corner of my eye, I noticed Louise's mouth set in a grim line and saw Ginette raise a plucked eyebrow. A blush heated my cheeks, and I hurried to wrap the scarf around me before anyone noticed. I gave it a surreptitious sniff. It smelled like Ivory soap and Mike. He grinned at me, his dimple popping into sight.

Oliver was talking about our section's quarterly performance. As he berated the staff, I considered his opportunity for murder. With blanket access to the vaults, he could have easily slipped in and killed Thibodeau. What's more, he knew a great deal about art, history, and everything else, at least according to him. I settled into a lovely little fantasy of Oliver being hauled away in handcuffs, his cape waving in the breeze as they bundled him into the squad car. Eventually, I tuned back in to his monologue.

"Appraisal work is down, and we haven't acquired much new material. I'm most displeased."

Barry O'Quinn yawned in response, but Ginette raised a hand. "Olivier." In his presence she always pronounced his name with a French inflection. I saw him smile slightly; he must like it. She continued. "You're not forgetting my acquisition of those papers belonging to John Graves? He was president of Beverly Steel for years. His records are quite important, you know."

I examined Ginette. Could she be the killer? She was in the Art Vault last month. She was in charge of business and industry papers; there was no reason for her to be in there.

"Yes," Oliver frowned. "But it was only two feet of material."

Ginette waved a hand. "It's the importance of what I acquire that matters, not the volume. You can't judge archives by meters!"

Louise interrupted. "He'd actually said 'feet.'"

Ginette turned on her, not bothering to hide her annoyance "What?" she demanded.

Louise coughed, seemingly unperturbed. "Oliver used the imperial system of measurement, not the metric. He said you'd brought in only two feet. He wasn't judging you by meters."

I barely caught Ginette's muttered reply, "Pedantic old cow."

The slightest snore eased out from Barry O'Quinn's slack mouth. I considered him as his head bobbed forward. I had heard him placing bets. Maybe he'd lost all his savings on the ponies and was in debt to the mob. Maybe to a biker gang. Somehow, he'd found out about the Rembrandt and got into bed with Thibodeau, only to have his scheme go horribly wrong.

I turned my detective gaze to Louise. She was a good friend, but she'd stonewalled me about Gilbert Jarvis's address. Could she have been hiding something with her adamant refusal to divulge his whereabouts? She'd also claimed to be sick the day after the murder. Louise was angry and bitter with the institution. Could the theft of the Rembrandt be revenge? She certainly knew the institution and was undoubtedly the best researcher at this table. If anyone could have found out about the Rembrandt, it was her. I remembered that I'd seen her name on the Art Vault access list. She had no reason to be in there.

"People," Oliver clapped his hands, and Barry's head snapped upright. "Let's get back to the task at hand. What do you have to show for three months of work? Mike?"

He looked up, startled. "What's that?"

"What have you done these past months?"

Mike answered slowly, his deep voice creaking a little. "Well, I went on the Vancouver acquisition trip. Met with some potential donors. Appraised a dancer's collection. Nothing major there, mostly old programs and some film of past performances. That might be interesting. I'll have to talk to AV about it."

Oliver seemed impatient. "Just list what you've acquired, okay?"

"Right." He scratched his head in a thoughtful gesture. "There were the papers from the Group of Seven niece, the accrual to the National Dance Theatre, and the works of Wilson Burroughs, a minor poet."

Mike acquired artists' papers and had valid reasons for going into the vault. Still, his knowledge of the art world, however limited, made him a prime suspect. The fact that he was a nice guy and an even better kisser shouldn't throw me off his scent. I took another sniff of the scarf.

Oliver jumped in. "Great. Ginette, what about you?"

"As I said, I acquired John Graves's papers. I also brought in some lovely watercolors, painted by Lise Leduc, one of the country's first female CEOs."

Aha, presumably this was Ginette's reason for being in the vault. Maybe she wasn't trying to steal my Rembrandt story—or worse, cover up a murder.

I was concentrating so hard on my detective musings that I started when Oliver addressed me. "Jess, you're looking hale and hearty despite feeling so poorly yesterday. I'm sure you've got a few items to tell us about?"

I stared at him. He had never let me acquire anything, telling me I wasn't ready for the responsibility. He knew I hadn't brought anything in and was asking so that he could reinforce my junior status. Out of the corner of my eye, I saw Ginette lean forward, a smirk crawling over her face. Mike caught my eye and tilted his head in sympathy.

I opened my mouth to speak, but Louise jumped in. "Jess was invaluable on my acquisition of the Doucette papers two months ago. She did a ton of research and was a big help in my decision-making."

I shot Louise a grateful look. She continued talking, obviously hoping to distract Oliver from preying on me. "I've done a lot of acquisition lately . . ."

Louise listed what she brought in. My ears perked up when she mentioned the acquisition of a series of political cartoons. Those would be stored in the Art Vault. I was relieved Louise had good reason to access the vault. Despite her bitterness, Louise couldn't kill anyone. She'd saved me from Oliver. She was a saint in combat boots.

Oliver moved on to Barry.

The meeting dragged on, with Oliver alternating between insufferable pomposity and "motivational" diatribes about how poorly everyone was working.

I glanced at Mike as Oliver exhorted us to "step up to the plate," "think outside of the box," and "break free of silos." Mike scratched at his ear, and it took me a moment to realize he was circling his finger around it, to indicate that Oliver was crazy. I stifled a giggle and looked down.

The meeting was finally winding down when Ginette spoke. "We forgot to mention something. I'm surprised that Jessica didn't bring it up, actually."

I braced myself. I didn't know what was coming, but I was sure I wouldn't like it.

CHAPTER THIRTY-THREE

THE HUM OF THE FURNACE WAS THE ONLY SOUND AS WE ALL STARED AT Ginette, waiting for her to explain herself. She smiled serenely.

Finally, Oliver prompted her. "What do you mean, Ginette?"

"The state visit? The prime minister of Belgium?" Ginette said.

Everyone looked at her blankly until she sighed with impatience. "The dead body?"

My mind whirled. Ginette was bringing this up to put me on the spot. I realized the insincerity of her earlier kindness and was glad I hadn't told her anything. There was an awkward silence. I hadn't killed the guy, yet they were treating me as if I were somehow re-sponsible. My throat tightened, although my feelings were more anger than embarrassment.

Oliver actually took pity on me and broke the tense silence. "I don't think Jessica wants to talk about it, Ginette."

I recalled my impending meeting with Stephen. What did it matter what my colleagues thought of me? I was probably getting fired anyway. "No, it's okay, Oliver. I don't mind. I'm sure there have been a lot of rumors, and I'm happy to tell you what I know." I matter-of-factly recounted the story I had told a dozen times already. I concluded, "So I ran back and got the commissionaire, and then the police came."

There was a silence as everyone absorbed my tale. Ginette spoke first, zeroing in on my weak point. "And why were you in the Art Vault?"

"Like I said, I'd forgotten a notebook." I couldn't keep the edge from my voice. "I won't do it again."

"Good, good," she said. "Valuable paintings are stored there. Even parts of my collections."

"I know," I said impatiently. "Stephen Nguyen told me that."

"You spoke to Stephen?" Louise sounded surprised.

I turned to her. "Yeah. He wanted an explanation."

"What did he say?"

"The standard things you'd expect—'Don't do it again' was the gist of it." I flushed. I had done it again, and I was soon going to pay the price.

Oliver must have noticed my face, because his earlier kindness disappeared, and he pressed me for more information. "Are you telling us everything, Jessica?"

Everyone in the room looked at me with expectation. If I was fired they'd find out about my second foray into the vault soon enough, but I was damned if I was going to tell them about it. Instead, I blurted the first thing that came to mind. "The police think the murder's related to biker gangs, but I'm not convinced." Damn it. That was going to lead to even more uncomfortable questions.

Everyone seemed taken aback at my statement until Barry O'Quinn, muffled in his duvet, broke the silence with a guffaw. "What are you, some sort of latter-day Columbo?"

Normally I would have been annoyed at being patronized in such a manner, but I was actually grateful to Barry. Everyone laughed, and my loaded statement was forgotten. The meeting adjourned, and I walked back to my office, my limbs and fingers tingling with the return of warmth.

Happily, Mike soon arrived at my door.

"Hi," I smiled and unwound the scarf from my neck. "Thanks for this."

"Maybe I shouldn't have given it to you. It seemed to attract attention. I'm very new to this kind of thing."

"What is 'this kind of thing'?" I asked.

He grinned. "I don't know. An office romance, maybe?"

My stomach sank. Our office romance was about to come to a premature end. I should give him a heads-up. "There's something I need to tell you." I took a deep breath, looking away from him to prepare myself to tell him I was being fired. That's when I noticed a letter on my desk.

"What's this?" I asked, picking it up. When I spotted the spidery handwriting and the return address indicating Westmount, Quebec, my heart fluttered. It was a reply from Gilbert Jarvis.

I ripped it open and read quickly:

> Dear Miss Novak,
>
> Your letter has intrigued me, and I would be delighted to meet and talk about my cousin. The older I get (and I'm now quite, quite old), the more I find myself fascinated by history, especially my own. I have some family photographs and stories I could share. I'm unable to travel but will gladly welcome you to my home. Please make arrangements with my housekeeper at a time that is convenient to you. I do not get out much anymore, and you are always sure to find me at home.
>
> Cordially,
>
> Gilbert Jarvis

"Is everything all right?" Mike asked.

I smiled radiantly. "It's fantastic. Look." I handed him the note and watched as he read it.

"This is about the letters you found?"

"Yes, isn't it great? It's my first real break!" Impulsively I threw my hands around Mike's neck, squeezing him in a hug. In an instant, I realized what I had done.

Mike's head was already descending toward mine. This kiss, like the other two, started out gently, but when I leaned in to return it, Mike deepened the pressure, pulling me to him. His lips were soft and sweet, but I hardly noticed. I was desperate to feel him as close to me as possible. The anxiety crouching over me since Monday night evaporated. For the first time in days, I felt like nothing more than a woman. I kissed him, sliding my hand down his back to grasp his bum. He groaned, pressing ever more firmly against me.

A noise in the hall brought me back to my senses, and I pushed away from Mike, looking nervously out the office door. I couldn't see anyone from my vantage point.

Mike stared at the door. "Did someone spot us?"

"I'm not sure," I replied. "I thought I heard something."

He ran a hand through his hair. "That was probably stupid, but I couldn't resist. You were so excited."

I grinned back at him and spent a moment lost in his eyes before remembering the reason for my impulsiveness. I took the letter from Mike's hand.

Reality came crashing back. I couldn't meet with Gilbert Jarvis. I had written him as an archivist at the Dominion Archives, and in two days I probably wouldn't be an employee. My eyes filled with tears. It was so frustrating. I was so close to learning Jem and Victoria's fate, and yet it was going to be denied me. It wasn't fair.

Mike read the turmoil in my face. "Hey, is everything all right?"

I didn't want to tell him about my stupid trip to the vault. I didn't want to tell him that I was going to be fired. I wanted him to like me, to admire me. I shrugged. "I don't know when I'll get to meet him. I'll have to go to Montreal."

"I could give you a lift," Mike offered.

"What?" I asked, surprised.

"Sure, I could drive you down. We could stay overnight. Maybe make a weekend out of it?"

I looked into his eyes and saw what he was offering. Damn it all, it wasn't fair that I was going to have to give up Mike, Jem and Victoria, and my career. The least I could do was take a final crack at solving the mystery and spend one night with Mike. I smiled at him. "Let's be completely crazy. I know it's Wednesday, but let's go tonight. We can stay over, and I'll meet with Mr. Jarvis tomorrow. What do you say?"

Mike looked momentarily startled by the suggestion, but he met my eyes and smiled. "Are you sure you want to do this? I know you're on probation, and Oliver is a stickler for work attendance."

"I'll call in sick," I said. Stephen was going to fire me. I had nothing to lose.

Mike hesitated. "I'd hate to get you in trouble."

I took a step closer to Mike, putting my hand on his neck. "I suddenly don't mind a little trouble." Then I kissed him.

CHAPTER THIRTY-FOUR

FROM THE FOURTEENTH FLOOR, I LOOKED DOWN AT RENÉ-LÉVESQUE BOU-
levard as a bus sped past a stop, spraying the waiting passengers with
slushy water. While I didn't hear the angry curses, I could imagine
them from the graphic gestures the soaked people aimed at the re-
treating vehicle. Montrealers tended to be a lot more animated than
polite Ottawans. I turned back to the bed, where Mike still slept,
wrapped in the one sheet that hadn't been kicked off during last
night's activities.

We'd driven down after work. Climbing into his car, I'd had a few
misgivings. After all, I didn't know Mike very well. In fact, my second
thoughts were so strong that I'd been tempted to back out, but then,
the idea of spending the next thirty-six hours obsessing about my Friday meeting with Stephen Nguyen was too depressing.

Before leaving Ottawa I called the number the police had given
me to report my whereabouts. There was no answer. Instead I got
a message telling me that the voicemail box I was calling was full.
This wasn't exactly a confidence boost, but I refused to be concerned.
Lemieux was probably right and Malone was long gone. I relaxed
when we hit the highway, speeding away from Ottawa. The worn seat
of Mike's car was comfortable, and he brought along some mellow
jazz for the CD player. His conversation, like the music, was low-key
and soothing. We spent the two-hour drive talking about everything
except what we both knew we were going to do when we arrived at
the hotel.

It was dark by the time we pulled into the city, its skyscrapers
gleaming in the winter night, the streets filled with the same melting,

slushy snow that was swamping Ottawa. I was surprised when Mike pulled up to the swanky entrance of the Queen Elizabeth hotel. We exited the car, and a uniformed valet sped it off to underground parking.

We walked into a luxuriously appointed lobby, complete with plush red carpeting and gleaming chandeliers. "Wow, Mike."

He grinned, his eyes crinkling. "I thought I'd better do it up right. I don't plan seductions every day."

My knees went a little weak, and the last of my doubts vanished. This was going to be fun. "You picked a good spot," I said.

"Yeah," he said. "I got it on points from my gas card. A real deal."

Our room was gorgeous, with big windows and expensive finishings. We changed for dinner, shyly taking turns in the marble bathroom, and then went to the hotel bistro. Our meal was wonderful, hushed, candlelit, and intimate. We ordered a bottle of wine, and Mike surprised me by hardly touching his glass. We held hands on the elevator ride back to the room and I liked how mine felt wrapped in his.

Unlocking the door to the room, I hesitated for a moment. The bed seemed to dominate the whole space. "Now what?" I laughed uncomfortably. Our journey from friendly coworkers to people about to lie down naked together seemed surreal.

Mike stepped forward. "I guess we do this." He pulled me toward him, kissing me deeply. Awkwardness dissolved with that first touch.

When we came up for air, he tugged me to the bed. Off came my shirt, and I wiggled out of my skirt. I lay down, watching Mike strip. He took off his shirt, throwing it on the floor and stood before me in his boxer briefs. He looked good nearly-naked and I took a moment to appreciate him.

Up to now, the few men I'd slept with were all in their twenties. They'd had patchy chest hair and a gawkiness about their limbs that suggested they were still coming to terms with their last adolescent growth spurt. Mike wasn't like that. He was thicker, but in a good way. He was substantial and more real.

He seemed to enjoy my stare, and he moved purposefully to the bed. He reached for my shoulders, as he drew me into a long kiss. "You're beautiful," he murmured.

The evening was like nothing I experienced before. Mike was a calm, confident lover who took the time to get to know what I liked, actually paying attention to how I responded. Most breathtaking of all, he acted as if we had all the time in the world to get where we were going. This was completely different from the testosterone-addled twenty-year-olds I was used to. One ex-boyfriend actually resorted to reciting the captains of NHL teams to slow himself down. This worked well for him, but it was pretty hard to enjoy myself with someone panting "Niedermeyer," "Koivu," and "Alfredsson," in my ear. Mike savored me, and I liked how that felt. Unlike previous boyfriends, he also handled the usual condom awkwardness smoothly by producing one at the appropriate moment without fuss or comment.

The night was amazing, but now it was time to get moving. I was due to meet Gilbert Jarvis soon. I took a quick shower. When I came out, wrapped in a thick white towel, Mike was awake and grinning. His hair was even more of a mess than usual. "Hey, come back to bed." He patted the place beside him.

I smiled but shook my head. "I've got to meet Mr. Jarvis in forty-five minutes."

"Right!" he exclaimed. "The reason we're here."

"Not the only reason," I said, bending down to kiss him.

Mike pulled me toward him, and for a few moments I forgot all about my meeting. "I've got to get over there," I sighed.

"I can drive you."

"It's okay. I've looked at the map. I can grab a bus, no problem."

"You sure?"

"Absolutely. I need a little quiet time to go over what I'm going to ask him. Besides, this way I get to leave you naked in bed. I want you to be well-rested when I come back for round two."

Mike looked disappointed. "Actually, we have to be checked out by noon. Otherwise they'll charge us for another night."

I laughed. "Okay. Why don't I meet you in the lobby? I should be done by about one o'clock."

"Perfect."

I got dressed and left before I was tempted back into bed.

◇◇◇◇◇◇

STEPPING OFF THE 24 BUS ONTO THE STREETS OF WESTMOUNT, IT FELT like I was in another world from the fast-moving, grimy downtown. Here the homes were old and still single-family. Trees lined the streets, which all seemed to pitch steeply upward, climbing the mountain. Westmount lorded over the city of Montreal as its first white settlers, the nineteenth-century captains of trade and industry, had done.

The warm weather left the sidewalk clear of ice, and my walk up Rosemount to Mountain, although steep, was not slippery. As I climbed the street, I also mounted the social ladder. The higher I rose, the nicer, bigger, and more private the homes became. Things were hushed up here: no noisy buses, no hustling pedestrians, no children playing street hockey.

Eventually, I reached the top of the hill—and the Jarvis home. Like its neighbors, it was a mansion of gray stone sitting behind a large stand of trees. It wasn't the biggest house on the block, but its location meant that it commanded a glorious view of the city with the Saint Lawrence River glittering beyond.

I announced my presence by rapping a large lion-head knocker. The door was opened by a substantial woman in a T-shirt and jeans. I blinked. I had expected a starched white maid's uniform.

"Oui?" she asked.

"Je suis ici pour rencontrer Monsieur Jarvis," I said in my tortured French.

"Come this way."

The house was immaculate. Floors gleamed, windows sparkled, and there was nary a dust bunny to be seen. Despite this rigid cleanliness, however, it felt warm and lived-in. We walked down a long wood-paneled hall. The walls were covered with paintings: portraits, landscapes, still lifes. I stared at them eagerly as I passed, but I didn't spot a "Jeremy Crawford" signature among them.

"Ici," said the woman, gesturing to a doorway. The room was bright after the dark hall, and I blinked once or twice as my eyes adjusted. I first noticed the smell, a strong antiseptic odor masking something more earthy and human: the scent of sickness. A bank of windows on the far wall looked out over a huge expanse of soggy brown grass to the neighbor's stone gate. Despite the day's warmth, a fire crackled to my left. Paintings hung along all the walls. This room must have once been an office or a library but had been converted into a bedroom. On my right, where one would normally expect to find two deep leather armchairs and a man smoking a pipe, was a white hospital bed. It was incongruous, like a boat that floated into the library on a particularly high tide.

A shriveled man lay in the bed, his head resting on a stack of pillows. He stared at me with keen eyes. "You must be Miss Novak," he called in a weak voice.

"Yes, I am." I walked forward and shook his hand. His grip was loose, and his skin was dry and papery.

"Gilbert Jarvis," he said in his near whisper. "Sit." He gestured feebly to a chair against the wall, and the woman who let me in brought it forward. "You can leave us, Sylvie. I'll buzz if I need anything."

"Yes, monsieur."

Sylvie withdrew, and we were left alone, the ticking of a clock the only sound in the room.

"I'm grateful you're able to meet with me," I began.

"Happy to do it, my dear. I'm so old now, I hardly get out." He paused, taking a deep wheezing breath before continuing. "The advantage of being rich, of course. I should be in one of those homes. Too depressing, though. You never leave those places except in an ambulance or a hearse. When I go, I want people to notice before I start to smell."

"Oh," I said, unsure of how to respond.

He saw my discomfort and laughed, a surprisingly joyful sound. "My kids say I'm morbid, and my grandkids think I'm crazy. Don't ask me what my great-grandchildren think. They don't talk to me. Too busy with their iPod machines."

I smiled. "As you know, I wanted to talk to you about your cousin, Victoria. I'm writing an article about her."

"Of course. She lived with my family for a time."

"What was she like?"

Jarvis blinked. "Well, I can't give you a firsthand account. She died before I was born."

"What!" I exclaimed. I felt dizzy. My throat tight. "When did that happen?"

Jarvis regarded me quizzically, obviously puzzled by the force of my reaction. "I don't remember the exact date of her death, but it should be in the family Bible." He gestured to a shelf along the far wall, which was covered in rows of old-looking hardcover books. I rose and rifled through them carefully, noting what must have been first editions of Hemingway, Fitzgerald, Joyce, and Woolf jumbled in with ancient leather-bound volumes of Shakespearean plays and Edwardian poetry. If I hadn't been so consumed processing confirmation of Victoria's death, I would have asked him about his collection. As it was, I concentrated on finding the Bible. I needed to learn Victoria's fate. I lugged back the big leather-covered tome to Jarvis and placed it on his bedside table.

His age-spotted hand rubbed the cover meditatively. "My mother tried to record all of our significant events here. In a way, perhaps you could say she was our family's archivist."

I forced a smile and opened the book. A faintly musty smell greeted me. Jarvis noticed it as well and grimaced. "That scent betrays the book's lack of use, I'm afraid. My parents were deeply religious people, but I lost their faith. I don't know how I ended up with the family Bible—by rights it should have gone to my older brother, Andrew. He was a much more dutiful son."

I barely registered his words, focused as I was on reading the delicately inked names and dates on the first few onionskin pages of the book. The birth, death, and marriage dates of Gilbert's father, uncle, and an aunt who died in childhood were all recorded. Victoria's and her brother's birth dates were there, as were Andrew's and Gilbert's. But, while Victoria's brother's death in April 1917 was recorded, hers was not.

"It's not here," I said. Was I doomed to never get any answers?

CHAPTER THIRTY-FIVE

JARVIS PEERED OVER AT THE BIBLE I WAS HOLDING. "NOT RECORDED? That is odd. Mother said Victoria died in the spring of the year I was born."

I glanced at the book. "That was 1915?" I asked.

"Yes."

Jem wrote that he was on his way home in February of 1915. Victoria might have died before he got back. They may never have been reunited. My carefully constructed fantasy about a blissful Tahitian life crumbled before my eyes. Jem had probably been too overwhelmed with grief to reclaim *Paris 1915*. That must be why it stayed with the Jarvis family. Victoria's death explained almost everything. "How did she die?" I asked softly.

Jarvis shrugged. "I'm not entirely sure. My mother said she took sick. There was a great deal of illness back then, and not a lot of doctors. It could have been any number of ailments, I suppose."

I kept my voice steady. "She stayed with your parents for a time, I think."

"That's right. Uncle sent her out to us. My mother always hinted that she'd got into some mischief here in Montreal, maybe something to do with a young man."

I leaned forward. "You don't know the name of that young man, do you? Or anything about him?"

Jarvis smiled, motioning to his side table, where I noticed the letter I had written to him. "You want me to tell you it's this Jeremy Crawford you're researching, don't you? Well, I can't. I know very little. Only that Victoria came to stay on the farm for a number of months. She was unhappy. She was a city girl, and she hated country life."

"How do you know that?" I asked.

"My mother talked a lot about Victoria. I think she was deeply affected by her death. Mother said that Victoria was always a worry to her father. She was a suffragette, you know, which was very scandalous at the time. She was artistic, and my uncle didn't understand that and it worried him, almost as much as her agitating for the vote. She took some lessons at the Art Association of Montreal, which was the forerunner of the Museum of Fine Arts. Uncle was worried she would turn to socialism, I think. That's why he sent her to the farm, to get her away from city influences."

Jem had mentioned the Art Association in his letters. "But it didn't work, did it?"

Jarvis shook his head weakly. "Not according to Mother. Victoria was miserable. She missed the city terribly. I've sometimes wondered if perhaps she committed suicide. It would explain why Mother seemed so affected by her death."

"I'm sure she wouldn't have killed herself," I said decisively.

"Oh?"

I hesitated. I was loath to reveal Jem and Victoria's full story, at least not until I sorted it out for myself. I wanted to tell him something, however. "The reason I'm researching Victoria is because I've come across some letters between her and her lover. I've only read Jem's side of things, but from the tone I don't think Victoria was suicidal."

"I'd love to read those letters." His rheumy eyes sparked with curiosity, but nothing more. If Jarvis knew about the Rembrandt, he concealed it well.

"I'd be happy to share them. I'm doing some research with them at the moment, but as soon as I'm done I'll send you photocopies."

"Don't wait too long," he said with a grin. "I don't know how much more time I've got on this planet."

I smiled back, becoming accustomed to his gallows humor. Then a thought occurred to me. Maybe Jem made it out to the farm after all. Maybe he'd seen her before she died. "Do you know if anyone visited Victoria on the farm?"

Jarvis furrowed his brow. "Mother never mentioned anything like that. Visitors were a big event, so I'm sure she would have talked about it."

Disappointment seeped into my voice. "Well, thanks so much for everything."

"I don't think I helped that much. I have a photograph of her, if you're interested."

"I'd love to see it!"

He gestured to the bookshelf. "It should be in that box, by the dictionary."

I returned with an old cigar box tied with a white string. I placed the box next to him on the bed, and he lifted a feeble hand. He couldn't unwrap the string, however, so I untied it before handing it back to him. He sorted the photos carefully.

"Here it is. This is August 1914, when she first arrived."

I held the sepia-toned photograph at its edge, and stared at the image. The photo was taken outside. A dusty barn could be seen in the distance, while chickens pecked at the dirt to the right of the four figures who made up the foreground. A man and a woman with a toddler clinging to her skirts flanked a girl of about eighteen. The man and woman were both tall, big-boned, and sturdy. They looked almost like they were guarding the girl, who stood behind a large steamer trunk. She was much shorter than her aunt and uncle and wore a dark wide-brimmed hat and a light-colored blouse tucked into a long dark skirt. I peered at her face. She was unsmiling, but I could see her high cheekbones and wide eyes. She was beautiful.

I said as much to Jarvis.

"Yes, she was lovely, at least that's what my mother said. But you can see how little she was, how weak. I guess farm life was too much for her. My brother and I both took after that side of the family. We were quite runty. I had it worse, however. I was sickly. After a few hard winters out West, my mother became convinced I'd not survive another one. That's how I ended up here." He gestured to the room.

I looked surprised, and he smiled. "That's right—I'm living in my uncle's home. From the time I was five I spent every winter here, close to the country's best medical care. Uncle lost Victoria in 1915, and his son was killed at Vimy in 1917. I became his adopted son in a way, and his heir. It drove Andrew crazy of course. He was always a greedy bugger and thought he should get Uncle's estate. Primogeniture and all that." Jarvis chuckled.

For the first time I felt a twinge of sympathy for Victoria's father. His wife was dead, he drove his daughter away, and then he lost his son. He must have been lonely. No wonder he adopted his nephew. I placed the photograph back into the box.

"Are there any other of your relatives who might remember Victoria? Maybe even a friend?"

Jarvis thought a moment but then shook his head. "It was a long, long time ago. I'm afraid anyone who might have known Victoria is dead."

I nodded. It was a long shot.

"I do have a painting of her, though."

"Really?"

"Yes. It was painted by one of her Art Association friends. Uncle hated all 'modern art,' and he especially hated anything to do with the Art Association. After he died I discovered a chest full of paintings by these artists, some never even unwrapped. Presumably Victoria didn't dare hang them, and then she was shipped off to Alberta." Jarvis sighed and continued to talk. "Uncle would never have believed the 'crude' paintings his daughter collected were of any value, but it was actually quite farsighted of him to stow them away. A few of those artists went on to prominence, and now some of the paintings on my walls are worth a lot of money. They'll be keeping my great-grandchildren well supplied with ear pod music for years to come."

I smiled. "May I see the portrait?"

"Oh, it's not a portrait, really." He gestured to the mantelpiece above the fire, where a number of smallish paintings hung. I walked over.

The painting was not large, about a foot by a foot and a half. The colors were muted, and the style was jagged and expressionist. It was a winter scene. Dark trees denuded of leaves loomed over a gray pond upon which a figure could be seen, bathed in the glow of moonlight. The figure was a couple of blotches of paint, impossible to identify. It was a beautiful painting. There was something almost erotic about the figure's movement. I turned to Jarvis. "How do you know it's Victoria?" I asked.

"Look in the right-hand corner."

Sure enough, the artist had written "Victoria skating in moonlight. Montreal 1914." Beneath that, I could make out the signature: "J. Crawford."

I gasped. Jem must have painted it that first winter he met Victoria. I stared hungrily at the image, my eyes filling with tears. At least Victoria would have held this image, tangible evidence of Jem's love. It must have been hard to leave it behind when she was sent to Alberta.

Jarvis interrupted my thoughts. "Is the painter the unsuitable man that Uncle disapproved of?"

"Yes. From the letters I've found, it seems like your uncle ended their affair. He sent Victoria to your father. Jeremy Crawford went to Paris to paint, and then the war broke out and I lost track of him."

"I wish I could help you, my dear. It looks like Victoria's early death ended their relationship."

"Yes, it does." I was depressed. I hadn't wanted their story to finish like that. From the point of view of my article, tragic death was as good, if not better, than blissful reunion, but I didn't feel any better about it. I straightened my spine. "I want to thank you very much for meeting me. I enjoyed talking with you."

Jarvis's wrinkled mouth stretched into a smile. "And I you, my dear. It's wonderful to revisit old times with someone who is genuinely interested."

We shook hands again, and he summoned Sylvie to guide me to

the door. I lingered over the paintings in the hall, despite Sylvie's obvious impatience. I'd learned enough from my recent art research to identify them as mostly modernist. Bright, strong lines, not necessarily representational. It was nice to know that these were paintings that Victoria cherished and loved. I liked thinking that a part of her, her passion for art, still lived on.

◇◇◇◇◇◇

MIKE AND I HAD A LOT TO TALK ABOUT ON THE DRIVE BACK TO OTTAWA. I gave him a brief description of my visit with Jarvis, ending with a sigh. "Victoria died without being reunited with her love. I wish I knew what happened to him, but I think I'm at a dead end."

Mike cheered me up. "I know research. When you think you've hit a wall, something turns up. I remember when Melvin Perkins was poring over Edward Hauver's records, desperate to prove that he'd had an affair with some young poetess. He didn't find the evidence, but instead he found an unpublished poem. Look at your case—you didn't expect to find love letters in those old ledgers, but you did. That's the thrill of the hunt. That's what research is all about."

I smiled at his passion. "I guess it's all serendipity, then?"

"More like knowing where to look and being open to the unexpected." He reached over and patted my thigh, and I felt comforted as much by his words as by his warm hand on my leg.

I thought about the serendipitous nature of research and frowned. Something was nagging at the corner of my consciousness. Something about my visit with Jarvis. That room, its strange mixture of cozy den and clinical hospital. The crackling of the fire, the old man's whispery voice, my disappointment to learn of Victoria's death. I was missing something.

Heavy rain on the windshield distracted me. We were almost at the provincial border with Ontario. The road was running with melted snow and rainwater.

I noticed Mike slowed down a bit. "How's the driving?" I asked.

Mike frowned. "Not great." He placed both hands on the wheel. "It's a bit slick." A semitrailer passed us at high speed, spewing slush and dirt onto the windshield. Mike put the wipers on and glanced in the rearview mirror. "I wish other people would slow down. I've got someone riding our tail."

"You're doing fine," I said. I looked back, and there was indeed a big black SUV right behind the car.

I returned to the subject of my visit, hoping to distract Mike from the road hog. "I'll come up with a new game plan to track down Jem," I said. I'd made a resolution on the bus back to the hotel. If Stephen did indeed fire me at tomorrow's meeting, I would not return to Toronto. Instead, I'd find another job in Ottawa. I'd write my Jem and Victoria article. I wouldn't give up.

Mike's grip on the wheel tightened, and he was glancing continuously between the rearview mirror and the road. "What did the boyfriend in Paris do for a living? You might be able to track him through a professional association," he suggested distractedly.

I never got the chance to reply, because in that instant the SUV chose to pass. The car bombed up alongside us. Even through the driving rain, I could tell that it was too close. I stared at the driver as I heard the scrape of metal. Mike's little Hyundai swerved toward the ditch.

"What the hell!" he shouted, struggling to regain control of the wheel.

I gripped the side of the seat. The SUV did not correct itself; instead, it leaned more heavily into Mike's car. There was the sickening sound of metal against metal, and the next moments became a blur of images as we rolled into the ditch. I saw the windshield, the SUV, and Mike's white, drawn face. We stopped with a lurch.

I gasped for air. Just before veering off the road, I got a good look at the driver's face. Ray Malone was at the wheel.

CHAPTER THIRTY-SIX

THE CAR LAY ON ITS ROOF NEXT TO A MUDDY EMBANKMENT. WE WERE upside down, held in our seats by our belts. Mike put one hand down onto the car roof and released his belt with the other. His knees fell forward. "Don't move," he muttered. "I'll get you out." He fumbled for the car latch, struggling to open the door from upside down, and then he crawled out.

As I waited, the significance of what happened hit me: Malone tried to kill us. Maybe he'd come back to finish the job. I clawed at my seat belt, desperate to get out of the car.

"Hey, hey. Take it easy." Mike's face was pinched. He reached my side of the car and tugged open the door. "Put your hands on the roof and ease your legs down when I undo the belt. Okay?"

I obeyed his command and forced myself to stop panicking. I crawled out, my hands sinking into half-frozen mud. Stumbling, I looked around, fearing I'd see the black SUV. It was gone, but several other cars stopped. A gray-haired man stepped out of his truck and walked toward us. "Êtes-vous blessés?" he called down.

"Are you hurt?" Mike asked, looking at me. My chest felt bruised from the seat belt, but otherwise I was okay.

I laughed, a tinge of hysteria in my voice. "Never better."

"We're okay," Mike called back to the man, who switched to English.

"Thank God. I saw that maniac running you off the road. I got his plate number and called the Sûreté. They'll be here soon."

In the distance, I heard the wail of a siren and felt relief. The Sûreté's involvement surely meant Lemieux's as well. It was oddly comforting to know that he would soon be on the scene.

Mike's shoulders were tense, and he stared at me. "Are you okay?"

I was grateful for the intensity of his concern. "I'm fine," I said. "How are you?"

"I can't believe we were run off the road," his voice cracked.

This was my fault. Malone had been trying to murder me, and he'd nearly killed Mike. I stepped forward, wrapping my arms around him, leaning against his comforting strength.

When the cop car arrived, I strode toward it. It was time I took responsibility for my actions. I would never have forgiven myself if something happened to Mike because I wouldn't trust the cops. I gave the officer my name and address and then said with authority, "You should contact Daniel Lemieux with the Gatineau PD. This accident is connected to a case that he is currently working on."

Both the cop and Mike did double takes.

I spoke calmly. "We were deliberately run off the road by a man who has assaulted me in the past."

"What?" Mike's eyes bulged, but I ignored him. I needed to make sure that the cop listened to me. "Lemieux is familiar with the case. You should contact him immediately."

"Jess, what's going on?" Mike demanded.

I looked at his face—part anger, part bewilderment. He hadn't deserved any of this. I led us a step away from the squad car. "I recognized the man who tried to kill us. His name is Ray Malone. He's been following me ever since I discovered Thibodeau's body. He broke into my apartment earlier this week and threatened me with a knife."

"What?"

As I told him about Malone's attack on Monday night, the ambulance arrived. I continued my explanation while we were checked over by paramedics. Neither of us was hurt, although Mike looked like he was going to be sick by the time I finished my story.

"My God," he stuttered. "I can't believe you've been shouldering all of this. You should have told me."

"I'm sorry. I didn't want to freak you out." I laughed. "I guess that plan backfired, huh?"

He laughed and pulled me into an embrace. "You had a knife to your throat," he said, his voice muffled in my hair. "You must have been terrified."

I melted into his bear hug. It felt so good to have told him. In a way, it was more intimate than the night we had shared.

The rain stopped. We waited for Lemieux's arrival, leaning against the squad car in the watery sunshine. We talked of inconsequential things, but I felt a tenderness toward Mike I hadn't felt before. It seems true that you appreciate people more when you think you might lose them. I snuggled closer to him. We were interrupted by the arrival of a familiar low-slung black car. Lemieux stepped out, his head sheathed in a pair of reflective wraparound sunglasses. He looked like RoboCop. I assumed it was intentional. He didn't approach us right away, instead conferring with the officer. They walked back up on the road, and I could tell by their hand movements that they were re-creating the accident. I saw the duty officer reading something to Lemieux, probably our statements and the witnesses'. Lemieux made eye contact with me as he finally approached us. I couldn't read his expression. He shook Mike's hand, giving him an appraising stare.

"That is your car?" he asked Mike. There was the faintest hesitation before he said the word "car." Obviously, a cheap Hyundai didn't count for much in Lemieux's books.

"Yes," Mike nodded, oblivious to the undertone.

"You can't drive it. I've instructed the officer to have it towed to the nearest garage. I think it is good only for scrap."

The three of us stared at the car. The roof was completely bashed in and the frame bent from the force of the SUV's impact. Mike looked thoughtful. "Insurance will probably give me more than its value, even factoring in the deductible. It wasn't worth much to begin with."

"I imagine not," Lemieux said. "I'll drive you both back to Ottawa, and we can discuss the accident on the way."

Mike spoke for both of us. "Of course, officer. Whatever you think is best."

I was startled to hear such formal politeness from Mike but re-flected that average people probably reacted to the police that way. I should have realized by now that my knee-jerk desire to make "smells like bacon" jokes was not normal.

Lemieux held the passenger door open for me, and I slid into the front seat, Mike took the back. The detective pulled onto the road, wasting no time in firing the first question at me: "You're sure you saw Malone?"

I nodded.

"You were moving fast on a highway, and you had only a few sec-onds to make the identification."

I flared. "It was Malone. I'm never going to forget that face. It was him." Unconsciously, my hand reached for my throat, touching the place where his knife jabbed me. Lemieux cast me a sidelong look, and I let my hand drop.

"Okay, I ask simply for the confirmation. We've already located the SUV. He abandoned it in Gatineau. It was stolen in Montreal, so he's been following you."

I didn't respond. I'd been secretly hoping that I was wrong about it being Malone at the wheel.

Mike filled the silence. "That was quick work on the identifica-tion, officer. Well done."

Lemieux allowed himself a self-satisfied grin. "Yes, my team is on top of this case."

I couldn't let that pass. "What do you mean? You told me Malone was in New York!"

Mike must have been startled by my belligerence, because he intervened. "Don't get angry, Jess. I'm sure the detective is doing his best. She's had quite a shock," he explained.

I turned and glared at Mike. I didn't need his condescension.

Lemieux responded to my question. "For a woman who prom-ised to inform the police of her movements and then snuck off to Montreal, you're being quite hostile, mademoiselle."

"I called the damn number. I got voice mail. I couldn't even leave a message. Stellar victim services from Ottawa PD."

Lemieux frowned at this but didn't defend his colleagues. "Malone knows he's wanted in connection with his cousin's murder, so he should be staying away from here. I don't know why he would come back." He glanced in the rearview mirror, and I correctly interpreted his gaze.

"It's okay. I've told Mike everything. We can talk in front of him."

"I see you trust some people with your secrets."

"I would have more faith in you, Lemieux, if you'd actually protected me from Malone."

"I'm sure the police did everything they could," Mike said. "This fellow sounds like an unpredictable madman."

I knew that his attitude toward Lemieux was reasonable, but I needed Mike to have my back. Why were men never as supportive as women? Adela would have been on my side in this conversation, pointing out the ways the police had failed me and subtly mocking the crunchiness of Lemieux's gelled curls. Did he sculpt each one separately?

Lemieux's warm chuckle interrupted me before I could snap at Mike. "Thanks, Monsieur Roy. Jess is sometimes a bit of a pain."

"Now, that's not fair," Mike responded. "She's had a terrible scare."

Why was I being discussed like I wasn't even there? My teeth ground together.

Lemieux acted like he hadn't heard Mike. "Yes, it is good to have someone else see her when she gets all roared up."

"It's 'riled up,'" I snapped.

"You see?" Lemieux asked Mike, their eyes meeting in the rear-view mirror.

Thankfully, Mike didn't rise to Lemieux's attempt at old boy's chumminess. He spoke almost absentmindedly. "I would never have forgiven myself if something happened to her."

"What do you mean?" Lemieux's voice was sharp.

Mike seemed startled by Lemieux's change in tone. "I mean if she'd been hurt in the car accident. I was driving. I should have realized what that man was trying to do and prevented the crash."

"Mike, there was nothing you could do. It wasn't an accident. Malone was intent on killing me, or at least sending me a message." I shivered. "Who knows, maybe your driving saved my life."

"Do you think so?" he asked.

I shrugged. "I'm still here, aren't I?"

CHAPTER THIRTY-SEVEN

LEMIEUX RETURNED TO THE ORIGINAL TOPIC. "WE HAD CONFIRMATION that Malone was in New York. If he came back and risked arrest, it must be because he has not yet found the painting that interests him so much."

"What painting?" Mike interjected.

I took a deep breath. It was time to lay my cards on the table. I felt good about my decision. I had figured out what happened to Jem and Victoria. While it wasn't the happy ending I wanted, at least the mystery was solved. In a halting voice, I told Lemieux and Mike about finding the letters and what they contained. I concluded, "So you see, Victoria died before Jem returned to her. He never recovered the painting. The Rembrandt is beneath *Paris 1915*. Thibodeau must have stashed it somewhere after the auction, and that's what Malone is still looking for."

Mike, who had been listening avidly, leaned back. "That is quite the story, Jess. To think those letters and that secret were just sitting in our vaults."

"Exactly," I said, turning to him. "It's like what you said about research and serendipity. You never know when you're going to stumble across something magical."

He smiled in response.

Lemieux surprised me by keeping his anger in check. When he did speak, it was in a quiet voice. "Despite what you promised, you kept this secret. I will not tell you again, mademoiselle—do not keep information from me."

"I am sorry," I said. "I realize now how right you were. I could have got Mike and I killed. I won't keep anything from you anymore, I promise."

Lemieux grunted. "How much would a Rembrandt be worth, do you think?"

"It would be millions," I said. I turned to Mike. "You know the art world better than I do. Do you have any idea?"

He shrugged. "I'm not an expert, but you're right—a Rembrandt self-portrait would be in the millions."

"That's a good motive for murder. I've seen people killed over a hundred-dollar bar tab," Lemieux said.

Mike nodded knowingly, as if he, too, was familiar with life's mean streets. His eagerness to please Lemieux was off-putting. I suddenly noticed a few stray dark hairs sprouting from his ears like a hobbit.

I returned to the case. "So Thibodeau stashed the painting somewhere, and Malone is desperate to find it. That still doesn't explain why he tried to kill me."

We were winding our way through Ottawa now. "Mr. Roy, you gave your address as Grove Avenue. Should I drop you there?"

"Yes, that's fine."

I quizzed Lemieux. "The painting wasn't at Thibodeau's, correct?"

"Non. We searched his house top to bottom. Now that we know how much the painting is worth, we'll go back and make sure we checked everywhere. It would have been helpful to know about the Rembrandt right away, but I'm getting used to your habit of keeping little secrets."

Mike came to my defense. "I think you're being hard on Jess. After all, she discovered the existence of the missing Rembrandt. That's your motive, isn't it?"

Lemieux sighed. "Oui, but it would have been much better if she came to me at the beginning."

It was the "me" that said it all. Lemieux's ego was bruised because he hadn't figured it out for himself.

I concentrated on the matter at hand. "If the painting isn't at his home, where could it be?"

The three of us lapsed into thoughtful silence, until Lemieux pulled into Mike's driveway. He lived in an old home in Ottawa South, a respectable, middle-class neighborhood. It was a small brown brick place with a pitched red roof. Ottawa real estate had started to get pricey. Knowing Mike, he must have bought it long before property values skyrocketed. The house had a tiny patch of front yard, dominated by a big maple.

"Here we go," Lemieux spoke cheerily. "The Sûreté will be in touch to get further details about the accident. I think the officer at the scene gave you the forms for insurance and all of the rest?"

Mike climbed stiffly out of the car. I got out as well, anxious about saying goodbye to him. It was early evening, and winter darkness closed in. We were silent for a moment, the splash of water dripping from the eaves the only sound.

"Well . . ." I began. At that moment, a light turned on in Mike's house. I jumped. "Is someone in there?" I asked.

Mike jumped as well, before relaxing with a smile. "No, no—it's my automatic timers. Cheaper than a burglar alarm." Mike looked at me tenderly. "Malone has you spooked, eh?"

I didn't want him to see how touched I was by his concern. "I'm okay," I said gruffly. I couldn't meet his gaze, staring instead through the lit window at his kitchen; it needed new wallpaper. I blurted out what was uppermost in my mind. "I'm so sorry I put you through this, Mike. I mean, you nearly died and your car is totaled, and it's all my fault . . ."

Mike grabbed my hand. "Shh," he said. "It's okay. You have absolutely nothing to be sorry for. Don't beat yourself up."

I felt shy, knowing that Lemieux was watching. "Thanks so much for giving me a ride." I blushed as soon as I said the words, realizing the double entendre.

"Last night was amazing, Jess. I hope we can do that again."

I smiled up at him. "Absolutely." I thought of my meeting with Stephen tomorrow. I hadn't told Mike about it, but nothing had changed. My career was likely over.

"I'm glad," he said softly. Then, ignoring Lemieux's beady little stare, he pulled me into an embrace.

Maybe it was the residual adrenaline from the accident, maybe some small part of me got satisfaction in the fact Lemieux was watching, or maybe it was that Mike was a damn good kisser, but I responded passionately, wrapping my arms around him and pressing my body to his. Mike pulled away first. "I've got a quick acquisition trip to Toronto tomorrow, but I'll be back by evening. Can I call you when I get home, even if it's late? I want to make sure you're safe."

I smiled. "That would be perfect."

I returned to the car and Lemieux reversed out of the driveway without a word. We drove in silence for a minute.

"I guess you weren't in Montreal on business, then?"

"Like I said, I wanted to meet Gilbert Jarvis to investigate the painting."

"Yes, but I think you were investigating other things with this Michael Roy."

Lemieux made it sound so sordid. I stared out the window.

"How much do you know about that guy?"

"I've worked with him for months. I know him very well. How's this any business of yours?"

Lemieux's voice was edgy. "It's my business because you are wrapped up in a murder that happened on my watch. Anything that affects you, affects my case."

"Mike has nothing to do with this case."

We were at a stoplight, and Lemieux turned to face me. "I'm not saying he has anything to do with anything, but you should still be careful. He's much older than you and has seen the world. He could hurt you."

I stared at Lemieux. Was he seriously giving me relationship advice? I stifled the urge to laugh. I seemed to have moved from being a pain in Lemieux's butt into a "little sister" category. I employed the tone I used on my mother when she said something completely unforgivable. It was a voice that closed down all conversation and let the other person know what a heel they were. It never actually worked on my mother, but I tried it on Lemieux. "I can handle myself."

He seemed to take the hint and drove me in silence to Adela's apartment. His voice was neutral when he spoke. "The Ottawa PD assigned another officer to your case. They're taking this second attempt seriously and have freed up additional resources. You will be escorted to and from work, and I request that you abide by a strict schedule to accommodate the officers. I know that this is restrictive, but Malone has threatened you twice now and we're not taking any chances."

"Okay, thanks." I was out of the car when I remembered my meeting with Stephen. I leaned back in. "I have to go to the Conservation Facility tomorrow morning."

Lemieux cocked an eyebrow.

"It's work related," I explained. "Nothing to do with the murder." At least I hoped that was the case.

CHAPTER THIRTY-EIGHT

ERNIE WASN'T BEHIND THE SECURITY DESK THAT MORNING, AND THE stocky commissionaire barely looked up when I flashed my badge and strode to the elevator. Unlike the vaults, the small number of offices and work spaces at the Conservation Facility weren't closely monitored. Perched on top of the five-story cement mass of the vaults, a glassed-in elevator whizzed employees up to the area, providing an incredible view of the modern architecture. Zipping up to the top, I worried about the forthcoming meeting. Either Stephen was going to fire me or he wanted to pump me for information about the Rembrandt because he was the murderer. Whatever this was, it wasn't going to be fun.

Leaving the elevator, I walked along a shiny steel catwalk. I glanced over the railing and saw the bald spot on the commissionaire's head five stories below. Once I reached the security doors, I was on top of the vaults. Beneath my feet lay four hundred years of history. Picking up the phone attached to the wall, I called Jaleel, Stephen's assistant; my pass didn't open these doors.

He arrived promptly to let me in. "Come right this way. Stephen is waiting for you."

That didn't bode well. A man as important as Stephen Nguyen should be making me wait, not the other way around.

I tried to calm my anxiety by taking in my surroundings. I didn't get many chances to visit these work areas. The roof of the Conservation Facility soared another two stories above us, like a glass-rimmed sky. The architect designed the space like a village. Rather than being open concept, each cubicle had a little roof. Corridors between offices had street names, usually after prominent historians or archivists. The lunch area and central meeting space was designated the "Town Center." The colors were bright, with reds, blues, and oranges bouncing off the metallic furnishings.

I couldn't distract myself from the meeting ahead, however, and I addressed Jaleel as we wended our way past the rare book treatment area and the photo conservation labs. "Do you know what this is about?"

He turned back and smiled at me. Was there a trace of pity in his look? "No, I don't. I think it's important, though. Stephen had me clear his morning schedule."

His morning schedule? How long did it take to fire someone?

We left behind the conservation and treatment areas and faced a bank of offices fronted with tinted glass. Jaleel sat down at a wide white desk in front of a door and gestured to it. "You can go right in."

My first impression was of vast space. Stephen's office had no back walls; instead, it opened up over the long drop to the concrete floor below. A wide guardrail prevented anyone from accidentally falling. The rest of the room was simple. It contained a white desk similar to the one out front, three chairs, and one thin bookcase. The walls were painted white, and the warm sun poured in from the east. Stephen was sitting at his desk, basking in the light, looking angelic.

"Hi," I said.

To my surprise, he sprang up as soon as he saw me. "Jessica, have a seat."

He sounded almost friendly, and I allowed myself to relax slightly. I sat in one of the chairs he gestured to, and he took the one opposite.

"I've been looking over your employment file."

My neck stiffened. "Oh?" I asked, sounding calm.

"Yes. I see that you have not been upgraded to 'secret' security clearance yet."

Oliver had only requested "enhanced" clearance for me because I didn't work with government documents or sensitive materials. "Probationary employees aren't usually given 'secret,'" I said.

"Well, its absence gave me pause, but I think I'll proceed as I initially intended."

Stephen usually spoke with precision, but this time I had no idea what he was talking about. I stared at him, waiting for elucidation.

"I'm taking a chance and trusting you with something, Jessica—something only I and the chief archivist are aware of. Given your activities over the past month, I hope you might be able to shed some light on the situation."

My shoulders unknotted. He wasn't yelling about my second trip to the Art Vault. In fact, it didn't sound like he knew about it. "What can I do?" I asked.

Stephen leaned back. "Let me commence at the beginning. Always a useful place to start." He smiled tiredly. "As you know, the murder in the Art Vault was a huge blow to our reputation and generated negative publicity. Questions have been raised in Parliament about our security and whether we should be entrusted with the care of valuable paintings. We are now under review by the government's auditor general."

I hadn't known any of this. Indeed, I was so concerned with Jem, Victoria, and Malone that I hadn't been following the fallout to the institution. I'd never even considered how my actions—from uncovering the body to uncovering a Rembrandt—would affect the archives. Maybe Oliver was right; maybe I wasn't a team player. I didn't want to look foolish in front of Stephen, however, so I nodded.

"Reviewing our procedures and answering the charges of lax security have fallen to me, as the head curator. Of course, we did an inventory of our most valuable holdings in the immediate aftermath of the murder, to ascertain whether anything was stolen—"

"Which it wasn't," I interrupted, remembering my conversation with Ernie.

"Correct. It appeared that none of our most precious and costly items, the obvious targets for thieves, had been taken. However, I deemed it prudent to conduct a complete survey of all our art holdings. As you know, we have over half a million items stored here. The murder occurred on January nineteenth, and I'm sorry to say it took us nearly a week to wade through the red tape in order to put the vault in lockdown mode. We managed to sort out the final clearances and shut the vault down to all nonessential staff and researchers last Wednesday."

I blushed and looked down. I'd been in the vault Tuesday night.

Stephen didn't notice my expression. "I received the final tally only last week. The results have been surprising and, despite our excellent tracking system, I'm afraid to say highly irregular."

I furrowed my brow. Thibodeau bought *Paris 1915* two weeks ago, but what if he had been looking for the Rembrandt for longer? What if he hadn't known which Crawford painting it was hidden under? Could Thibodeau have been stealing art from the archives? "Is something missing from the vault?" I asked.

"Quite the contrary. I was hoping you might have an idea why there are four more paintings in our collection than there should be."

"What?"

Stephen raised a thin eyebrow. "From your reaction I take it you are not responsible for our surprise acquisitions. I thought, with the interest I know you have in the artist, you might shed some light on the matter. The four additional paintings are all by Jeremy Crawford."

Why would Thibodeau bring Crawford paintings to the archives? None of it made any sense. Could he have stashed *Paris 1915* at the Conservation Facility? "Can I see the paintings?" I asked.

"I'd appreciate hearing what you can tell me about this issue, beforehand."

Jem and Victoria's painting could be in this very building. My voice betrayed my anxiety. "I promise, I'll tell you everything I know. Please, let me see the paintings first."

The eyebrow again. A long pause. Finally, he said, "Certainly, if that will help resolve the issue."

We took the elevator down to the Art Vault, and Stephen swiped us in. He shooed away a junior conservator toiling at one of the preservation tables and waited until the heavy steel door closed behind her before speaking. "The chief archivist and I are in agreement—we're keeping this anomaly in our inventory absolutely confidential until we can sort out what happened. We're under enough scrutiny about the management of our holdings as it is. I'm trusting your discretion."

I nodded. On my walk down, I had tried to puzzle out Thibodeau's actions. All the evidence pointed to him knowing that *Paris 1915* concealed a Rembrandt. But maybe he, or whoever he was working for, was like me and hadn't possessed all the information. Maybe Thibodeau knew a Crawford hid a Rembrandt, but not which one. That explained why he had extra paintings, but not why he brought them to the Art Vault. Surely there were better places to stash them?

Stephen put on a pair of white cotton gloves and indicated that I should do the same. "I'll show you the paintings." He confused me when he strode over to the far corner of the vault.

"I thought Crawford was stored here," I said, pointing to the shelf I was familiar with.

"Yes, that's another odd thing. My staff located the four paintings tucked in behind some early floral watercolors. They couldn't have picked a better hiding spot. I checked the tracking system, and the watercolors hadn't been touched in years. If I hadn't ordered the complete inventory, the Crawford paintings would never have been found." He pointed, and I could see how the canvases were stashed in the shelving that held the larger framed art works not in boxes. They would be invisible unless someone removed all of the watercolors.

He tugged out a canvas. "Have a look and tell me what you think." It was a scene from Montreal, with Mount Royal foregrounded. This was probably *Landscape 12*, one of the paintings that Thibodeau bought at the auction. I didn't recognize the other two paintings, although one was certainly more modernist. Jem's attempt at cubism, by the looks of it.

Stephen reached in and slid the last canvas out. "I've been able to identify this one," he said. It was a Parisian street scene, painted in a modernist style. The figures in the foreground were mere black dabs of paint, but the shape of the Eiffel Tower was clear.

I knew it as well. I'd seen it in *Canadian Modernism*. My mouth was dry. This was the Rembrandt. "Let me guess, *Paris 1915*?"

"I see your Crawford research paid off."

Stephen carried the painting to the conservator's table. "Let's sit. I think you can help me by explaining what you know. Both the chief archivist and I would be very grateful."

I nodded again, following him. Stephen pulled up two stools, and we sat at the wide, flat table. I owed it to the institution to make a clean breast of things. If telling Stephen about the Rembrandt would help the archives, I'd do it. I recited the facts of Jem and Victoria's story and my involvement. I thought it prudent to leave out a few things, like my second visit to the vault and the degree of Malone's scariness. Stephen listened, and I was surprised by his lack of reaction. "You don't seem shocked to learn that a painting in your holdings conceals a Rembrandt."

Stephen shook his head. "There have been rumors floating around to that effect for decades. No one has ever been able to pin it down to an exact artist or to a specific time or place, but I've heard whispers that there might be an old master hidden beneath a twentieth-century Canadian canvas. The art world in Canada is very small, and no one can keep a secret."

My shoulders sagged. In a couple of sentences, Stephen had completely deflated the thrill of my discovery.

He must have read my expression because his tone turned stern. "You could have learned all of this, Jessica, had you thought to share your discovery with your manager. The Dominion Archives is a collegial environment, with no room for glory hogs. You must learn to trust your colleagues."

I was startled. Since starting at the archives, no one had ever spoken about trusting or sharing. Everyone told me it was a dog-eat-dog world. Was I approaching my colleagues with too much suspicion, or was Stephen out of touch? "I wasn't trying to conceal anything. I wanted a chance to publish the article myself," I explained.

His voice softened. "I wouldn't worry about that," he said. "It's a fascinating story, and I'm sure it will make a first-class article." He turned back to the canvas. "You think *Paris 1915* conceals the Rembrandt, don't you?"

"I'm sure it does."

"Let me show you something." Stephen stood. "Turn off the lights, will you?" He pointed to the panel at the far wall.

"Why?" I asked.

"I want you to see what the painting looks like under ultraviolet light." He pulled a heavy-looking lamp across the table and positioned it over the painting.

I turned off the lights and plunged us into darkness. For a moment I was disoriented. The blackness was oppressive, and memories of my last two visits to this vault tightened my stomach.

CHAPTER THIRTY-NINE

when I heard a click and saw him bathed in the glow of the ultraviolet light.

"John Ruskin, the nineteenth-century art critic, said of Rembrandt, 'It is the aim of the best painters to paint the noblest things they can see by sunlight, but of Rembrandt to paint the foulest things he could see by rushlight.' This wasn't fair to poor Rembrandt, of course. What Ruskin didn't realize is that the master's paintings have been victimized by well-intentioned restorers over centuries."

I looked down at the canvas, seeing only blackness under the ultraviolet light.

Stephen continued, his voice dreamy. "These 'restorers' shellacked his works in layer upon layer of varnish. For instance, when the Rijksmuseum restored the *Night Watch* a few years ago, they removed centuries of grimy shellac and revealed that the painting is actually a vibrant day scene."

I shifted impatiently, squinting at the canvas. "I don't see anything."

"Precisely. If there was a Rembrandt under there, we would see it."

"What do you mean?"

"Ultraviolet testing is the easiest means of spotting the existence of alterations to a painting. Dark blotches mean relatively new paint. This is what we see now. The existence of an underpainting would be revealed as a chartreuse haze, indicating the presence of old varnish. As you can see, there is nothing."

I tried to process what he had said. "Jem's painting must conceal the Rembrandt. His letter described it."

"What exactly did it say?" Stephen asked.

I furrowed my brow. I'd reread the copies of the letters many times and remembered them well. "He wrote something like, 'Paris inspired me, but I haven't forgotten the past either.' He said that he thought about Victoria the whole time he painted it." I stopped. There was a thought, tantalizingly close, that I couldn't quite grasp. "He painted it in 1915, while he was in Paris." I stared at Stephen through the gloom, my voice almost pleading. "Maybe one of the other paintings . . ."

Stephen spoke quietly. "Remembering the old rumor of a hidden Rembrandt, I checked all of the Crawfords already. It's not there. Turn the lights back on, Jessica."

I walked to the wall, adjusting my thinking and grappling with my disappointment. I switched on the light, a thought occurring to me. "Is that why the paintings are here, do you think? Thibodeau was smuggling them in to test under the UV?"

"It makes sense. We've got state-of-the-art equipment, the best in the country. We've also got an X-ray machine, which he could have used if a Crawford revealed the presence of old varnish under the light. Then he would have been able to actually see the painting beneath."

I tried to imagine the scene. "Maybe Thibodeau and his partner tested those four paintings, realized that none contained a Rembrandt, and Thibodeau's partner killed him in frustration."

Stephen sniffed delicately, obviously uncomfortable with talk of murder.

I continued, ignoring his distress. "I'd been working under the assumption that Thibodeau found the Rembrandt when he successfully bid on *Paris 1915*. Now it looks like he didn't know which painting concealed the Rembrandt. He, or his partner, must have been buying them for a while. That points to someone who knows the art market. The cops' number one suspect is Thibodeau's cousin, Ray Malone. He doesn't fit that profile, though. There has to be someone else."

"I imagine you're looking for someone with a keen interest in art history."

"How would they have smuggled the paintings into the vault, though? There are cameras everywhere."

Stephen shrugged. "It's winter. Everyone's wearing big parkas. The loading dock camera footage from the night of the murder shows two figures entering in bulky coats. They could have easily hidden them under their parkas."

"That fits," I said. "Hopefully this information helps the police with their investigation." I wanted Malone and this unknown man locked up as quickly as possible.

Stephen coughed. "Your tale confirms what I suspected. I'll speak with the chief archivist as soon as possible. These paintings are connected with the murder investigation, and we can't keep such information from the police, much as it will damage us in the public eye."

"At least it's a question of us having extra art, as opposed to losing some," I tried to joke.

Stephen shook his head. "The perception that we lost control of our inventory will do us immeasurable harm. There's been an increased questioning of our role in collecting art in the first place. Because we've always acquired material that had documentary rather than artistic value, we weren't seen as competing with fine art galleries. Indeed, a large portion of our collection is by women, Indigenous peoples, and immigrants, groups that have traditionally not been considered 'artistic.' Yet now there's growing interest in art by these people, which means our collection suddenly has an 'artistic' value and many other agencies want it. This might be the stick they use to get it."

"Gee, Stephen, I'm sorry. Is there anything I can do?"

"Well, I have to ask you something, Jessica, and it requires you to trust me as I've trusted you."

I leaned forward. "Yes, absolutely."

"From what you've told me, you're working fairly closely with the police on this case."

I opened my mouth to deny this heinous accusation but realized it was true.

Stephen continued. "The chief archivist and I would appreciate it if you kept news of the extra paintings to yourself."

Seeing my troubled frown, he hastened to explain. "I grant you it's an unusual request, but this whole situation is delicate. We can do much more effective damage control if we can manage the message about the extra paintings. It will give the art program a fighting chance."

"I don't know, Stephen. The paintings have probably been handled by the murderer. I bet they've got DNA or fingerprints all over them. They're evidence."

"I've thought of that, and I've worn gloves whenever I've touched them. I'll put them back in their spot right now and seal up the vault so no one can access it. Please, Jessica. An extra day would make all the difference. You could help save our art program."

I bit my lip. I'd kept a lot of secrets from Lemieux that were a lot more important to the investigation and a short delay could help the institution. "Okay, Stephen. I can hold off for one day, but if you haven't contacted Detective Lemieux by this time tomorrow, I will."

"I thank you, and the Dominion Archives thanks you. You've been a tremendous help. I'll put in a good word for you with Oliver. We need your kind of people working here."

I nodded absently, processing all I had learned. The Rembrandt was still out there. Jem and Victoria's story wasn't over yet.

CHAPTER FORTY

feeling good after my meeting with Stephen. I hadn't been fired, and the fact that *Paris 1915* didn't conceal the Rembrandt put a whole new spin on Jem's story. He could have retrieved the painting and restored it, as he and Victoria planned. Although she had died, maybe he lived their dream and fled to Tahiti. Maybe he sold the painting and became a philanthropist, donating huge sums of money to the causes that Victoria held dear. I was determined to learn his fate.

I rounded the corner on my floor and stopped in surprise. The door of my office was ajar. I had locked it when I left, knowing I would be calling in sick and going to Montreal with Mike. I hurried forward.

Oliver was leafing through some files on my desk.

"Can I help you?" I asked.

He turned with a jump. "Ah, Jessica. So glad you could grace us with your presence today. I hope you weren't too 'sick' yesterday." He made air quotes around the word *sick*. "You're an hour late, young lady. I trust you have a good excuse, otherwise I'll start to think you're quite the delinquent."

I stepped into the office, glancing down at the desk to make sure that I hadn't left anything revealing on it. It held only information about a few inconsequential projects Oliver had assigned to me. I relaxed and answered, "I do feel better, thanks, Oliver. I was meeting with Stephen Nguyen this morning. I told you about it when I called in sick on Wednesday night. Remember? I left you the message on your voice mail?"

"Did you? I don't recall that. I must be having a 'senior moment,' although I'm too youthful to be worried about those." He paused, obviously expecting me to agree.

"You're a real young buck, Oliver."

He beamed. "That's right, still virile." He pushed a hand through his hair in a nervous, jerky movement. "It's all real. Not many men have manes like this. I'm a lion."

"Uh, sure you are," I said. "Did you need anything from me?"

He shook his head. "No, no," he said breezily. "I thought I would find out how you are progressing. I care for my protégés, you know."

He was checking up on me, hoping to catch me slacking off. "Things are going really well," I said. "I've finished processing the Jarvis collection." I tried to smile, even though the knowledge that there were no more letters to find depressed me.

Oliver didn't notice my demeanor. "Excellent," he said. "I'd like a final report and the finding aid on my desk first thing Monday morning, then."

"Okay," I said, gesturing to my desk. "I'll have to get to work."

He took the hint and moved to the door. "I must be going. I'm spending the day in meetings. What a bore." He was almost at the door when he turned back casually. "Find anything interesting in those ledgers?"

I hesitated, remembering Stephen's words about sharing my findings. I couldn't stomach going over it all with Oliver now, however. "I'll put everything into the report," I promised.

"Excellent."

He was almost out of my office when a thought occurred to me. "Oliver, how did you get in here?" I asked.

"Your door was ajar this morning. Ginette noticed that you weren't in but your office was open and alerted me. I came down to investigate. So many untoward things have been going on here lately, I wanted to ensure that nothing was amiss."

I kept a smile plastered to my face until he was gone. The only reason my door would have been open is if someone broke in. I yanked open the filing cabinet, scrambling through the folders, searching for the photocopied letters. They weren't there. I went back and combed through each file methodically but found nothing. I sat in my chair. I thought of my office as a haven, away from the craziness of the past few weeks. Now my sanctuary had been invaded. I breathed deeply but couldn't stop a few tears from trickling out.

Someone knocked, and I looked up. Louise stood in the doorway. "Want to go for coffee?" She saw my face. "Hey, you okay, kiddo?"

I shook my head, another tear rolling down my cheek.

Louise came into the office, closing the door behind her. "Has Oliver upset you? I saw him in here earlier."

"No," I mumbled.

She didn't hear me, though, and continued. "That jerk has it in for you. He's getting worse too. Rumor has it," Louise's voice dropped to a whisper, "that he's sending his salary up his nose."

"What?" I asked, momentarily distracted from my lost letters. "Oliver's a cokehead?"

She shrugged. "That's what I hear."

That would explain his hyper behavior, if not his fashion choices. "It's not Oliver," I said more clearly. "Someone has stolen one of my files."

"Is it those letters you were asking me about?"

I nodded. "How did you know?"

"I could tell you cared about them. What happened?"

I shrugged. "I'm not sure. I locked the office on Wednesday night, but Oliver told me that Ginette found it open this morning. The folder containing the copies of the letters is missing."

Louise's nose quivered. "You see," she said almost triumphantly. "It's as I told you. There are people here who will stop at nothing to steal your ideas. It's significant that it was Ginette who found your office like this."

I wasn't interested in feeding into Louise's paranoia. "I'm so sorry, but I have to take care of this missing file. Do you mind if I get a rain check on the coffee?"

234 · AMY TECTOR

"Yeah, yeah." She coughed, a long hacking sound that wracked her frame.

"Are you okay?" I asked.

"Fine," she snapped. "Perfectly fine." She glowered at me and turned. "Thanks for your concern," she said grudgingly as she was leaving.

I stared after her for a moment, wondering what was going on. I didn't have time to deal with that now, however. Instead, I called Lemieux. He told me he was in the middle of something but he would alert Ottawa PD and send over one his own officers to get the details. Given the uncertainty of the identity of the "professor," he urged me to keep quiet about the theft for the time being.

Call made, I thought about what the loss of my copies meant. The originals, which had been sent back to the Conservation Facility, were now the only clues to the painting's existence. Why hadn't I brought copies of the letters home as I had planned? If the thief was after the missing Rembrandt, he possessed the same information as I did. Did that matter? The letters led me to believe the Rembrandt was beneath *Paris 1915*. I thought back to the correspondence, trying to recall the specific sentences about the painting.

A young constable from the Gatineau PD interrupted my thoughts. He spoke no English, so we struggled along in my broken French. Following Lemieux's orders to keep the break-in quiet, he worked quickly. He examined the broken lock, dusted the door and the filing cabinet for fingerprints, and tried to make notes of what I said.

After he left, I sat at my desk, but couldn't concentrate on work. My thoughts were gloomy. Certainly, part of my feeling was fear. I shivered to think that Malone might have been in my office. More than that, however, I felt violated. I had avidly followed Jem's arrival in Paris, his discovery of the painting, and his love for Victoria. Their story belonged to me. I was angry and sad to think that someone was pawing through Jem's words and learning the couple's secrets.

Pushing those thoughts away, I concentrated on writing up the report on the Jarvis collection for Oliver. I knew I should include details about finding the letters and the Rembrandt, but I justified their exclusion by reminding myself that they were part of an ongoing murder investigation. A few hours later, there was a soft knock at the door. I looked up. Gus, the circulation guy, stood before me.

"Sorry to bug you, Jess, but I've got that last box from the Jarvis acquisition."

"I've seen that box already," I said.

Gus checked his circulation sheet. "No, I don't think you did. This one was sequestered when they brought it in two weeks ago. One of the circ guys thought he detected mold. The last box in a series can be vulnerable like that. They're usually the ones pushed up against some damp basement wall or whatever. Anyway, he stuck it in the dirty room at the Conservation Facility until they could test it. It was released today. It had water damage, but no nasties."

My spirits rose. If this box was sealed up in the "dirty room," no one would have accessed it. "You've made my day! Thanks."

He placed it on my processing table and was about to leave when a thought occurred to me. "Hey, Gus, has anyone else requested those Jarvis boxes?"

"Funny you should mention it. Ginette called up the early boxes. Fifteen in all. Is she checking up on your work or something?"

"Something," I agreed, my lips tightening.

As soon as Gus left, I started examining the ledgers for slits, turning pages eagerly. Despite my impatience, I forced myself to slow down. I didn't want to damage anything. I had opened the mid-March ledger when my phone rang.

"Ms. Novak, it's the commissionaire downstairs. Your police escort is waiting."

I looked at my watch. It was five after six. I had to go. "I'll be right down." I hung up the phone, hesitating. The day's events proved how insecure my office was. There was one more ledger to look at, from April 1915. I opened it and felt the binding . . . something was in there. I stuffed my hand in and took out a bundle of letters. One was in Jem's hand. Two others were written in a different handwriting, and my pulse quickened. It looked like Victoria's. The last item was small and square shaped. I could tell by its thin paper that it was a telegram. I placed them in a folder and grabbed my coat. I stopped at the door to my office. What I was doing was highly irregular. Removing original documents from the building was tantamount to theft, and even Stephen Nguyen's endorsement wouldn't keep me from being fired.

My mother wouldn't have hesitated in taking them, but I knew that the records belonged to the Dominion Archives and I couldn't bring them home with me. If something happened to them, I would be responsible for destroying a piece of history. I cursed myself for being a Goody Two-shoes at the same time as I rushed to the photocopier and hurriedly copied the letters and their envelopes. Most people had gone home, and the hall echoed as I raced about. I ran to my office and placed the originals back in the proper ledger as the phone rang again. "Ms. Novak. It's the commissionaire. The police officer is getting most impatient."

"I'm coming," I nearly screamed.

I was running down the hall when a voice called to me. Ginette sat in her office, typing at her computer. "I didn't want to bother you today, but I found something of yours."

"Yes," I said coldly, remembering Louise's suspicions and Gus's words.

"I wasn't snooping in your office, if that's what you think." She sounded sincere, but I didn't want to be lulled. I said nothing.

She continued. "I knew you were sick yesterday, and when I saw that your door was open I wanted to ask if you were feeling better. That's why I looked in. When I realized you hadn't come in, I told Oliver."

I frowned. I seriously doubted this newly kind version of Ginette.

She ignored my expression and continued. "Anyway, I saw this on the floor. It looked a lot like the letters I saw you photocopying lately, so I thought it might be important."

THE FOULEST THINGS · 237

Damn, she had noticed the copies I was making. So much for being discreet.

"I figured I should hang on to it and give it back to you, but I wanted to wait until no one was around," she said.

She held out a sheet of paper, and I recognized it at once. It was my photocopy of the third letter from the day Oliver called me into his office, in which Jem described buying the painting. I snatched it from her, scanning it quickly to make sure I remembered it correctly. Yes, there were Jem's loving words to Victoria and a bit about buying the painting because the refugee was so pathetic, but nothing at all about the Rembrandt. I looked at Ginette.

"I couldn't help but read it," she said. "It's a fascinating story. Are there more letters?"

I spoke grudgingly. "A few."

"With your inexperience, someone might scoop you. If you want, I could help you. We could collaborate. You write up the article and give it to me. I've got a good name in academic circles. It would help get the article published quickly, and we'd both come out winners."

In other words, I would do all the work and she would get the credit. My contribution would probably be relegated to a footnote. I was in a hurry and didn't have time for niceties. "No way, Ginette."

"Think it over." She smiled, but I didn't fall for her false warmth.

I hurried down the hall, adding Ginette to my list of worries.

CHAPTER FORTY-ONE

I WAS SURPRISED TO SEE LEMIEUX'S CAR WAITING AS I EXITED THE building. He unrolled the passenger window. "Get in," he said.

"Am I being arrested?" I asked tiredly.

He grinned. "That depends—have you been bad?"

Was Lemieux flirting? I preferred to think of it as a linguistic misunderstanding.

"Since I couldn't come earlier today, I thought I'd pick you up myself, make sure you're not too frightened about Malone. We'll catch him."

"Thanks. You know, I've been thinking about it, and I don't think Malone burgled my office."

"Why?"

"Security is fairly tight in our building. You have to get past the commissionaires and use a swipe card to access my floor. If it was him, someone would have had to explain how to bypass security."

Lemieux sighed. "Malone is still our number one suspect."

I hesitated. If I told Lemieux about what I discussed with Stephen today, he'd see that Thibodeau's murderer must be an insider; but I'd promised I'd give the archives twenty-four hours before revealing the extra paintings. I glanced at my watch. Stephen still had fourteen hours. I thought about my career and how important it was to stay on Stephen's good side. Surely one night wouldn't make a difference. "Uncovering the Rembrandt would be painstaking work that would take years. Do you think Malone has that kind of patience? Isn't he the sort of guy who wants a quick payoff? Besides, how would Thibodeau or Malone even know about the masterpiece?"

"You suspect someone you work with?" he confirmed.

"Yes."

"That might explain why Malone came back. He needs to protect his interests. Maybe his partner is screwing him over," Lemieux said.

"Well, they haven't found the Rembrandt yet."

"Non?" Lemieux looked inquiring.

"If they had the painting, then they wouldn't need to steal the letters."

"Maybe they want to prevent anyone else from tracking it down. I bet that's why Malone is after you. He wants to stop you from finding it first."

I shivered.

"Another thing, how would Malone know about the letters?" Lemieux asked. "Have you told many people of their existence?"

"My colleague Louise and Gilbert Jarvis know that I found some letters, but not the full story. Only Adela and Mike know the Rembrandt association," I said. I bit my lip. I couldn't tell him that Stephen knew too.

"Maybe it's that Mike guy, then. I thought there was something off about him."

"That's because you think he's too old for me," I retorted.

"Maybe." Lemieux flashed a grin, and he looked so boyish that I almost liked him for a moment.

I rolled my eyes. "It could be anyone I work with. I haven't been as discreet as I thought about the letters." I told him about my conversation with Ginette.

"You should give me a list of those people," he said.

I nodded. We were outside of Adela's now, and I undid my seat belt.

"I had another reason for picking you up today," he said.

"Oh?"

"Yeah. They've arrested two of Malone's pals on drug charges. Apparently they've got some information on what he's been up to, and they're willing to talk in exchange for a plea."

"That's fantastic," I said. "I bet they know who Thibodeau's partner, this third man, is."

"Maybe. The only thing is that they're in Detroit. I'm flying out now and won't be back until tomorrow afternoon. I wanted to let you know."

I hugged my chest. Lemieux leaving the country made me feel surprisingly vulnerable.

"You've got my cell number. Call me if anything happens, or if you remember new information. Got it?"

"Yes, sure," I said. Lemieux waited until I was in Adela's building and then drove away.

The elevator was slow, but once inside the apartment I dead bolted the door and stepped onto the balcony. Looking down, I could see there was an Ottawa PD squad car parked outside. I was safe. It was only six thirty, and Adela would be at work for a while. This gave me lots of quiet time to study the last batch of letters.

I opened the first. It was from Jem.

February 10, 1915

Darling,

I know I am interrupting our regular pattern of correspondence by sending you a letter before receiving your reply, but I have wonderful news. We leave next week for England. Once there, Teddy's aunt has us booked on a merchant ship departing for Halifax on March 9. Now, don't fret darling. I know the crossing will be as safe as houses. Why do I write with such confidence? Because the name of the ship is the *Princess Victoria*! Is that not a fortuitous sign?

It was impossible to get the necessary travel documents in time—war has certainly brought out the bureaucratic red tape! Nonetheless, Teddy secured a couple of sets of identity papers. I shall travel as Herbert Morse, and Teddy is to be known as Leonard Jones. It should be a jolly lark and as simple as remembering to call one another "Herbie" and "Lennie" when anyone else is about.

You must have received the painting by now. What do you think? Are you proud of me, darling? Your opinion is the only one that matters. You sometimes accuse me of being too romantic, but surely I'm innocent of the charge. Any man, if he had you waiting on the opposite shore, would be as lovelorn as I.

Yours,

Jem

So he returned home and Victoria should have received the painting. My mind returned to my visit with Gilbert Jarvis and my sense that I was missing something. An idea, tantalizingly close, flitted through my thoughts. I closed my eyes. *Paris 1915* was not the Rembrandt. Jem told Victoria he'd been thinking of her the whole time he'd painted it. He said it recalled the past and also looked to the future. My eyes flew open. I had a new theory about the location of the missing Rembrandt. Maybe the next letters would confirm my suspicion.

I turned to the rest of the correspondence. Back at the archives I'd slit open the envelopes in order to photocopy them because they were still sealed. Someone had scrawled on both: "L'addresse postale n'est plus valide, Retour à l'expéditeur." I looked at the copies I made of the envelopes, both addressed to Jeremy Crawford in the strong, spiked handwriting I knew from the ledger entries. They must be Victoria's letters to Jem, returned to her after he left Paris. This was my chance to finally hear her voice.

The first was dated February 14, 1915. Jem's missive was written only four days earlier. The two letters must have crossed paths.

Please forgive me for my delinquency, darling. It is only that I have been feeling so frightfully unwell, and Aunt and Uncle are horrid to me. They insist that I stay confined to my bed, where Aunt sits, staring at me balefully. Her bulging blue eyes remind me of the jellied eels the street vendors sold in London when Papa, Freddy, and I did our European tour two years ago.

The only chance I have to write to you is when I am allowed to help Uncle with his farm accountancy, and then only in fits and snatches because they insist that I do so in the evening, when all of the farmhands have turned in for the night.

Oh! I must stop. I am sure you hate receiving my fretful letters. I shall be positive and cheerful. Honestly, I expected to hate the West. All we hear about Alberta back home is how primitive and rough it is. While it's true that compared with Papa's grand house on Mountain, Uncle Henry's home is not luxurious, but there is a beauty to the countryside that I cannot convey to you. The landscape, so raw and wild, invades the soul. What paintings you could create here! I tell you, if it weren't for the people being as judgmental and war-mad as the rest of the dominion, I would be tempted to stay.

Today I find myself as sappy as a maple tree in springtime; perhaps you are rubbing off on me! This is St. Valentine's Day, a day for lovers. How I wish you were here with me. I miss your capable hands, your quick smile, and your dreamy eyes. When will I see you again? Write soon and tell me your sailing date.

Now, I have thrilling news to tell you, darling. *I have the painting.* I have been frantic to get into town this past week, knowing from your last letter that it would soon be arriving. It took some conniving. Since winter arrived in earnest, I have been enlisting George, one of the farmhands, to collect your letters for me on the sly, but I did not dare trust him with such an important parcel. I was determined to fetch the painting myself. Unfortunately, Aunt has been draconian about allowing me to leave the house and was quite resistant. Finally, after days of pleading for fresh air and a change of scenery to no avail, I took a desperate step. I became quite hysterical. I ripped out my hair, gnashed my teeth, and generally behaved like the madman of the Gadarene (or as Aunt would have it, Mary Magdalene before Christ banished her seven demons). At any rate, after threatening suicide if I wasn't given a buggy ride into town immediately, she relented, making sure, of course, that I was wrapped against the cold in her enormous beaver-fur coat.

It truly was glorious to get out into the winter sunshine and see people again, different people from Aunt, Uncle, and little cousin Andrew. Getting to the post office was easy as pie. I solemnly promised to stay put as Aunt ran errands and then promptly broke my promise the instant she was out of sight! I'm certainly a sinner, Jem, but you love me for it, don't you, dear? I concealed the little painting beneath the great coat and was back in the cart before Aunt realized I was gone.

Oh Jem, darling, you are so right. This painting is wonderful. It is so special to me, dear, and I, too, am loath to strip its paint away. The way you have captured the sense of the cold and yet the pure joy of the moment. It was last year at this time, wasn't it? When we met at the skating pond? The style is positively electric. It reminds me of the pictures you showed me from that New York art catalog. Everything bold and strong, none of those weak colors or attempts at "realism." You've captured the truth on this canvas, Jem, and you should be very proud of yourself. I know I am. I can't bear to part with the painting, and so I've hidden it under my bed. I peep at it whenever I get the chance, although, as I said, Auntie Eel Eyes is making those moments rare indeed.

I long to see you, darling. Please hurry home.

Love and kisses,

Victoria

I put the letter down with shaking hands. Victoria had described the painting concealing the Rembrandt. There was the confirmation of what I suspected. At this moment, it hung over Gilbert Jarvis's mantle. I was two feet away from it yesterday and never realized. The inscription written on the canvas, "Victoria skating in moonlight. Montreal 1914" referred to the date of the event Jem had painted rather than the date he created it. It made sense, after all—the vibrant, modernist painting was quite accomplished, and the critical assessment of Jem's career was that he didn't become a good painter until after he moved to Paris. I groaned aloud, frustrated that my insight had come a day late. I needed to tell Gilbert Jarvis. If Malone and his partner figured out what I knew, the old man could be in danger. I'd also have to inform Lemieux. I reached for the phone, but my eye caught the other two letters. I should check to see if they yielded further information.

CHAPTER FORTY-TWO

I OPENED VICTORIA'S NEXT LETTER. IT WAS DATED FEBRUARY 21, ONLY a week after she'd written the earlier one. She still hadn't received Jem's letter from February 10 giving his sailing date, or she wouldn't have written to his Parisian address.

Darling, forgive the abruptness of this letter, but Aunt is outside, and I have a small window of time before she returns. I cannot conceal my secret from you any longer. This will be a great shock to you, and I wish that I could cushion the baldness of my statement, but I cannot: I am expecting a child, our child. I know this news must come as a horrible shock. I don't know what I can write, beyond begging for your pardon.

Perhaps you could forgive me if you knew how difficult these past months have been. Living with Aunt and Uncle has been stifling. They have made it clear that they disapprove most heartily of me. I have endured months of admonishing prayer. It has done nothing to make me feel shame; indeed, I have become more rebellious. Was what we did so scandalous? We love one another and would surely have married had not father's oppressive class-consciousness intervened. Had he not chased you from Montreal, we would be together right now.

I think Papa almost relished it when I told him of my condition; it confirmed the terrible opinion he held me in. I don't believe he has ever forgiven me for being born and killing my mother. Perhaps that is why we have clashed so violently over the years. Poor Freddy was always the peacemaker, but now he has taken up a commission . . . Like every other foolish boy in this country, my brother is off to war.

Papa sent me to Uncle's as soon as he learned of my condition, so that I would be out of his and, more importantly, the neighbors' sight. Aunt and Uncle took me in out of "Christian charity." Although, I am certain it was more to preserve the family name from scandal. They agreed to care for me and conceal my confinement in exchange for the child.

It pains me to confess this now, but at the time I agreed to the plan willingly. Indeed, I was happy to have the problem resolved so simply. I thought it would be best to keep this secret from you. There was no point in you knowing. You were marooned in France and could not support a family even if you did return. Most importantly, I did not want you to sacrifice your painting to fulfill a duty that was thrust upon you.

Then war broke out, and you seemed even farther away. I felt so alone, my darling. Gradually, I came to hate those loving letters I wrote to you; letters where I could not reveal the secret weighing upon my soul. When you discovered the Rembrandt, I saw a glimmer of hope. Money has a way of smoothing out even the most devastating scandal. We would flee Canada and start anew. For the first time, I allowed myself to imagine our reunion. It was not too late.

Then the doubts started to plague me. Perhaps it is because I have been so isolated and alone on this farm, but I began to wonder if this is what you wanted. I am not the same girl you left in Montreal, darling. I have become so ugly, so big and unwieldy. Perhaps a squalling infant is not what you envisaged for your life, for us. I do not know anymore. I am so confused.

One thing has happened to me in the past week, however; I've become attached to this child growing inside me. I cannot give the baby up to be raised by Aunt Therese with her watery all-seeing, all-judging eyes and by Uncle Henry with his sanctimonious speeches. I want to love and care for this baby, our baby. I feel it move, and my heart swells.

Every day I hope the post comes with news of your sailing date. Write to me soon, dearest, and tell me that you forgive me this secret. Tell me you want me. Tell me you want our child.

Waiting for your letter,

Victoria

I looked at the dates of the letters I had in hand and rushed to my notes. Victoria made her confession on February 21. Gilbert Jarvis was born April 4. Gilbert said that Victoria died in the spring of 1915. She must have died in childbirth, like her mother. Gilbert Jarvis was Jem and Victoria's son. Did Jem ever know about his child?

I turned to the final piece of correspondence, the telegraph, hoping for an answer. I was surprised by its length. Obviously, the sender wasn't too concerned about cost. It was from Liverpool, England, and was dated April 2, 1915.

Dear Miss Jarvis, deeply regret to inform you Jeremy Crawford was killed on 9 March [Full stop] Merchant Ship Princess Victoria torpedoed sixteen miles northwest of Liverpool by submarine [full stop] I was meant to be aboard, but a sudden illness kept me ashore [full stop] Forgive delay in relaying this information, but illness prevented me from doing so earlier [full stop] Heartfelt condolences [full stop] Jem was a good man and a true friend [full stop]

Sincerely, Teddy Hauver

I blinked back tears. Victoria was dead. Jem was dead—sunk to the bottom of the icy Atlantic and all but forgotten. I hadn't found any mention of Jem's death, because he was traveing under a false identity. The telegram arrived two days before Gilbert's birth. Had the shock of Jem's death sent Victoria into labor? She must have died heartbroken. I remembered my conversation with Gilbert. It was clear that he knew nothing about his parentage. Their story wasn't over yet. I needed to tell their son the truth. It was extraordinary to think that he had been living under the Rembrandt concealed by a portrait of his mother, painted by his father. Indeed, he lived in the very house of his grandfather, the man who had separated the lovers all those years ago.

I found Gilbert's phone number and dialed quickly.

"Bonsoir?"

Damn, I'd forgotten that the maid always answered. "Hello," I responded. "Can I speak with Mr. Jarvis?"

"I'm sorry; he does not come to the phone. I will relay a message."

"I need to talk to him personally. Please, it's urgent."

The nurse's voice took on a stricter tone. "I'm sorry, mademoiselle. He is far too ill to move. He cannot hear. He will not come to the phone."

"It's a matter of life and death," I pleaded.

"Impossible," she said.

"It's Jess Novak. I visited him yesterday. What if I came there? Could he speak with me tonight?"

"I will inquire with monsieur and let you know. Your number please?"

I gave her the number and hung up. Fifteen long minutes passed, and I was about to call again when the phone rang. "Yes, you can come. Monsieur Jarvis says he is not too tired to speak with you tonight."

"I'm in Ottawa," I explained. "That's two hours away."

"Monsieur Jarvis usually retires at ten o'clock. I'm sure if you arrive before then he will be able to see you. He would like to talk to you. He has remembered something he wishes to tell you."

It was a little after seven. Buses left for Montreal every half hour. I could catch the seven thirty bus and be there by nine thirty. It would be tight, but I'd make it. "Okay, expect me in two and a half hours," I said, hanging up.

I called Lemieux next, but his cell went straight to voice mail. He must have switched off his phone for the flight to Detroit. I left him a message, telling him of my plan. He couldn't accuse me of not keeping him informed this time. I scrawled a note to Adela—"Gone to Montreal on the case. Back late tonight." —and raced to the door.

Reaching the lobby, I spotted the squad car. I didn't want to be seen by the cops, who might delay me, or even prevent my trip. I scooted back into the elevator, descending to the building's parking garage.

Under normal circumstances, racing through the dimly lit, shadow-filled parking garage would have filled me with dread. I was so intent on getting to Gilbert, however, that I didn't give myself the chance to get the willies. I emerged in an alley and hurried to the street. I never made it.

Instead, a strong arm grabbed me from behind. Someone pressed a knife into the back of my spine. Malone's whisper hissed in my ear, "Where you sneaking off to, honey? Move."

If I'd been thinking straight, I would have broken away and ran. The self-defense course was clear: never allow yourself to be taken to a second location. It was always better to take your chances by fighting back and running. Unfortunately, Malone's voice filled me with such sick terror that it drowned out those survival rules.

He marched me back into the alley. I moved like a zombie, unable to think of anything but my own deafening heartbeat.

A car was parked, engine running and trunk popped open. I saw a dim figure in the front seat. He turned, and a blinding pain burst into the back of my head. The man's face was the last thing I saw for a long time.

CHAPTER FORTY-THREE

I CAME TO IN THE TRUNK OF THE CAR. A TINY PIECE OF LIGHT SEEPING
through the door latch illuminated my plight. The car was moving
quickly, bumping along uneven terrain. My head ached with a tight
throbbing, and I moved cautiously. I didn't have a lot of room.

Fumbling, I found the latch. The metal was hard, and I tried
to twist it open. I felt around for a tool, something left in the
trunk, but I found nothing. I searched in the dark for my leather
purse, groping like a blind woman. It wasn't there, which probably
meant that it was in the front along with my cell phone. I needed
something to bash in the latch. I had to get out of the trunk. If I
didn't . . .

My boots had a hard rubber heel; maybe that would dislodge the
latch. I pulled off a boot, wriggling desperately in the tight space. I
moved against the far wall of the trunk, trying to get enough force
to crack it open. I was about to strike when I realized I could hear a
murmur of voices in the front. If I could hear them, they would hear
me smashing at the latch. I tossed the boot aside in despair. If I had
any suitable tool, I could try to pick the lock from inside, but I didn't
even have a bobby pin on me.

I'd read somewhere about disabling a brake light. Maybe I could
do that and cause them to be pulled over. I yanked at the thin carpet
covering the trunk floor, exposing the plywood. I hauled that up and
reached into the car's cavity, feeling wires. Somewhere down there
was the electric circuit for the taillights. I clutched willy-nilly, but the
effort made my head pound even more. I became nauseous from the
pain and the car's movement. The dim light of the trunk faded for a

moment as I fought against blacking out again. It was probably futile. The way the car was bouncing up and down, we were off the main highway, maybe on a dirt road or even a track.

I lay on my side in the fetal position, cradling my head from the car's jostling, and tried to quell my queasiness. I breathed deeply.

In my stillness, it was easier to hear what was being said in the front. Malone was speaking. "She knows where it is. Why else would she take off like that?"

"We shouldn't have grabbed her before we saw where she was going," said a male voice.

"What did you expect me to do, dumbass? Snatch her in the street with the cops out front? I had to be discreet." Malone said.

"Yeah, but how are we going to get her to talk now?"

Malone's voice was confident. "She'll talk."

I shivered.

"Still, I don't think—"

"You're not meant to think. I brought you in on this because you're good at what you do."

The other person chuckled and I strained to hear more, but they must have shifted position, because their voices were muted. I heard them again when Malone raised his voice to say, "I don't care what he fucking says."

The other voice was angry as well. "Shit, chill out, okay?"

I realized who was in the front. The dim figure I spotted before being knocked unconscious came into focus. It was Joe, the biker Adela talked to at Leo's.

The car roared over a big bump, and the tender spot on my head smashed the floor. The pain was excruciating, and I couldn't stifle a groan.

"She's awake," Joe said to Malone.

"Doesn't matter," he replied. "We're nearly there. The lake's up ahead."

I remembered something Adela reported about her conversation with Joe. He'd said that if Malone had murdered Thibodeau, he would have disposed of the body in a remote lake. Oh God.

I was shivering uncontrollably now, almost convulsing. Was this what my life had come to? I thought of my mother and my sister. Would I ever see them again? I remembered Mike and choked back a sob. How could this be happening? My head was in agony, and my nausea returned in full. Unable to stop myself, I threw up, gagging and coughing as I expelled the contents of my stomach, right down to bitter bile.

When it was over, I rested, exhausted. Then the car stopped moving. I heard doors slam and footsteps.

I wiped my mouth and tried to focus. I wasn't dead yet.

Malone opened the trunk, pointing a gun at me. He and Joe were lit up by the taillights, satanic in their red glow. I glanced around. A stand of dark conifers stood like implacable witnesses in front of me. To my left was the lake, a great glimmering white sheet. It seemed like there was no one around for miles, and the stars hung down, full and ripe.

Malone spoke. "Hello, Jess. How was the ride?"

I looked up, not saying a word.

He continued, obviously enjoying his role as my torturer. "I guess you already know my buddy. You saw him when you were spying on me."

Joe no longer looked like the slow-witted muscle head from the bar. His face was twisted and mean. He also held a gun. "Your friend promised me a good time that night, but she fucking stood me up. I'm going to collect now, bitch." He leaned in to pull me out but then touched the vomit that spackled my right arm.

"Shit, she's puked everywhere," he shouted, stepping back.

"What?" Malone asked, peering at the mess I was covered in. "Jesus Christ." He turned away from me to address Joe. "Don't be such a pussy. Get her out of there."

"I've got it on my hand." Joe bent and began wiping it off in a puddle of melted snow. Malone watched in annoyance.

It was my moment, and I didn't hesitate. My headache disappeared, my nausea evaporated, and adrenaline coursed through me like a welcome dose of amphetamines.

The vague plan I formed as soon as I heard Malone mention a lake coalesced in my mind. I grabbed the boot I'd taken off and drilled it at Malone. Miraculously, it hit him full in the face.

He cried out as blood gushed from his nose. "You bitch!" he roared.

I hauled myself up and over the side of the trunk, the strength of terror allowing me to easily clear the car. I ran as best I could with one boot across the muddy grass. The sharp crack of a gun boomed through the air, and I ran all the faster.

"Don't kill her," Malone shouted. "We need her alive."

"I can hardly fucking see her," Joe yelled back.

I ran on, slipping in the melting snow, oblivious to the cold on my socked foot.

Someone barreled toward me, almost within striking distance. Frantically, I swerved and ran out onto the lake. My lungs were bursting, but I kept moving. We'd had days of warm weather. The canal was no longer frozen, and I hoped to God the same was true of this lake. "Please work, please work," I thought as I raced toward its center.

I snatched a glance back. Joe was a bit ahead of Malone, whose jacket was covered in blood. I ran on. While Joe's short legs didn't cover much ground, he was gaining on me. He grabbed at my shoulder, and I slipped, nearly falling. Reaching out made Joe lose his footing, and he dropped to the ice, bringing Malone down with him. They were up again in an instant and already closing the slim lead I had gained. I continued, heading straight to the lake's center.

Malone called out. "Big mistake, girlie. I can see you better out here. I've got a nice shot of your leg now. I'll bring you down like a fucking deer."

The first bullet went wide, but the second found its mark, hitting me in the calf. I dropped to the ice, my leg on fire.

"Got you, bitch."

The adrenaline faded, and all I could think of was the pain spreading up in bands of fiery agony. Doggedly, I started crawling.

Malone and Joe were swaggering now, strutting over to me as I continued my agonizing way across the ice.

"Where you going?" Joe jeered.

I stole a glance back.

He was one hundred yards from me when what I hoped would happen finally did; the ice beneath him began to crack. "Oh fuck!" he shouted.

Malone watched as the crack under Joe spread between his own feet. "What the hell?"

I crawled on, away from the increasing fissures around the two heavy men, leaving a trail of blood behind me. I was careful to keep my weight evenly distributed as I began working my way back to the safety of the shore's thicker ice.

Malone and Joe had obviously not benefited from my Girl Guide leader's wise winter camping advice; they were doing everything wrong. Joe tried to run, which only strained the ice further. With a sickening splash, I heard him fall in. He screamed, his breath wheezing out in a horrified gasp.

Malone lasted a little longer. Seeing my example, he slipped to his knees, but he was too close to Joe's frantic thrashing and grasping. I heard the second splash. Malone went under.

I could see the outline of the shore now. The trees, which had looked so ominous only minutes earlier, were welcoming me back like old friends. My knees ached, and my hands were bleeding from the rough surface of the ice. My leg throbbed. I plowed on. Not far now.

It was then that I heard the sound. It was all around me, like bones breaking, and I knew what it meant. The cracks that swallowed Malone and Joe were spreading out over the rotten ice. I felt the surface beneath me buckle and sway, and I was plunged into the frigid water. The shock of cold was like being electrocuted. Everything was black. I lost my bearings, flailing instinctively.

My foot touched something—the muddy bottom of the lake. I looked up with burning eyes. I could see starlight through the hole. I was closer to the shore than Malone or Joe, and it wasn't as deep.

I pushed off from the lake's soft bottom and propelled my head out of the hole, coughing and choking in the night air. I remembered to thrust my head back to stay afloat, but too late to prevent going under again. The surface fell away from me, and I sucked in a mouthful of black water.

I swallowed death.

It would be easy to stop right now. No more worries about boyfriends, jobs, Rembrandts, or mothers. I could take in a few more lungfuls of water and drift away from everything. The pain of the cold would end, and I would be free.

I gritted my teeth. I was going to get out of this. I pushed off from the bottom again but slowed my ascent so I wouldn't pop out at the surface and immediately plunge back into the depths. Once my head was clear, I panted for air as the cold clawed at my lungs. I tried to stay calm and breathe evenly.

Waving my arms out, I found a handhold on the rough ice. I treaded water and hung on. The most important thing was to get as much of my body out of the water as quickly as possible. I told myself that if I didn't panic I had at least two minutes.

I could do this.

The pain in my fingers and toes was excruciating, but I did my best to ignore it. I couldn't feel the bullet wound anymore, and I was thankful for the numbing cold. I located the thickest edge of the hole and kicked the dark water with all my strength.

I threw my torso onto the ice, praying it would hold my weight. Water sloshed out of the hole, but the ice held. Kicking and clawing, I pulled myself painfully out of the water. Once clear of its dark, sucking power, I didn't allow myself to catch my breath. Instead, I pulled myself to the shore's edge on my belly. The ice was so weak, I didn't dare crawl. I don't know how I managed it, but I slithered to shore, my triceps and thigh muscles screaming with the strain.

When I felt the safety of the shore's icy mud, I gave an exhausted cry. I allowed myself a rest then, slumping for a moment on the half-frozen earth. I stayed like that for only a few seconds, however.

While unseasonably warm, it was still cold and I was soaking wet. Stopping for long would mean death. I stood slowly, panting with the effort. My calf was numb as I blundered toward the car.

My boot was on the ground. The keys were in the lock of the trunk, where Malone left them. I picked everything up and returned to the driver's door. I sat heavily in the seat, turning the ignition and cranking the heat to maximum. A thick, heavy exhaustion overwhelmed me. All I wanted to do was sleep. Instead, I forced myself to take off my jacket, which was covered in a thin layer of ice. The zipper was completely frozen, so I tugged it over my tired shoulders. My jeans were icy as well, but they were so ripped and bloody from my wound and the crawl along the ice, I couldn't work up the energy to remove them. I slid my boot back on.

I was anxious to get away from this place. I'd seen enough thrillers to know that it was always a good idea to put distance between yourself and the baddie, even when you're positive he's dead. I was shaking so hard, however, that I couldn't slip the car out of park.

My teeth were chattering. It was a loud, angry clattering noise that I couldn't control. Frantically, I felt the car's heating ducts; they were beginning to pump out hot air. I hugged my armpits and rocked back and forth. At last, the car began to warm, and my shaking eased somewhat.

Thank God the car was automatic, because my leg could not have handled a clutch. I spun the vehicle around and followed the track back out of the woods. I was relieved when the trail turned into dirt road a few hundred meters along. After driving for some minutes, I came to a fork in the road. The car was hot now, and I was thinking more clearly. I pulled over and switched on the overhead light.

I noticed my bag on the floor of the passenger side and reached for it, fishing out my cell phone. I turned it on, but there was no signal. I had no idea how far out in the bush I was.

Before searching for a map, I decided to have a look at my leg. The pain changed to a dull throb; my head actually hurt more. My jeans thawed and were now soaking. I pulled the leg up gingerly. The bullet missed my calf bone, instead going in and out of the fleshy, muscled part of the leg. The wound looked small, so I imagined that the gun Malone used wasn't very powerful. It had actually stopped bleeding, and I decided to leave well enough alone.

I opened the glove compartment but found no map, so I turned to look in the back. What I saw brought me up short. There was a sharp, gleaming hunting knife, a coil of thick rope, and a metal box. I turned it over and realized it was a car battery, complete with cables. A wave of nausea washed over me as I remembered Malone's promise to make me talk. I'd thought that brutish Joe was enough of a threat, but no, they brought me up to the woods to torture me. My stomach heaved, and if I'd had anything left to throw up, I would have.

I grabbed the dirty gray blanket lying on the floor and wrapped it around myself. Between it and the overheated car, I began to feel a bit better. I needed to keep moving. I still didn't know which way to turn, but thinking of my mother, I decided to veer left.

It proved to be a good choice. I soon passed a road sign indicating that I was seventy-five kilometers from Ottawa. I pulled into a gas station and hobbled out. I must have looked terrifying, because the teenager behind the counter let me use the phone without a murmur and even stopped chewing his gum when he heard me explaining the kidnapping to the 911 dispatcher.

CHAPTER FORTY-FOUR

IT WAS THREE IN THE MORNING, AND I WAS BACK AT ADELA'S, SIPPING hot chocolate, with my bound leg resting on her coffee table. The cops had picked me up at the gas station and taken me to the nearest hospital. There my wound was pronounced "clean" and bandaged. They'd wanted to keep me overnight, but I dug my heels in and insisted on going to Adela's. I'd just sat down with her when the buzzer rang. It was Lemieux.

His presence didn't fill the room this time; in fact, he looked tired and a bit defeated. He came right over to the couch where I sat and stared down at me, his expression inscrutable. Then he held out a hand. I shook it, noticing how soft his skin was and how perfectly manicured the nails.

"I'm sorry it took me so long to get here. When I landed in Detroit, I heard you were missing. I caught the first plane back, but maudit de Air Canada does not make travel easy." He sat down on the couch next to me. "Now, tell me in your own words what happened."

When I finished talking, he said, "Mademoiselle, I am impressed. To remember how warm the weather has been and draw them out to the ice. That was good thinking."

I tried to assume an expression of modesty but failed completely, breaking into a big grin. "Yeah, it was pretty cool, eh? Winter camping paid off."

Lemieux's expression made me laugh, which hurt my chest and ribs. I was sore all over. "You said that you knew I had disappeared by the time you got to Detroit, but how?" I asked him.

Adela spoke. "That was my doing. Gilbert Jarvis's housekeeper called here. She said that you had been expected but hadn't shown up. She was mad and said that Mr. Jarvis was so agitated she couldn't get him to sleep. As soon as I heard that, I knew you must be in trouble. I called Lemieux on his cell, not realizing he'd gone to Detroit, and he called out the dogs. Every cop in Quebec and Ontario was looking for you when you made that 911 call."

Adela's voice quavered at the last sentence, and then she burst into tears. I'd never seen my tough friend cry before. "Oh God, Jess. I thought you'd died." She squeezed in beside me on the couch, stroking my hair and shoving me closer to Lemieux.

"It's okay, Adela. I'm here. I'm safe."

"Yes, it's all over now, mademoiselle. I expect you'll have to make a statement at the trial, but I'm sure it will take many months to come to that."

"Trial?" I asked. "Who's being tried?"

Lemieux blinked. "Didn't you know? Joe Lawson survived."

"But I saw him fall in. He was submerged in freezing water."

"Yes, it's true, but that's what saved him. When the body goes into severe hypothermia, it shuts down all but core functions. People can hang on for a long time that way."

Come to think of it, I did remember the Girl Guides mentioning that.

Lemieux continued. "He's in a coma now, and they're not sure what the extent of the brain damage will be, but he's expected to live."

"What about Malone? He's dead, right?"

"I'm sure of it. As soon as the body is recovered we'll—"

"Recovered?" It was Adela's turn to speak. "You don't have his body?"

Lemieux looked down. "They haven't been able to locate it. It went under the ice. They will, though."

"What makes you so sure?" Adela's vulnerability evaporated, and she returned to her aggressive self.

"There was no indication that anyone else made it out of the lake. Even if he had, there's no way he could have survived out there. He's dead. He's under the ice."

I shivered. No matter how illogical, I would continue to fear Malone until his body was recovered.

Lemieux stood. "The worst is behind you. Malone is dead, Joe is in the hospital under guard. After your statement to the police, the Montreal PD secured the painting from Gilbert Jarvis's home. It's over."

"What about the professor?" I asked.

Lemieux raised two hands. "That was speculation."

"In the car, Joe and Malone were talking about someone who might be angry at them for kidnapping me."

Lemieux sat back down. "You said nothing of this in your statement."

"I'd been shot in the leg and half drowned, so I wasn't thinking too clearly," I replied. I thought for a moment. "They were definitely talking about someone else."

"Who could it be?" Lemieux asked.

I considered everyone I knew at work. Had anyone expressed unseemly interest in what I was doing? Ginette was after the scholarly article, not the Rembrandt, and the men clearly said "he." Oliver? If he was a cokehead, he'd need a lot of cash to support his habit. I couldn't escape the feeling that the person was likely to be someone else. I flashed back to that jolt of fear I felt when I'd turned the lights off in the vault yesterday. "Stephen Nguyen," I said.

"The curator?" Lemieux asked. "We interviewed him after the murder."

"It makes sense. He's got blanket access to the vaults. He knows all about restoration techniques and exactly what equipment to use. If anyone at the archives looks and acts like a professor, it's him."

"Yeah," Lemieux sounded unconvinced.

I took a deep breath. "There's more."

"Oh?" he asked with a raised eyebrow.

I spoke in a rush, braced for Lemieux's anger. "I'm sorry I didn't tell you earlier. Stephen asked me to keep it quiet for a day to help the institution." I told him about the four extra paintings held at the Conservation Facility. I finished by saying, "Stephen knew about the Rembrandt, saying that there had always been rumors of its existence."

"Câlice, Jess. When are you going to stop keeping things from me?"

"I'm sorry," I stammered. "It didn't seem to matter much. Stephen said he'd speak to the chief archivist and they'd report it to the police right away."

"Not important? The man had the knowledge, the opportunity, and the motive to murder Thibodeau."

I nodded glumly.

Adela spoke. "What I don't get is why Stephen involved Thibodeau at all? There's nothing illegal in buying art. He didn't need Thibodeau's biker gang connections."

Lemieux replied. "He did if he was stealing Jeremy Crawford paintings."

"What?" Adela exclaimed.

"I've been doing some investigating. Turns out that five Crawford canvases have been reported stolen in the past six months. They were taken from homes and small museums across the country. The paintings don't have a lot of value, so it never made big news, but once we went looking, there was a definite pattern."

I glared at Lemieux. "Maybe you shouldn't be screaming at me for keeping secrets when you've got a few up your own sleeve."

"There's a difference," Lemieux said, returning to his usual smug complacency. "I'm a detective. Keeping secrets is my job."

Adela ignored our squabble. "So this Stephen guy knew that there was a Rembrandt under a Jeremy Crawford painting and brought Thibodeau in to do the dirty work. He was stealing the paintings, hoping to hit it big."

"That might be the case," said Lemieux. "Although I don't know why he would tip his hand to you like that."

"Maybe he was overconfident because he knew that Malone and Joe were going to finish me off tonight." I shuddered.

Lemieux shook his head. "Maybe. You've given me a lot to think about, Mademoiselle Novak." He stood. "You'd better get some rest. Now, I want you to stay here until Malone's body is recovered. Understand?"

"What about work on Monday?" I asked. I didn't think Oliver would tolerate my absence.

"We'll find Malone's body before then," Lemieux said confidently. He saw Adela's frown and added, "On the slim chance that we haven't, I'll let your boss know what's going on."

Lemieux turned to the door and Adela walked him out. They held a whispered conversation by the entrance, which I was too tired to even attempt to eavesdrop on. She locked up after he'd gone and then sat beside me. "It's over now, Jess. You're safe, and life can go back to normal."

I couldn't wait to return to my regular life and regular worries.

◇◇◇◇◇◇

THE NEXT MORNING ADELA HAD TO GO INTO THE OFFICE TO FINISH UP A bit of work, so I spent a glorious few hours eating Cap'n Crunch cereal and resting my leg while the childhood comfort of Saturday morning cartoons played in the background.

Around noon, the buzzer sounded. I answered, hoping it was Lemieux with news about Malone.

"Mike," I exclaimed when I heard his voice. "Come up."

I stood gingerly. Now that the adrenaline and painkillers had worn off, my leg ached. I wasn't meant to put any weight on it, but I couldn't sit around all day, and so I'd insisted that the hospital give me crutches.

I hobbled over to the door to unlock it, nearly biting through my lip in reaction to the throbbing from my calf. Luckily, Mike was already standing there when I opened the door, and he enveloped me in a strong, warm hug. I let the crutches fall to the floor so I could return the favor. Seeing how white my face was, he scooped me up and carried me back to the couch.

He got me settled and then spoke. "When I saw the news this morning, I was stunned. I called Oliver to see if he had heard anything, but he had no updates. Thank God you're okay." He stared at me searchingly. "You look like hell."

Not the most romantic words, but I smiled. "Matches how I feel."

"I brought you something." He retreated to the entrance, returning after closing the door with a huge bouquet of bright tulips, roses, and Queen Anne's lace.

"They're beautiful," I sighed.

"There's more. I figured you'd be recuperating for a while, so I brought you some reading material." He handed me a brown paper bag. I glanced quickly at the contents—a book on art history, a biography, and a thick issue of *People* magazine. I grinned when I saw the latter, yanking it out of the bag. "Oh, perfect!"

Mike smiled and sat in the chair opposite the couch. His grin faded, however, as he stared at me. "Are you really okay, Jess? What happened?"

I didn't feel like talking about Malone and Joe, so I told Mike about the painting instead. Gilbert Jarvis had called me that morning. Our conversation was difficult because I had to bellow into the receiver to be heard and Jarvis's quavering voice seemed to disappear down the line. I knew conditions weren't right to tell him about his parents, so I decided to wait with that news until I could speak with him in person. Instead, Jarvis told me that the Montreal PD's forensic lab X-rayed the painting and confirmed that there was a portrait of a man beneath it. The next step would be to recover the Rembrandt, but that would probably have to wait until the police investigation wrapped up.

"It's amazing," Mike said. "It was right there the whole time." He shook his head.

"I still can't believe I was staring at Jem's final gift to Victoria and didn't even realize it."

"Unbelievable," he said, still seeming to process the news. Finally, he roused himself. "It's a wonderful story, Jess. You will publish it?"

"I'm not sure now. You see, Victoria's last letter revealed something—she and Jem were Gilbert Jarvis's parents. She was sent out to her uncle's farm to hide the family shame."

Mike looked thoughtful. "That makes sense. Unmarried pregnancies weren't done in upper-class society back then."

"But Gilbert is still alive. It's not a story about history but about real, living people. I'm not sure I can tell it. Certainly not without talking to him first."

"That's wise." He gestured to the paper bag he brought. "I know when I was working with the Hauver biographer, we had a number of conversations about the ethics of writing about living people."

"Oh," I said, looking into the bag more carefully. "Is that what you've given me?" I pulled out the heavy hardcover book, *Edward Hauver: A Life Uncovered* by Melvin Perkins. I flipped it open to the first page. There was a handwritten inscription: "To Mike, thanks for all of your help and advice, Melvin." I was touched. "Are you sure you want to give me the copy he signed for you?"

"Absolutely," he said. "I hope you enjoy it. Hauver's the man who inspired me to study history, you know."

"I remember," I said, recalling our conversation at Hy's. It seemed like a decade ago. My smile faded as I remembered something; I had seen Hauver's name recently. "Did Edward Hauver have a nickname?" I asked.

Mike nodded. "He was usually called Teddy. Why?"

CHAPTER FORTY-FIVE

HIS NICKNAME WAS TEDDY. THAT WAS TOO MUCH OF A COINCIDENCE.
"You said that Edward Hauver lived in Paris, right?" I frantically tried
to recall the details of our discussion at Hy's. "That was during the
First World War?" I confirmed.

Mike sat up straighter, but his conversational tone didn't change.
"That's right. He was there at the beginning of the conflict and then
spent some time in England recuperating from an illness."

I closed my eyes for a moment. When I opened them, I strove
to keep my voice light. "By the way, how did you know I was here,
Mike?"

He didn't blink at this change in topic. "Oliver gave me the
address."

Lemieux would not have told Oliver that I was staying at Adela's,
not with Malone's body still unrecovered.

"What's going on, Jess?" Mike asked.

"Jem and Teddy were in Paris at the same time. They were friends.
I think Teddy knew about the Rembrandt."

Mike seemed to consider the question. "It's possible, I guess."

"Stephen Nguyen said that there have always been rumors in art
circles that a Canadian painting might hide an old master. You're the
archivist for artists, so you must have heard them. Why didn't you
tell me and Lemieux about that after Malone drove us off the road?"

"There are lots of rumors floating around. I didn't want to confuse
things with old gossip."

The lies came too easily. When telling the truth, Mike was never
glib; he stumbled over his words like an awkward teenager.

I was sitting across from the professor.

His cords were worn at the knees, his jacket rumpled. I couldn't summon any fear. Instead, I was angry. "I remember you saying that when you worked for Edward Hauver he told you all sorts of tall tales. Things about his adventures. Did he tell you about meeting Jem in Paris?"

Mike stared at me, his large brown eyes sad. "Don't do this, Jess."

"Did he tell you that Jem found a Rembrandt? Did he tell you that his friend had painted over it and then died? Maybe Hauver tried to find the painting but couldn't. Maybe he liked the story. I bet he told you all of it."

The landline rang, and we both froze. "Don't answer that," Mike pleaded.

I spoke over the noise, the insistent ringing punctuating my question. "You and Thibodeau were working together to find the painting, weren't you? You killed him."

The ringing stopped.

Mike stood, pacing the room. "It was an accident. You've got to believe me."

I'd expected these words, but not the pain that bloomed in my chest. I said nothing.

Mike spoke as if relieved. "Teddy told me Jem's story about painting over a Rembrandt to smuggle it out of France. I still remember his words, 'Crawford was a foolish son of a gun, but he surely thought he was onto something.'" Mike stopped pacing, returning to his seat. His face had a faraway look. "I forgot about that story for years, and then Melvin started writing the biography. We'd sit and talk about Teddy for hours. Melvin said that Teddy was the originator of the 'old master' rumor but that he'd never revealed who the artist was. That's when it occurred to me that I had the jump on anyone else trying to find the painting, because I knew it was Crawford." Mike's voice quickened as he told this part of the story, and I was drawn into the excitement in spite of myself.

"I began buying up Crawford canvases. He was never a big name, so it took a lot of work tracking them down. I bought everything that was available."

The phone rang again, but I ignored it. I wasn't even sure if Mike heard it, he was so engrossed in his own story.

"I'd sneak them into the Conservation Facility to test them under the UV light," he continued. "After a couple of months, I hadn't found anything and was ready to give up. I knew there were other Crawfords out there, but most were held in private hands or museums. Then one evening Thibodeau was doing his rounds and caught me coming out of the Art Vault with a painting under my arm. His shift was ending, so I promised to buy him a beer if he'd keep quiet. I didn't want to draw attention to my activities. Anyway, we went for a drink . . ."

I doubted it was one drink, but I let it slide, not wanting to interrupt Mike.

"I ended up telling Thibodeau about the Rembrandt. He said that he could steal the other Crawfords, the ones that weren't for sale, and we could test them. As crazy as it seems now, I thought his idea made sense. He was in charge of getting the paintings, and I was supposed to handle the testing, find a restorer, and broker the sale. If it panned out, we'd split the money down the middle."

I watched Mike as he recounted the events. His eyes were bright, his hair fell in front of his eyes, and his dimple appeared and disappeared. I couldn't reconcile this calm, kind man with the criminal he described. My thoughts must have shown in my face, because he met my eyes and broke off his tale.

"You have to understand my state of mind, Jess. I'd spent three years nursing my wife through breast cancer. I'd given her everything, but she had died anyway. I was in a state of shock. I was empty, broken. I had nothing in my life. The mystery, the allure of finding the Rembrandt was what reanimated me. It gave me a sense of purpose."

I considered his words. "I can understand what you're saying. I feel a bit like that with Victoria and Jem's story. But what you were doing was against the law."

"Come on, Jess. We stole a few almost valueless paintings. I'm sure the owners were insured. They probably never even noticed that their Crawford was missing." Mike's justifications came easily, as if he'd told himself the same things many times.

He returned to his account. "With Thibodeau's help, I'd sneak into the Art Vault at night to use the equipment to test the paintings we acquired. I know I could have bought my own UV lamp, but I was already spending so much on the paintings, it seemed like a needless expense."

I actually smiled. Mike's cheapness extended to his criminal life as well.

Mike noticed my expression and smiled back. "We stored some of the paintings on site. I found a good hiding spot, and didn't have to risk bringing them back out of the Conservation Facility."

My cell phone rang. The noise was angry, like a wasp in the room. Rather than throwing Mike off, however, it seemed to goad him into finishing his story.

"Things started to go sour about two months ago. I couldn't locate any more Crawford paintings, and Thibodeau was getting antsy. I began to think that maybe Teddy was wrong and there was no hidden Rembrandt. It came to a head the night of the auction. Thibodeau had wanted to steal the paintings, but the auction was too close to home, and I didn't want to attract attention. I insisted that we buy them legally. I'd read the title of the one work, *Paris 1915*, and hoped it was the jackpot. Still, I told Thibodeau not to spend more than $2,000 for the lot, because I couldn't afford any more. He didn't listen, though, and went way over budget.

"We smuggled the paintings into the vault that night and tested them right away. When neither revealed the Rembrandt, I threw in the towel. I had spent too much money and taken too many risks, chasing a dream. I was ready to move on. Only Thibodeau didn't see it that way."

Mike paused, reaching into his breast pocket for a small silver flask. He took a long slug.

"What happened, Mike?"

His words came slowly, as if his tongue was thick. "I told him that I didn't want to keep doing this, that there might not even be a bloody Rembrandt. He got angry. Stomped around the stacks. Told me I'd promised him a sure thing. He said that he had a cousin in a biker gang, and that the cousin had helped out in the robberies. This man wanted a cut of our profits and wasn't going to abandon the project. Thibodeau pulled a gun on me, and for once in my life, I fought back. We struggled, and the gun went off."

Mike buried his face in his hands. "It was an accident, Jess. I never meant for this to happen. If only I had seen those letters. How was I to know that the Jarvis family was connected to Crawford? One stupid piece of information would have changed everything. In retrospect, I should have instructed Thibodeau to buy everything from the Jarvis lot. Then it would have been me who discovered the letters, not you. I would have figured out that Gilbert Jarvis owned the painting, and none of this would have happened."

His voice was bitter, and I marveled that he was focusing on his failure to detect the Jarvis connection rather than the murder.

"I actually felt better about things after"—he paused, stammering—"after the incident in the vault. At least it was over." He sighed, thrusting a hand through his hair. "Except it wasn't. Because you found the body, and I found you. At first I wanted to learn if you knew anything, but soon I was falling for you."

I tried to analyze my feelings about hearing all of this. In books and movies, the bad guy always reveals his true character at the end, when he explains how he did it. The villain's voice changes, he starts to sneer, he exposes his evil nature. This didn't happen with Mike. I could understand his position. I could see why he made the choices he did. Some of it even seemed reasonable. He wasn't crazy; he was still Mike. His voice was the same, his manner still hesitant. He was still kind. He still had his dimple. This was the man who made me laugh, cheered me up, and been the best lover I'd ever had. He had also killed Thibodeau.

The frightening thing wasn't that I couldn't reconcile these two Mikes, but that I could.

He was still talking. "I knew I had to get the Crawford paintings back from the vault. I'd panicked and hidden them in our usual spot after the . . ." His voice trailed away, and then he continued. "I waited until Tuesday, when the police finally stopped scouring the facility. I slipped in a back entrance that Thibodeau and I normally used, but while I was in the vault someone else came in."

I gave a start. It was Mike, not Malone, who was in the vault with me that night. He was probably as frightened as I was.

"Anyway, Stephen put the vault in lockdown after that, and I couldn't access it at all. At the same time, Malone started threatening me. He said I owed him. It didn't matter that I hadn't found the painting. He told me I had to get it, or he'd kill me the way I'd killed Thibodeau. He was interested in you too. He thought you might know more than you were saying."

Mike looked urgently at me, his eyes radiating honesty. "I tried to shield you from him, but he was convinced that you knew where the painting was."

Mike punched his fist into his hand. "Malone was after me when he drove us off the road. It was a warning. He came to my place the night of the accident. He told me that if I didn't deliver the goods by today, he'd kill me and he'd come after you. He said that he knew you were staying at your friend Adela's place. I was still processing everything you told me. I was stunned that those letters existed. I told Malone about them and snuck into work that night to steal the copies for him. Once he had those, he knew exactly what you did and I thought he'd leave you alone."

Mike paused and took a deep breath. "This is hard for me to confess, Jess, but when I went to Toronto on the acquisition trip, I had every intention of running. I'm a weak man, I admit, and I was terrified. But I came back. I needed to know if you were safe."

The room was silent again. The pause stretched between us, a physical thing that pulsed with the unspoken.

Mike stared into my face. "Do you believe me that Thibodeau's death was an accident?"

"Yes," I said unreservedly.

"Then you see that I haven't done anything so terrible. We don't have to tell anyone. The police never need to know. This can be our secret, Jess. I'm a good man, you know that."

I hesitated. I knew what my mother would do. Cassie would damn conventional justice and encourage him to atone for his misdeeds by giving unto others or purging his sins in some crystal-lined healing lodge. She'd think of something creative, something regenerative, something "Cassie." If she truly believed the death was accidental, as I did, she certainly wouldn't hand him over to the rough justice of the criminal courts. To the "man."

I thought about my pain and fear. I thought about what would have happened to Gilbert Jarvis if Malone and Joe had shown up at his door. I thought of Mike's desperation and the way he dismissed Thibodeau's murder. I also thought of his dimple.

I wasn't my mother, and I needed to do things my way. "I'm sorry, Mike. I have to tell the police."

As if on cue, someone pounded on the door. "Mademoiselle, are you there? It's Lemieux."

Mike stared, his face taut with tension. "They're already here. They've found me." He edged away from the door, as if he could hide from the police.

I tried to stand, but the pain in my leg made me dizzy.

"I can't go to jail, Jess. Do you know what will happen to me there?"

Lemieux's voice was rough now. "Jess, let me in."

I stood. The pain was intolerable, but I limped toward the door. Tears poured down my face. I stopped, my hand on the doorknob. "If you cooperate with the police, they will go easy on you."

"Please don't do this, Jess."

"I'm sorry," I said. Then I opened the door to Lemieux.

MORE TEA, MISS NOVAK?"

"No thanks," I declined Gilbert Jarvis's offer and leaned back in the hard seat, letting the watery late-March sunlight wash over me. A square of dark wallpaper was the only indication that Jem's painting once hung on the wall. The room looked different with its absence. It was like a person you're used to seeing wearing glasses, suddenly without them. I said as much to Jarvis.

He chuckled. "Yes, I miss the portrait. The police say they will be done with it shortly. The painting wasn't key to their investigation, from what I gather."

"No, and I guess they've got all of the evidence they need." Malone's body had been recovered, which was what Lemieux had been calling to tell me on that day with Mike. Knowing my immobility, he realized something was wrong when I didn't answer the phone.

"You've had quite a time of it, my dear," said Jarvis.

I nodded, remembering that day. Mike hadn't met my gaze when, in a few short sentences, I'd told Lemieux what he confessed to me.

Lemieux said to Mike, "I bet we get good fingerprints and maybe some DNA from those stashed paintings in the vault, eh?"

Mike looked old as Lemieux handcuffed him and ushered him out of Adela's apartment. The case against him was sealed when Joe awoke from his coma and confessed everything in an effort to save his own skin.

Jarvis pulled me out of my reverie. "How have you been getting along since our last visit?"

I didn't mention the nightmares where Malone pulled me under the icy water. I didn't tell him that every time I closed my eyes, I saw Mike's face crumple as I opened the door to Lemieux. I didn't say that it took me three weeks to return to work. "I've been hired on permanently at the Dominion Archives."

"That's wonderful news."

And it was. Stephen and the chief archivist told Oliver that I had been invaluable to the institution in a time of crisis. What's more, the lurid stories in the press of my battle with art thieves and the identification of a lost Rembrandt overshadowed any further investigations into the Dominion Archives. Our holdings were safe, at least for the time being.

Jarvis looked over from his hospital bed, his eyes twinkling. "Now, as much as I'm enjoying this social visit, I'm sure it's not the only reason you wanted to see me."

In the last few weeks, I avoided thinking about Jem and Victoria. Their story was tied up with so much pain for me that it was hard. Still, I knew that I owed them, and Gilbert, the truth.

I'd wrestled with how best to break the news of his parentage, finally deciding that he should read the proof himself. I cleared my throat. "In doing research on Jeremy Crawford and Victoria Jarvis, I discovered some interesting facts about their relationship. There was the story of the Rembrandt, of course, but there was also a more personal narrative—one that concerns you." I handed him a copy of the last letter Victoria wrote. I'd blown it up so that Jarvis would have no trouble seeing it.

He read the document wordlessly, then handed it back to me. "It's a very touching note," he said. "I wish I had known my mother." There was a slight moistness at his eyes, but no other sign of emotion.

I was surprised by his lack of reaction. "You don't seem shocked."

"Should I be?" he queried.

"I thought discovering who your real parents were would be greeted with a little more surprise."

"Oh, I was very surprised when I first found out," he replied placidly.

"First found out?"

"Yes," he said. "When your colleague came around. I forget her name now—Jeanne or Jennifer."

The hairs stood up on the back of my neck. "Ginette?" I suggested to him.

"Yes, a lovely woman. She visited here about three weeks ago, shortly after all the police excitement. She told me about my parentage. We had a marvelous chat."

"I bet you did," I said through gritted teeth.

"I'm surprised you didn't know she visited. She said you were working on an article together."

Ginette scooped me. If she knew about Gilbert's parentage, she must have seen all the letters, even the last ones that I made such an effort to copy and replace. I was surprised to realize that after everything I'd been through, this last betrayal stung.

Gilbert continued talking, unaware of the emotions his statement churned up. "There was one thing that I didn't get to discuss with that charming woman. It is what I meant to tell you the evening you were coming to see me. I'm sure it doesn't matter now that the Rembrandt has been found, but something tells me you're a girl who enjoys tying up loose ends."

"Yes?"

"It's about the painting. When we spoke the first time, I told you that I discovered it with all of Victoria's other Art Association paintings. That's not the case. After you left, I remembered that this painting used to hang in our parlor in High Plains. I loved it as a child. My mother gave it to me when I moved to Montreal. It was a way for me to remember home."

Therese must have discovered the painting after Victoria's death. Knowing it would have meant a great deal to her, Therese made sure to pass it along to Gilbert, Victoria's son. My eyes filled with tears. Suddenly, I didn't care that Ginette stole my story; I knew the truth. I had closed the circle, and that was enough.

Gilbert didn't notice my tears. "The older I get, the better I recall the past, so it's surprising I didn't remember that when we first

THE FOULEST THINGS · 275

chatted. My only excuse is that talking to a pretty girl must have jumbled my brain."

I smiled at his flirtatiousness. We spent the rest of the afternoon talking about Victoria and Jem. I think they would have been pleased to see their child tucked into a warm blanket, next to a comfortable fire, enjoying the final days of a happy life. At the end of the visit, I asked him when he would be getting the overpainting removed to reveal the Rembrandt.

"I'm not sure I will, to be honest. As I told you, they've confirmed that there is an underpainting, but I think I value the painting on top more. My mother has been watching over me for decades, and I never knew it. I might leave it as it is. My children can discover the next chapter, after I'm gone."

I smiled again, thinking of how proud Jem was of that painting. It had enjoyed nearly a hundred years of appreciation and affection. That would have pleased him.

◇◇◇◇◇◇

I RETURNED TO OTTAWA, AND MY LITTLE APARTMENT, ON THE AFTER-noon bus. Now that I was hired on permanently, I was planning on moving to a better place, one without so many bad memories.

My mother called that night. "Salali? Darling, how are you?"

Ever since I'd made the national press, Cassie had been calling on a more regular basis. In the early days, she'd tried to get me to give her an "exclusive," but I took enormous satisfaction in telling her "no comment." If only I could do that with all aspects of my life.

"Fine, Mum. You?"

She talked for twenty-five minutes, telling me about her latest article, her latest lover, and her latest hair color. Finally, she wrapped it up. "Listen, sweetie. It's not too late for you. Joel Beaker says he can get you something at one of his weekly magazines. Leave your musty books, and come back to the city."

I wasn't angry. I wasn't even annoyed. I spoke matter-of-factly, but from the heart. "What I do isn't musty, Mum. I don't deal with books—I deal with records. They aren't old papers that no one cares about, but things that matter. My work is important. I'm never going to be a journalist. I'm an archivist."

There was a long pause on the other end. "Let me know when this idea of yours runs its course. Don't wait too long, though, or you'll only be good for a small-town paper."

I restrained the urge to throw the phone through the window, instead bidding her an impressively polite goodbye.

◇◇◇◇◇◇

I TRIED NOT TO THINK TOO MUCH ABOUT MIKE IN THE FOLLOWING months, but it wasn't easy. He was around every corner at work. His case wound its way through the court system, occasionally making headlines.

Old feelings were further stirred up when Ginette's article came out in the *Journal of Historical Research*. She was generous enough to credit me: the first footnote stated, "Jessica Novak's research assistantship was helpful in the completion of this article."

Adela was around less than usual in those months because she and Lemieux started dating. I realized that the one thing worse than trying to convince the preening detective that I wasn't a murderer was dropping by Adela's place to discover her giving him a manicure.

I had no real friends at work. Most colleagues treated me like a pariah, or worse, tried to get to know me better because of my notoriety. Louise was on an extended sick leave. Her years of smoking had caught up with her and she was being treated for Stage 2 emphysema. I visited her often. Though her prognosis wasn't good, she was determined to get back to work. "Mostly to piss Oliver off," she confessed. We spent our time together speculating about his supposed coke habit. I'd snapped a photo of his new hairdo and we analyzed whether his decision to scrape his thinning locks into a ponytail was bad taste or evidence of a drug-fried brain.

One morning in June, we went for a slow walk outside Louise's apartment. It had been a bad week. More news had come out about the case, and my colleagues were whispering behind my back. I looked at Louise in despair. "Will it ever get easier?"

She took a shallow breath and let out a short cough. "When I first started and I was having a tough time of it, I had one colleague who was decent to me. He was a grizzled old fart who'd started at the archives during the Second World War. He took me aside one day and said, 'Louise, don't worry. It will get better eventually.'"

"And did it?"

"Sure, sure."

"How long did it take?"

She hesitated and then grinned. "Well, remember, we're archivists, kiddo. We think in terms of decades, not days."

Maybe it was a sign that I was finally figuring things out, because her answer actually made me feel better.

ACKNOWLEDGMENTS

THANK YOU TO THE CREW AT TURNER PUBLISHING: STEPHANIE BEARD for signing this book and being my champion. Thanks to Ryan Smernoff for guiding its progress and being a great sounding board; Claire Ong for keeping everything on track; Kathy Haake for her thoughtful and thorough editorial insight; Andrew Clark for his helpful copy edits; and Lauren Ash for her fabulous marketing savvy. Huge thanks to Emily Mahon for another gorgeous cover.

Thank you to my amazing critiquing group, Alette Willis, Wayne Ng, and Chris Crowder, who sharpened and shaped this story while learning far more about archives than they bargained for.

I wrote the first draft of this novel way back in 2006. It has evolved a great deal since then, but my delight and fascination with the world of archives has remained constant. This is a work of fiction. While my time at Library and Archives Canada has inspired me, the Dominion Archives, its backstabbing and murderous staff members, lax security, poor human resources practices, and occasional blatant disregard for proper archival technique are all entirely fictional. I want to thank my colleagues at Library and Archives Canada for being such wonderful coworkers and such dedicated guardians and disseminators of Canadian history. Special thanks to Karen Linauskas, Lisa Tremblay-Goodyer, David Clement, Kathleen Talarico and Marie Peron who were amazing teammates during the enormous challenges of the pandemic.

Thanks to my best friend, Kathryn Moore. She probably doesn't remember this, but I worked out a tricky plot issue on a long run with her one wintery morning years ago. For that, and a thousand other reasons, thanks KJM!

Big thanks to the other friends who have been limping along with me through these (hopefully) final days of the pandemic: Dara Price, Johanna Smith, Meghan Hall, Amy Turner, Serena Manson, Christa Peters, Christine Barrass, Laura Madokoro, Martha Copestake, Michelle Reimer, and Kaia Ambrose. Special thanks to Sara Trew. #ComingOutOnTop.

Thanks to my brother and sisters, their partners and kids and to all my lovely Horrall family. I feel very lucky to be related to all of you.

I thank my husband, Andrew, the best husband, father, and yes, archivist. Lastly, thanks to Violet, my staunchest fan . . . You don't have to work at the archives when you grow up!

This book is dedicated to my mother, Sarah Tector. She raised five children through some tough times and put up with our incessant teasing about her Australian accent. I love you mum—thank you for everything you've done for me.

ABOUT THE AUTHOR

AMY TECTOR WAS BORN AND RAISED IN THE ROLLING HILLS OF QUEBEC'S Eastern Townships. She has worked in archives for the past twenty years and has found some pretty amazing things, including lost letters, mysterious notes, and even a whale's ear. Amy spent many years as an expat, living in Brussels and in The Hague, where she worked for the International Criminal Tribunal for War Crimes in Yugoslavia. She lives in Ottawa, Canada, with her daughter, dog, and husband.

CPSIA information can be obtained
at www.ICGtesting.com
Printed in the USA
JSHW061952300822
29828JS00002B/2